Queen of Queens

ALAN HINES

Trafford rev. 06/03/2015

 www.trafford.com

North America & international
toll-free: 844-688-6899 (USA & Canada)
fax: 812 355 4082

Books of poetry already published by Alan Hines,
1. Reflections of Love
2. Thug Poetry Volume 1
3. The Words I Spoke

Urban Novel already published by Alan Hines,
1. Book Writer

Upcoming books of poetry by Alan Hines,
1. Reflections of Love (Volume 2, and 3)
2. This is Love (Volume 1, 2, and 3)
3. Founded Love (Volume 1, 2, and 3)
4. True Love (Volume 1, 2, and 3)
5. Thug Poetry (Endless Volumes)
6. When Thugs Cry (Volume 1, 2, and 3)
7. A Inner Soul That Cried (Volume 1, 2, and 3)
8. Visionary (Endless Volumes)
9. In My Eyes To See (Volume 1, 2, and 3)
10. A Seed That Grew (Volume 1, 2, and, 3)
11. The Words I Spoke (Volume 1, 2 and 3)
12. Scriptures (Volume 1, 2, and 3)
13. Revelations (volume 1, 2, and 3)
14. Destiny (Volume 1, 2, and 3)
15. Trials and Tribulations (Volume 1, 2, and 3)
16. IMMORTALITY (Volume 1, 2, and 3)
17. My Low Spoken Words (Volume 1, 2, and 3)
18. Beauty Within (Volume 1, 2, and 3)
19. Red Ink of Blood (Volume 1, 2, and 3)
20. Destiny of Light (Jean Hines) (Volume 1, 2, and 3)
21. Deep Within (Volume 1, 2, and 3)
22. Literature (Volume 1, 2, and 3)
23. Silent Mind (Volume 1, 2, and 3)
24. Amor (Volume 1, 2, and 3)

Upcoming non-fiction books by Alan Hines,
1. Time Versus Life
2. Timeless Jewels
3. The Essence of Time

Upcoming Urban Novels by Alan Hines,
1. Black Kings
2. Playerlistic
3. The Police
4. Scandalous
5. The West Side Rapist
6. Shattered Dreams
7. She Wrote Murder
8. Black Fonz
9. A Slow Form of Suicide
10. No-Love
11. War Stories
12. Storm
13. Ghetto Heros
14. Boss Pimps
15. Adolescents
16. In The Hearts of Men
17. Story Teller

Acknowledgements

First and foremost I'm thanking the Father of the Heavens and Earth. I thank you Father for showing me love regardless, for blessing me to be in the likeness of yourself, marvelous. Thanking you for blessing me to awake to live to see another day. Thank you Heavenly Father for always being there in my times of need your love surely feeds. Thank you for blessing me with the talent to write, it's truly a blessed gift from you to me.

Special thanks to my grandmother Jean Hines, I love her all the time as in Heaven she resides. Special thanks to my mom, and dad, thank God they got together and gave me this life. Special thanks to my sister Alicia for being there in my time of need, and being the one that initially gave me the idea to write books. Special thanks to Julie Hull (attorney), John Fitzgerald Lyke (attorney), and to Mr. Marasa (English Teacher). Special thanks to anybody else that showed me any love, and support throughout life.

As always I thank the entire Hines, and Laughlin family, all my co-workers, even the phony ones that's always going behind my back to those in charge saying bad things about my performance, what they don't know is that, that's motivation for me to keep writing books focusing on bigger and better things in life than working for someone else's company, I'm a boss. Thanks to everybody that read one of my books awaiting on the next one. Thanks Ricardo Sanchez, for being helpful when I was going through troublesome times I never forgot or will forget your help. Roscell Hines(Cel), Alan White(Block), Shamon Miller(Pac), although you may not hear from me sometime, but know it's love I know what each one of you gentlemen are going through it's rough. I pray for each one of you everyday knowing that the Heavenly Father is the only one that can wash that problem away allowing you to freely see the light of days.....

Thanks to any and everybody that will decide to read this book, and I hope everybody enjoys it, and all my other books.

Prologue

It was the summer of 1971, fourth of July, 11:30 p.m., in Chicago as the fireworks lit up the skies.

Chapter 1

"You sure this the right spot, man?" Slim asked.

"I'm positive this is the right spot. I wouldn't never bring you on no blank mission," Double J said.

With no hesitation, Double J kicked in the door and yelled, "Police! Lay the fuck down!"

Double J and Slim stormed into the crib with guns in hand, ready to fuck a nigga up if anybody made any false moves.

As they entered the crib, they immediately noticed two women sitting at the table. The women were getting ready to shake up some dope.

One of the women laid on the floor facedown, crying out, "Please, please don't shoot me."

She had seen many TV shows and movies in which the police kicked in doors and wrongfully thought an individual was strapped or reaching for a gun when they weren't, and the police hideously shot them, taking their lives from 'em.

The other woman tried to run and jump outta the window. Before she could do so, Double J tackled her down and handcuffed her.

Double J threw Slim a pair of handcuffs. "Handcuff her," Double J said.

As Slim began to handcuff the other chick, he began thinking, *Where the fuck this nigga get some motherfucking handcuffs from?*

The woman who was on the floor, crying, looked up and noticed that Slim wasn't the police.

"You niggas ain't no motherfucking police," she said.

Double J ran over and kicked her in the face, and busted her nose. "Bitch, shut the fuck up," Double J said.

She shut up, laid her head on the floor. As her head was filled with pain while tears ran down her face, with blood running from her nose, she silently prayed that this real-life nightmare would come to an end!

Simultaneously, Slim and Double J looked at the table filled with dope. Both Slim and Double J's mouths dropped. They'd never seen so much dope in their lives. Right in front of their eyes were one hundred grams of pure, uncut heroin.

Both women laid on the floor, scared to death. They'd never been so scared in their natural lives.

Double J went into the kitchen found some ziplock bags, came back and put the dope in them, and then stuffed the dope in the sleeves of his jacket 'cause it was too much dope to fit in his pockets.

"Man, we gotta hurry up. You know the neighbors probably heard us kick the door in," Slim said.

"The neighbors ain't heard shit 'cuz of all the fireworks going off. That's why I picked this time to run off in here, while the fireworks going off, so nobody won't hear us," Double J said.

"Shiit, they could've still heard us. The fireworks ain't going off inside the building," Slim said.

"Don't worry about it," Double J said.

"Lord, let's search the rooms before we leave. You know, if all this dope is here, it gotta be some guns or money in here somewhere," Double J said.

"Yep, Jo, I bet you it is," Slim said.

Double J walked over to the woman whose nose he busted, knelt, put a .357 to her ear, and clicked the hammer back. The woman heard the hammer click in her ear. She became so scared that she literally shit on herself.

"Bitch, I'ma ask you one time, where the rest of that shit at?" Double J asked in a deep hideous voice.

She began crying out and yelling, "It's in the closet, in the bottom of the dirty clothes hamper."

Double J went into the closet snatched all the clothes outta the hamper and found ten big bundles of money. He saw a book bag hanging in the closet, grabbed it, and loaded the money in it.

Double J went back into the front room. Without second-guessing it, he shot both women in the back of their heads two times a piece.

Double J and Slim fled from the apartment building, got into their steamer, and smashed off. As Double J drove a few blocks away, Slim sat in the passenger side of the car, looking over at Double J, pissed off.

"Lord, why the fuck you shoot them hos?" Slim asked with hostility.

"Look at all the money and dope we got," Double J said.

"What that gotta do with it?" Slim asked.

"You know that that wasn't them hos shit. They was working for some nigga, and if that nigga ever found out we stuck him up for all that shit, he'd have a price on our heads. Now that the only people who knew about us taking that shit is dead, we don't gotta worry about that shit," Double J said.

Yeah, you right about that, Slim thought as he remained silent for a few seconds. "You just said something about dope and money. What money?" Slim asked.

"Look in the book bag," Double J said.

Slim unzipped the book bag, and it was as if he saw a million dollars. His mouth dropped, amazed by all the money that was in the book bag.

They hit the e-way and set fire to a lace joint as they began to think of all the things they'd be able to do with the money and dope.

Double J and Slim were two petty hustlers looking for this one big lick, and they finally got it. They had various hustles that consisted of robbing, car thieving, and selling a little dope. All their hustles revolved around King Phill. King Phill was a king of a branch of ViceLords, the Insane ViceLords (IVL). They'd rob, steal cars, and sell dope through King Phill, one way or the other.

Double J and Slim were basically King Phill's yes men. Whatever Phill would say or wanted them to do, they'd say yes to.

After forty-five minutes of driving, they parked the steamer on a deserted block where there were no houses, only a big empty park.

Double J began wiping off the inside of the car. Slim began to do the same.

"Make sure you wipe off everything real good. We don't wanna leave no fingerprints," Double J said.

"You ain't gotta tell me. The last thing I wanna do is get pinched for a pussy-ass stickup murder," Slim said.

Double J put the book bag on his back. They left the car, wiping off the inside and outside door handles, and they began walking to Double J's crib, which was about thirty minutes away.

"Lord, fire up one of them lace joints," Slim said.

"Here, you fire it up," Double J said as he passed the joint to Slim.

Slim instantly set fire to it. They walked swiftly to Double J's crib, continuously puffing on the lace joints. Once they made it halfway there, out of nowhere, Double J stopped in his tracks.

"What the fuck you stop for?" Slim asked.

"Lord, we gotta get rid of that car," Double J said.

"Why?" Slim asked.

"'Cuz like you said, we don't wanna get pinched for no stickup murder. If somebody seen that car leave the scene of the crime and they tell the police and the police find the car and dust it for fingerprints and find one fingerprint that matches one of ours, we booked. We'll be sitting on death row saying what we should've, would've, and could've done," Double J said.

"How we gone get rid of it?" Slim asked.

"Here, take my gun and bookbag and meet me at my crib. My girl there, she'll let you in," Double J said.

"You still didn't answer my question," Slim said.

"What's that?" Double J asked.

"How we gone get rid of the car?" Slim asked.

"Don't worry about it. I got it," Double J said.

"Let's get rid of it together," Slim said.

"Naw, man, we need to make sure the money and dope is safe, and we need to get these hot-ass guns off the streets," Double J said.

"Where is the dope?" Slim asked.

Double J reached into his sleeves, pulled out the dope, and handed it all to Slim as they departed and went their separate ways.

I hope this nigga don't get caught fucking around with that car, Slim thought.

Double J went back to the car, looking for something to use to set it on fire. He ended up finding some charcoal fluid in the trunk of the car, squeezed all the fluid out of the bottle all over the car, struck a match, and threw it on the car as it instantly began burning. Double J took off running. He ran halfway home and walked the other half.

Once Double J made it home, before he could even knock on the door or ring the doorbell, Slim opened the door. Double J rushed in nervously and slammed the door behind himself and frantically locked it.

"Nigga, what the fuck took you so long?" Slim asked.

"What took me so long? Shiiit, I ran halfway back, but anyway, I took care of the business. I burned the car up," Double J said.

"How much dough we got?" Double J asked.

"I don't know. I ain't even open the book bag up, I was waiting to you get here," Slim said.

"See that's why I fuck with you. Anybody else would've played me for some of the money and dope," Double J said.

"You my nigga. I wouldn't never try to get over on you. To keep it real, you didn't even have to take me on the lick with you," Slim said.

They went into the bathroom, locked the door, and began counting the money. Each bundle of money was a G.

"Damn, Lord, we got ten stacks and all this dope," Slim said.

"How we gone get rid of all this dope?" Double J asked.

"We gone sell it in grams," Slim said.

"Naw, man, we need to sell it in bags. We'll make more money selling it in bags. The only problem is where we gone sell it at. You know anywhere we try to open up at, they gone close us down," Double J said.

"We gone sell it in the hood," Slim said.

"Stop playing! You know damn well we dead in the hood. You know if we open up in the hood, they gone close us straight down," Double J said.

"We gone have to go through Phill," Slim said.

"Yeah, we'll get up with Phill tomorrow," Double J said.

"Man, don't tell nobody where we got the dope from."

"Nigga, do I look like a lame to you? What the fuck I look like, telling somebody about what we did," Slim said.

"I'm finna go to sleep. You might as well spend a night," Double J said.

"Yeah, I might as well spend a night," Slim said.

"I'll holla at you in the morning. I'm sleepy as hell," Double J said as he started to yawn.

Slim went and lay on the couch in the living room. Double J went into his bedroom, undressed down to his boxers and T-shirt, and got into bed with his wife, who he assumed was asleep. As Double J pulled the covers back, he noticed that his wife was in bed asshole-naked. *I'm glad I married her,* Double J thought while enjoying the view.

Slim and Double J stayed awake for a little while, thinking about the money they had and the profit they was going to make off the dope. As Double J closed his eyes to go to sleep, he felt his wife's hands gently slipping into his boxers, rubbing his dick.

"I thought you were asleep," Double J said.

"I ain't sleep. I was just lying here thinking about you," she said. She continued rubbing on his dick.

"Now you know you can't be rubbing on my dick without any lubrication. That shit don't feel good when you do it with dry hands," Double J said.

She got up and squeezed a little Jergens in the palm of her hand as he slipped his boxers off and lay back on the bed. She grabbed his dick firmly, began lathering it up with the lotion, and jagging him off at the same time.

As she thoroughly jagged him off, he pumped her hand until his nut unleashed on her titties, and she began rubbing the nut around on her titties as if it was baby oil or lotion. She then took his dick into her mouth, gobbling it and the lotion in all, swirling her tongue around it and sucking on it as if she was trying to suck some sweet nectar out of it.

Once it got rock hard, she began deep throating it, choking herself with his dick while rubbing on her own clitoris roughly while humming. In no time flat, he was releasing a load of nut down her throat. She stood, wiped her mouth, and slightly began growling. She then got on top of him and played with his dick for a few seconds until it got back hard.

She looked him in his eyes, as she grabbed his dick firmly and shoved it in her pussy, and began smiling. She began riding it slowly to get her pussy totally wet, while he grabbed her ass cheeks, guiding her movements.

Once her pussy got wet, he began slamming his dick in and out of her, enjoying the tightness of her moist pussy. She clawed his chest, moaning in the midst of pleasure and pain; she liked when it hurt.

It felt so good to him that every time he'd slam his dick up in her pussy, it felt like he was actually nutting.

As Double J began to nut, she was cumming simultaneously. As he began to slam his dick in and out her pussy rougher and harder, she began fucking him back. It was like a rodeo show as their orgasms exploded.

"Get up. Get on the bed so I can hit it from the back," Double J said.

She got on all fours on the bed. Double J got on his knees right behind her and began squeezing and rubbing her big brown pretty ass cheeks.

"Tell me you love me before you start fucking me," she said.

"I love your hot ass," he said. Double J then rammed his dick in her hot pussy, gripping her ass cheeks and slamming his dick in and out her pussy hard and fast while admiring the way her ass cheeks bounced. In no time, he was letting another nut explode in her pussy.

"Let me suck it," she said in a low seductive tone.

"Hold on, let me roll up a joint," Double J said.

"You know that I don't like the smell of lace joints. Why you got to lace your weed with cocaine? Why you can't smoke regular weed like everybody else?" she said.

Double J began smiling and looking her straight in the eyes. "Well, I'll smoke a regular joint just for you," Double J said. He rolled up a regular joint with only weed in it, set fire to it as she got on her knees with an aim to please.

As he inhaled and exhaled the potent weed smoke, she simultaneously sucked his dick, utilizing a suction method sucking mainly the tip thoroughly. The potent effect of the weed combined with her superb suction method and the moisture of her mouth felt so good that within seconds he released a glob of nut in her face.

He finished smoking his joint, and both of them lay on the bed. "You must really been wanting to fuck," Double J asked.

"I been thinking about you all day at work. I had to take off work because I creamed in my panties daydreaming about your dick going in and out my pussy and mouth. I been sitting in the house all day waiting on you," she said.

I done married a freak, Double J thought

They began to tell each other how much they loved each other and how their lives wouldn't be the same without each other, before both of them fell into a deep sleep.

The next morning, after Double J's wife had gone to work, Double J and Slim sat at the kitchen table eating breakfast, reminiscing about the stickup and the murders.

They glorified and celebrated the stickup and the murders as if they were professional athletes who just won a championship game or as if they had won the lottery.

It's sad how bloodshed make others glad. But this life some live in as thugs consist of no love. Other people were brought up to increase the peace and strive to earn college degrees, and live the American dream. But those who live the street life thrive on death and destruction. They rob, steal, and kill with no discretion, and glorify others' names who do the same.

"Hurry up and finish eating so we can go holla at Phill," Double J said.

"I'm already finished," Slim said.

"Well, empty the rest of that shit that's on the plate in the garbage and put that plate in the sink," Double J said.

Slim emptied the rest of the food in the garbage, put the plate in the sink, and went and grabbed the book bag.

"Naw, we gone leave the dope and shit here, unless you wanna take your half to your house," Double J said.

"It's cool, I'll leave it here," Slim said.

As they rode up the block in the hood where Phill was, they noticed many of the Insanes on Phill's security as usual.

Once they made it to where Phill was, Phill began smiling, 'cuz he was happy to see them. He needed them to take care of some business for him.

King Phill was a pretty boy. Stood about six feet five, half-Latino, half-black, with naturally curly black hair in his midtwenties. Those who didn't know Phill personally would've never believed that he was a king of a large street gang. King Phill looked like a pretty boy college student.

"Park the car. I need to holla at ya'll," Phill said.

They parked and got out to holla at him.

"I need ya'll to get some steamers for me," Phill said.

"We ain't on no car-thieving shit right now. We need your assistance on some other shit," Double J said.

"What ya'll need?" Phill asked.

"Let's step away from everybody. It's personal," Slim said.

As they stepped away from everybody else, Phill began trying to figure out what Double J and Slim wanted. *Maybe they finna ask for some shit,* Phill thought.

"Phill, we got some dope we need to get off," Double J said.

"What you talking about?" Phill asked.

"We need to pop it off in the hood," Slim said.

"What ya'll talking about, opening up a dope spot in the hood?" Phill asked.

"That's exactly what we're talking about," Slim said.

"You know ya'll can't work in the hood if ya'll ain't a five-star universal elite," Phill said.

"I told him," Double J said.

"Well, make us universal elites," Slim said.

Phill began laughing. "I don't just give out status like that. I ain't one of these phony-ass niggas that let people buy status. You gotta earn it fucking with me," Phill said.

Slim looked at Phill like he was crazy. "Earn it? All the shit we do for you and for the hood while them niggas you made universal elites be in the Bahamas some-motherfucking-where! We be doing all the shootings for the hood and all type of other shit for you and the hood," Slim said.

"Yeah, you do got a point, 'cuz ya'll do stand on nation business. This what I'm going to do for ya'll. I'ma let ya'll work in the hood under my name, but ya'll gotta pay," Phill said.

"How much we gotta pay?" Slim asked.

"That depends on how much dope ya'll got," Phill said.

"We got ten grams," Double J said. He was lying.

"Ten grams? That ain't shit. Ya'll work them ten grams for two or three weeks outta Argale park. In two or three weeks, ya'll should've at least doubled or tripled them ten grams. Once ya'll do, ya'll gotta give me a stack every week," Phill said.

Double J and Slim looked at each other smiling, knowing it was finna be on.

"A stack a week. We got you. We'll holla at you. I gotta go pick my girl up from work." Double J said. He was lying.

As Double J and Slim got into the car and rode off, listening to Al Green's "Love and Happiness." They were happier than a kid on Christmas Day.

Chapter 2

Three Days Later

"How much is that small black digital scale?" Double J asked the cashier.

"That one right there is a hundred dollars. But I'd recommend this white one right here if you're going to be weighing things over twenty-eight grams. A lot of customers usually buy that small black one, then later on down the line, the same customers come back and buy a bigger one, which is a waste of money to me," the woman cashier said.

"How much do the white one cost?" Slim asked.

"Two hundred," the cashier said.

"We'll take it," Slim said.

"Will that be it?" the cashier asked.

"Naw, we need five bottles of Dormin and a bundle of them little black baggies right there and two of them mac spoons," Slim said.

As other customers walked into the small record store, the cashier paused and began covering up the small area where contraband was being sold.

"Thomas, can you service the new customers?" the female cashier said to her coworker.

"Wait 'til these customers leave, then I'll give ya'll, ya'll items," the female cashier said to Double J and Slim.

"Ya'll sell scales, baggies, and all type of shit to everybody in the city, and now you wanna act like it's top secret," Slim said.

"Yeah, we do supply a lot of people with contraband, but those are only the people that come in here asking for it. We can't have contraband on display, because it's all types of people that come in here. A person might come in here with their kids. Or an off-duty police officer might come in here to buy some records. And if they see all this contraband on display, they'll report our ass to the city. We won't lose our store or anything like that, but we'll have to pay a healthy fine," the cashier said.

Within minutes, the other customers purchased their records and left the store.

"Your total will come out to three hundred seventy-five dollars," she said.

Slim paid her, and they left the store.

Once they made it to Double J's crib, they immediately weighed the dope for the first time.

"Damn, Lord, we got a hundred grams! I thought it'll be about fifty grams," Slim said.

"Yeah, me too," Double J said.

"Aw, we finna put up numbers if this shit is a bomb," Slim said.

"Showl is," Double J said.

"Why did you buy baggies instead of aluminum foil?" Double J asked.

"'Cuz we gone put the dope in the baggies. We don't need no aluminum foil," Slim said.

"But we need to put it in the aluminum foil so it can stay fresh," Double J said.

"Once we put it in the baggies then put some thick clear tape on the baggies, the dope will stay fresh," Slim said.

"We need to find us a connect on some quinine," Double J said.

"Naw, we ain't gone put no quinine or none of that other crazy shit on the dope. We either gone use dorms or sell it with no mix on it at all. We gone put three pills on each gram of dope," Slim said.

"How many grams we gone bag up the first time?" Double J asked.

"We gone bag up ten grams first and put it out there and see what it do. You know we can't bag up to much, 'cuz if it don't sell quick enough, it'll fall off," Slim said.

"That's my point exactly. That's why I ask," Double J said.

Double J weighed out ten grams on the scale. Then Double J and Slim opened up thirty dorms, which were actually capsules. Double J and Slim then grabbed two playing cards apiece and began mixing the dope with the dorms.

"How many mac spoons we gone use?" Double J asked.

"We gone give up two macs for a sawbuck and see how that go first. If the dope is a bomb, we gone drop down to one mac spoon or a mac and a half. That all depends on how good the dope is. And if it's real good, we gone put more dorms in it," Slim said.

Double J and Slim grabbed a mac spoon apiece and began measuring the dope and putting it in the bags.

"I got some thick clear tape in my room, in the closet," Double J said.

"Wait 'til we get finished before you go get it," Slim said.

After about an hour and a half, they'd finally finished bagging up the dope.

"Let's count it up to see how much we bagged up," Double J said.

"We gone put twelve blows in a pack. Whoever sells the pack gets twenty dollars and turns us in a hundred," Slim said.

"How much we gone pay people to run the joint?" Double J asked.

"We ain't worried about that right now. We gone run the joint ourselves. Once it picks up, then we'll put people in play to run the joint. We'll worry about what we gone pay them when that time comes," Slim said.

As they sat at the table counting up the dope, Slim began to wonder who they were going get to work the packs.

"Shiiit, who we gone get to work the joint?" Slim asked.

"My lil cousins gone work the joint. They been sweating me for the last couple days about when we gone open up the joint so they can work. They juveniles, so if they catch a case, they mommas can just sign them out from the police station," Double J said.

Once they finished counting the dope up, it came out to twenty packs and seven odds. They bagged up $2,070, not including the two blows in each pack for the pack workers to get paid.

Slim began doing the mathematics in his head. "So if we got two stacks off ten grams, then we gone get at least twenty stacks off of the whole hundred grams," Slim said.

"Shiit, we gone get more than that if the dope is a bomb and if it can take more than three pills a gram," Double J said.

"Yep, showl is. Go grab the tape outta the closet," Slim said. When he came back with the tape, Slim examined it. "Yeah, Joe, this tape perfect," Slim said.

They put twelve bags on a strip of tape then put another strip of tape over the bags. They put the tape over the bags in order for the dope to stay fresh, and so none of the workers wouldn't dip into the bags.

Double J and Slim grabbed the dope and a .45 automatic and went to pick up Double J's cousins and set up shop in Argale Park.

They posted up at the corners and in the park. One of Double J's cousins walked through the hood, telling all the dope fiends that they were passing out free dope in Argale Park. They dope fiends rushed to the park and spread the word. Two niggas who stood in the park, Double J's cousins, were passing out the samples to the dope fiends. A couple of hours later, the park was filled with dope fiends shopping for dope.

Double J and Slim couldn't believe how fast and how many dope fiends were coming to buy dope. Judging by the large amount of dope fiends who were coming to buy dope so soon, Double J and Slim knew they had some good dope.

"Damn, Lord, look how many dope fiends waiting in line to shop," Slim said.

"That's 'cuz the dope fiends that we gave samples to went and told everybody that we got good dope. Word of mouth travels," Double J said.

Within two days and one night, Double J and Slim sold the whole hundred grams.

"Lord, who we gone buy some more dope from?" Slim asked.

"That's a good question," Double J said.

As they continued to smoke and ride through the hood, they remained silent, trying to figure out who they'd start buying weight on the dope from.

"We gone have to start buying from Phill," Double J said.

"Phill got good dope, but it ain't a bomb," Slim said.

"How you know? You don't even use dope," Double J said.

"I can tell from the numbers his dope spots put up. His spots put up little numbers, but they ain't all that," Slim said.

"Who else we gone buy dope from? We gone have to get it from Phill," Double J said.

"Ride through Lexington and see if he out there," Slim said.

As they made it to Lexington, they saw Phill standing on the corner with a gang of niggas standing around him for his security.

"A Phill, check it out, Lord," Slim said.

Phill walked toward them smiling.

"Where's my money at?" Phill said.

"What money?" Slim asked.

"My g, what else? Money. I heard ya'll been tipping outta the park," Phill said.

"We'll get the money we owe you a little later on," Slim said.

"It ain't even been a whole week," Double J said.

"So what? I want my money ya'll been tipping," Phill said.

"A'ight we got you," Double J said.

"How much you'll sell us twenty-five grams of dope for?" Slim asked.

"Three thousand," Phill said.

"That's kinda high, ain't it?" Double J said.

"Naw, that's low. Anybody else I charge one fifty a gram. I'm only charging ya'll like one twenty-five a gram. At one twenty-five a gram, twenty-five grams suppose to come out to thirty-one twenty-five, but I just said an even three stacks. I ain't tripping over a hundred and twenty-five dollars. Look, right, I got shit I gotta do. Is ya'll gone need that twenty-five grams or not?" Phill asked.

"Yeah, we need it now," Double J said.

"I can't get it for ya'll right now, but I'll have somebody get it for ya'll later," Phill said.

"We gone have the g we owe you when you sell us the twenty-five grams, so we'll bring the whole four thousand with us," Slim said.

"I gotta go. I'll holla at ya'll later on," Phill said.

"Make sure we get them twenty-five grams today. Our joint is outta work," Slim said.

"I got ya'll. Don't worry about it," Phill said.

"A'ight, we'll holla at you," Slim said.

Later on that day, they were sitting in Double J's crib, chilling, when they got a call from Phill telling them that he was going to send his guy John over with the twenty-five grams, and that they needed to make sure the four stacks was counted up right before they gave it to John.

Once John delivered the twenty-five grams, they went straight to Double J's kitchen table and started bagging up.

"How many pills we gone use?" Double J asked.

"We gone use three first, to see how the dope fiends like it with three in it," Slim said.

Both of them began opening up the seventy-five capsules and dumping the inside of the dorms on the table, on top of the twenty-five grams.

"Lord, if this dope is any good, we finna be getting money like never before. Fuck spending our money. We need to stack our shit and get into some real estate, then we can leave the dope game alone," Slim said.

"Yeah, I agree with you on that. You know all these other niggas be spending their shit, then when it comes time for bound money, they can't even bound out for ten or fifteen stacks," Double J said.

As they continued mixing up the dope, they both imagined of riches.

They next day, they put the dope on their joint, and to their surprise, the dope fiends loved it.

They finished that twenty-five grams in one day, and was right back at Phill's buying fifty grams this time. Phill was a player who liked to see niggas doing good getting money, so he sold them fifty grams for fifty-five hundred.

Once they put that fifty grams out, their they thought it would slow down some because the dope fiends would know from the last twenty-five grams that they ain't selling the same dope they had originally when they first opened up.

Double J and Slim sat back at the end of the park, admiring the view of the customers swarming to buy dope. It was as if every time the pack worker would bring out a new pack, the dope fiends would swarm on him like flies to shit.

"How the hell is our joint tipping like this with Phill's dope, and his joint ain't putting up numbers like ours?" Double J asked.

"That 'cuz Phill and a lot of these other niggas be putting that crazy shit on they dope. That's why I told you we ain't gone use nothing but dorms. Phill nam still checking a bag, but their turnover rate is slower," Slim said.

Within a month, Double J and Slim were the men. Their joint was putting up numbers. They bought new Cadillacs, new sports cars, and all. Their team of workers constantly grew. Hos coming from everywhere were trying to get with them. Throughout it all, they continued to buy dope from Phill.

Chapter 3

One hot sunny day, Double J was simply bending blocks in the hood, listening to Al Green, puffing on joints that weren't laced with cocaine when he saw her from the back in those jeans.

Damn, this ho thick as hell, Double J thought.

He pulled up to her. Once he saw her face, he became disappointed. *Aw, this Cynthia dope fiend ass,* he thought.

Cynthia immediately opened the passenger-side door and just jumped in his car.

"Take me to your spot to get some dope," she said.

"I got a few bags in my pocket," Double J said.

"What are you doing, riding around with dope in your pocket?" Cynthia asked.

"What else am I doing with dope in my pocket?" Double J said sarcastically.

"I didn't know you shoot dope," Cynthia said.

"Tell somebody, and I'll kill you," Double J said.

They drove to a quiet block on the outskirts of the hood, pulled over, and parked.

Double J gave Cynthia the dope to hook it up and put in the needle.

Once she hooked the dope up and put it in the needle, she tried handing the needle to Double J.

"Naw, you go ahead. Ladies first," Double J said.

With her right hand, she shot dope into the veins of her left arm. As her eyes rolled in the back of her head, her entire body felt as if it were taken to a whole other planet. Afterward, she passed the needle to Double J.

With his right hand, he shot dope into the veins of his left arm. As Barry White's song "I'm Never Gone Leave Your Love" played on the radio, Double J felt as if he was soaring above the clouds.

Afterward, Double J dropped Cynthia off at home and went and met Slim at his crib to shake up some dope.

"I bought a hundred grams instead of fifty," Slim said.

"That's cool," Double J said.

"Start busting the dorms down. I gotta go use the bathroom. My stomach fucked up from smoking all them lace joints," Slim said.

Slim came out the bathroom and saw Double J sitting at the table, nodding and scratching.

"Damn, nigga, you look like you done had a dope," Slim said.

"Naw, man, I'm just sleepy," Double J said.

So they both began busting the dorms down.

Double J kept scratching and nodding at the table.

This nigga fucking around with dope, Slim thought.

"Lord, tell the truth. Ain't you getting high?" Slim asked.

"Nigga, you know damn well I been getting high ever since you've known me," Double J said.

"Nigga, you know what I'm talking about. Is you fucking with dope?" Slim said.

Double J paused for a little while. "Yeah, I fuck around with the dope a little," Double J said.

"What made you turn into a dope fiend?" Slim asked.

"I use to be seeing how dope fiends look after they get high. Some of them looked like it's the best feeling in the world. Some of them be looking like they're walking on the clouds or some shit. Then I start to see how the dope fiends do whatever it takes to get money for dope. That made me want to try some even more, 'cuz I knew it had to be some good shit. Once I tried it, it felt like heaven on Earth. No lie, I'ma be a dope fiend forever. I'ma get high 'til I die," Double J said.

Slim looked at Double J with a smirk on his face, thinking, *This nigga done lost his mind.*

"Niggas always trying to belittle dope fiends, when they get high they motherfucking self off all types of shit. A drug addict is a drug addict. It don't matter if you smoke weed, lace weed, toot cocaine, toot dope, or shoot dope—you still a drug addict," Double J said.

"I can agree with you on that 'cuz I smoke more lace joints than some people use dope," Slim said.

"We gone have to start paying somebody to bag up this dope. This shit a headache," Slim said.

"Straight up," Double J said.

In the days that followed, Slim began to admire how suave Double J was as he was high off dope. As he walked, talked, drove, ate, smoked cigarettes, every way he maneuvered was super cool when he was drunk off dope.

Before long, Slim began asking Double J a gang of questions on how it felt to be high off dope.

"You steady asking me about how it feels to be high off dope. My best answer is you won't know how it feels until you try it," Double J said.

"I'm scared of needles," Slim said.

"You ain't gotta shot it. You can toot it. But it ain't nothing look shooting it. As that dope run up your veins, it's the best high you'll ever experience," Double J said.

Slim was still hesitant to try dope. He let his pride get in the way. He knew certain people looked down on dope fiends.

A couple of days later at a club, with these two lesbian chicks he dated and paid for sex, he began wanting to try some dope again.

The lesbian chicks Tricey and Reese did it all besides dope. They snorted lines of cocaine, smoked lace joints and regular weed, and smoked leaf.

After downing a few drinks at the club. The girls sat at the table, snorting line after line of cocaine secretly, not in the public's eye.

"Damn, ya'll gone fuck around and OD," Slim said.

"That's only if you use dope. You ain't gonna find to many people OD'ing off cocaine, although you can OD off cocaine," Reese said.

"Have ya'll ever fucked around with dope before?" Slim asked.

"Hell naw, we ain't no motherfucking dope fiends," Tricey said.

"Shiiit, ya'll get high off everything else," Slim said.

"Everything besides dope," Tricey said.

"I heard that dope is the best high known to mankind," Slim said.

"Yeah, me too. But it takes control over your body. You gotta have it or your body won't be able to function right. And I heard the sickness is a motherfucker," Tricey said.

"I wanna snort a line or two to see how it feels," Slim said.

"So you wanna be a dope fiend?" Reese said sarcastically.

"Naw, I just wanna snort just one bag of dope to see how it feels. I want ya'll to snort it with me," Slim said.

"Hell naw," Reese said.

"Let's all three of us try it together," Slim said.

For almost an hour at the club, Slim tried convincing the girls to snort a bag of dope with him, and it worked. Slim pulled up to his dope spot.

"Tyrone, who working, Lord?" Slim asked.

"Ush working," Tyrone said.

"Why don't I see nobody shopping?" Slim asked.

"It's kinda slow right now, but you can best believe it'll be a gang of customers in line in no time," Tyrone said.

"Go get me three bags of dope, and hurry up, Lord," Slim said.

Tyrone rushed to go get three bags from Ush and brought it right back to the car. Slim took the dope and smashed off.

Slim parked a few blocks over from his joint. He tore open a bag of dope with his teeth and laid it on one of the girls' cigarette box. He tore a piece of the paper off his matchbox. He scooped up half the dope and snorted it like a pro. He sat the Newport box on the dash and leaned back in his seat to feel the total effect of the dope.

Within seconds, Slim had his door opened as he bent over, throwing up his guts.

If that shit gone have me throwing up like that, I don't even want none, Tricey thought.

30

After Slim finished throwing up, he snorted the other half of the dope off of the Newport box. He lay back in his seat and relaxed for minutes and began to feel the effect of being drunk off dope. The girls then snorted their bags.

As they lay there, high, they all thought within their own silent minds that dope was the best drug known to man.

Slim and both women wound up in a motel room. Slim's dick stayed on hard all the while. Slim had heard of the dope dick but didn't know that it was this intense.

For the entire week that followed, Slim snorted dope and smoked laced joints each day.

One morning as Slim went home, he got into it with his main girlfriend. She was tired of him spending nights out and cheating on her. She threw some hot coffee on him and swung at him a few times, leaving him with a few minor scars on his face. Slim stormed out the house and went to his joint.

Slim pulled on the joint, got two bags of dope, and pulled around the corner to blow them. He pulled back around to his joint sat on the hood of his car smoking a lace joint, thinking of all the good times, and the bad times he had, had with his girlfriend. He was still a little pissed off 'cuz she put her hands on him.

Double J pulled off, laughing.

"So I see you having problems with your girl," Double J said.

"How you know?" Slim asked.

"'Cuz I see you sitting there, faced all scratched up, looking crazy. I know you ain't let no nigga do it to you, because we'll be in war right now," Double J said.

31

Slim tossed the duck of the joint on the ground, bailed in with Double J, and Double J pulled off.

"Man this ho crazy. As soon as I walked through the door, she got to throwing shit, hollering, screaming, and swinging," Slim said.

"We all go through problems with women. That's been going on since the beginning of time," Double J said.

"Pull over for a minute. I need to take care of some business," Slim said.

Double J pulled over and put the car in park.

"What, you gotta piss or something?" Double J asked.

"Naw, I need to take care of something else," Slim said.

Slim pulled out his pack of cigarettes, then pulled out a bag of dope, opened it with his teeth, and poured it on the cigarette box. Double J remained silent. He couldn't believe what he was seeing. Slim then pulled out a small piece of a straw and snorted the entire bag of dope. Double J just sat there, looking at him like he was crazy.

Slim fired up a cigarette, looked at Double J, and asked, "Is my nose clean?"

"Yes, it's clean," Double J said.

"I can't believe you sat there and snorted a bag of dope after you been getting down on me after you found out I was getting high," Double J said.

"I been seeing how good you been looking when you high off dope. It be like you be walking on clouds or some shit, and I wanted that feeling. So I tried it, and I love it," Slim said.

"I told you it was a bomb, especially if you shoot it," Double J said.

Double J began smiling and pulled off, listening to Barry White's song "Ecstasy" as they drove to the mall.

Once they made it inside the mall, Slim became so happy at seeing all the hos there that he forgot all about what he and his girl had gone through earlier.

Slim wound up getting a gang of numbers from ho's.

When they entered this one shoe store, Slim couldn't take his eyes off this white chick. She was raw as hell. She was about five feet six, 140 pounds, a redhead, with black eyeliner around her hazel blue eyes, and red lipstick. She looked like a model or some shit. Slim decided to walk over and strike up a conversation with her.

Slim came to find out that her name was Angie. She lived on the north side of town. Twenty years of age with no boyfriend, no kids, or none of that. They exchanged numbers and went their separate ways.

All the rest of the day, Slim couldn't stop thinking of Angie. She just looked so good to him.

Slim went home that night and made up with his girl, and they got down from break-up to make-up sex.

Slim had never been with a white woman before but always wanted one. The next day, Slim wound up giving Angie a call. He thought she was gonna be on some phony shit, but he was wrong. She was real cool.

Slim and Angie starting hanging out together damn near every day. One of the things Slim liked about Angie was that she genuinely liked him for him. She wasn't like the other women that he'd fucked around with. They were only interested in money one way or the other. Angie wasn't.

Within a couple months, Slim left his main girl for Angie and moved in with her.

Within several months, Double J and Slim found their dope habits increasing. Having to spend more money to support their habits, for guns, for money on bonding their guys outta jail, and for having to pay more bills. This fortune and fame wasn't all what it seemed.

Chapter 4

"Roxanne you need a ride?" Slim asked.

"Naw, no, thank you. Here come my bus now," Roxanne said.

"Girl, get in. You ain't gotta wait on no bus," Slim said.

"No, it's okay. Thanks anyway," Roxanne said.

"Get in I insist," Slim said.

She wound up getting in. She looked around inside his Cadillac and noticed that it was super clean. The upholstery looked as if it was brand-new from the manufacturing place.

He put on some Teddy Pendergrass, "Turn off The Lights," as he pulled off. She immediately made herself comfortable.

"Where do you need me to take you to?" Slim asked.

"I need you to drop me off at the Cook County hospital," she said.

"What's wrong with you?" he asked.

"Ain't nothing wrong with me. I'm going to see my friend. She just had a baby," she said.

"Do you have any kids?" he asked.

"I don't have no kids, nor a boyfriend," she said.

Roxanne was one of Slim's grammar school friends that he'd only see every once in a while. On the rest of the short ride there, they began to reminisce about grammar school. They both admitted that they had been liking each other since grammar school.

As he pulled up in front of the hospital, he tried to park.

"Naw, you ain't gotta park. Just let me out in the front," she said.

"You need me to come back and pick you up when you get finished seeing your friend?" he asked.

"Naw, I'm straight," she said.

"What's up with later on? Let's go somewhere and fuck," Slim said as they both began laughing. "Naw, I'm just joking about fucking, but serious, let's get together and kick it later on," he said.

She reached into her purse and pulled out a little card with her phone number on it and handed it to him. "Well, here go my number just call me later on tonight," she said.

As she walked into the hospital, Slim just sat there, watching her in a daze, imagining what she'd look like naked.

Later on that day, Slim called her. The phone rang seven times. He didn't get any answer. He called her three more times, periodically, but still didn't get any answer. After calling her for the fifth time, he finally got an answer.

"Hello," she said.

"Hello, can I speak to Roxanne?" Slim said.

"Yes, this is me," she said.

"This Slim. Let me come through and pick you up," he said.

"Why you wait so late?" she asked.

"I been calling you all day. Ain't nobody answer the phone," he said.

"I been running errands for my granny. I been in and out the house all day. You got bad timing, you must been calling the times when I was out. Fuck it, come on over and pick me up. We'll kick it for a little while," she said.

He went over and picked her up. They rode around seeing the sights and reminiscing for about thirty minutes. Then he took her back home.

In the days that followed, he began sneaking off from Angie to hang with Roxanne almost every day for about two weeks straight. Each time they were together, she refused to give the pussy up.

One night, Slim was drunk off dope and liquor and had been smoking lace joints. He had his mind set on fucking the shit outta

Roxanne this particular night. He went to her house unannounced. She got dressed and decided to kick it with him anyway. As she entered his car, she smelled the smoke from lace joints.

"Why do you gotta smoke that stuff?" she asked.

"'Cuz it makes me feel good. You need to try it," he said.

"Never that. I'll never use drugs. I don't need drugs to make me feel good. I get high off life," she said.

"Getting high off life. I liked that. That sounded slick," he said.

As they cruised down the street, listening to Al Green's "Let's Stay Together," both of them became relaxed. She began slowly taking off her shoes to get comfortable. Outta the corner of his eyes, he looked at her, admiring her beauty.

"Let's go somewhere and chill out," he said.

"We already chilling out," she said.

"Naw, let's get a room or something," he said.

"Hell naw, we ain't getting no room or none of that until you get rid of her and let me become your main girl," she said.

"Who is *her*?" he asked.

"You know who she is. The woman that you go home to every night when you drop me off. The one you share your love and life with, the one you live with," she said.

He paused, trying to think of some good game to pop back at her but couldn't because he knew she was speaking the truth.

"But I been with her for a long time now and I just can't up and leave her," he said.

"Well, whenever you do decide to leave her, I'm willing to fill in her position and take on all responsibilities. And when I say all responsibilities, that's exactly what I mean," she said as she looked him in his eyes seductively.

As he cruised the streets, they peacefully listened to Al Green as thoughts of her in pornographic positions raced through his mind. He'd visualize his dick in and out her pussy, ass, and mouth.

He pulled up at a liquor store and parked. "Do you want me to get you something to drink?" he asked.

"A pink lemonade," she said.

As he exited the car, thoughts of him and herself walking down the aisle and getting married raced through her mind. She really liked him, but the only way he was going to get between her legs was if she was his main girl and only girl.

He came back into the car with two bottles of champagne, two cups, the pink lemonade, and a few bags of chips. He instantly popped open a bottle and poured some champagne in a cup. He handed her the other cup.

"Naw, I'm straight. You know I don't drink," she said.

"Try it out just for tonight. Just for me?" he asked.

"Thanks, but no thanks. I don't drink," she said.

She grabbed the pink lemonade, opened it, and began sipping on it like it was the best lemonade she ever had as they pulled off and began cruising through the town.

Roxanne reached into her purse and pulled out a pickle. She took the pickle out of its wrapper and began sucking on it like it was a dick. For a long time, she pulled the pickle in and out her mouth, sucking on it like she was trying to suck out all the juices from it.

Her reasoning for sucking on the pickle like that was to tease and entice him to wanna be with her and only her.

After cruising for a little, while Slim pulled into this vacant lot right next to this body shop where he use to get his cars spray painted at. The shop was closed because it was so late at night. As they began listening to Stevie Wonder's "Ribbon in the Sky" they started reminiscing about past times and began talking about things they'd like to do in the future. Slim began to roll a joint.

"Uhhhh, you ain't finna smoke that while I'm in here," she boldly said.

"Don't worry. I ain't gone lace it," he said.

"It don't matter if you lace it or not. You ain't finna smoke that while I'm in here," she said.

"I'ma crack the window," he said.

"You gone have my clothes smelling like weed," she said.

"I told you, I'ma crack the window," he said.

"Fuck it. Gone head," she said.

He finished rolling up the joint and set fire to it. He inhaled and exhaled the smoke harshly, which instantly boosted his dope high.

This shit a bomb, he thought.

He began to try to convince her for sex. She still wasn't interested. After he finished the joint, he downed a half bottle of champagne. As he was downing the champagne, he visualized her and him fucking and sucking each other. He began rubbing on her titties.

"Stop, boy! Don't put you hands on my titties. I ain't no ho. I don't get down like that," she said.

He then grabbed her left titty.

She snatched his hand away from her titties. "Drop me off! Drop me off!" she said.

In a frustrated, sex-craving rage, he locked his car doors and ripped off her shirt as she began yelling, kicking, and screaming.

He upped a .38 outta his jacket pocket and told her, "Bitch, shut the fuck up."

She immediately shut the fuck up.

Tears began to roll down her face as he snatched off the rest of her clothes then her panties in a storming rage. Craving for her pussy, he forced her to bend over the front seat and swiftly unbutton his pants and pull them down to his knees. He tried to force-feed her pussy his dick, but it didn't work because her pussy was too tight. His dick was too big to get in.

She continued silently crying and pleading inside her heart and mind for him to stop, but he didn't.

With the gun in his left hand, he spat in his right hand and rubbed it on the tip of his dick for lubrication. He worked on getting his dick in her pussy. After a minute, the tip of his dick finally slipped in. As he slowly worked his dick in and out her pussy to get it wet, he began thinking, *Damn, this ho pussy tight as hell.* Once her inner juices began flowing within, he commenced to slamming his dick in and out her pussy in a furious rage as she continued crying. To him it seemed as if every stroke, her pussy got wetter and wetter.

After the eighth pump, he put the gun in his jacket pocket and squeezed her waist, stopped pumping, and held his dick in her pussy until his entire nut was released in her guts. He took his dick out, grabbed her by the shoulders, and turned her body around to face him.

"Please, please, please stop," she cried out to him.

He backhanded her with his left hand.

"Shut up, bitch," he said.

She did exactly what he said. He pulled the gun back outta his jacket and put it to her head.

"Bitch, suck this dick," he said.

"Please, please, don't do this," she cried out.

"Bitch, suck this dick before I kill you," he said.

She began crying even harder and pouting like a little kid as her life flashed before her eyes. She wrapped her lips around his dick. She began to suck his dick like never before. The wetness of her mouth combined with her deep throat and his high made it feel so good that he instantly unleashed a glob of nut down her throat as she swallowed it all.

"Bitch, get in the backseat," he said.

"Please, please let me leave," she cried out.

He slapped her, busting her bottom lip.

She jumped into the backseat, frightened of what he'd do if she didn't do what he told her to do. She got on the backseat facedown, crying, lying flat on her stomach as he began raping her in the ass. She'd never felt so much pain in her life.

He never felt so much pleasure in his life. As he began nutting, he visualized the skies filled with fireworks similar to the Fourth of July.

He pushed her outta the car and threw her clothes on top of her. He smashed off, listening to "I'm Never Gone Leave Your Love" by Barry White.

At that very moment, Slim felt as if he ruled the world. He loved the power he achieved from raping her.

As Roxanne sat in the lot, scared to death and putting on her clothes, a car drove past slowly. There were two individuals in the car, an old lady and her daughter coming from church.

"Mom, it's a lady in that lot, naked," the little girl said.

"Hush up now. It ain't nobody in no lot, naked," the old lady said.

"It is, it is! We need to go back and help her," the little girl said.

Her mother looked at her, saw the sincerity in her words, and pulled over.

"Girl, if you have me to go back and it's not a naked woman there, Lord knows what I'ma do to you when we get home," the old lady said.

She made a U-turn and went back to see if there really was a naked woman. As she pulled up to the lot, Roxanne ran to her car with no shoes or shirt on—nothing but her skirt, with her hands over her titties—crying, "Please help me. Please help me." She jumped into the backseat of the four-door car.

"Oh my god, what happened to you?" the old lady said historically.

"He raped me!" Roxanne cried out in a loud voice.

The old lady immediately drove off. She and her daughter were in shock. They'd never experienced being in a situation like that before.

Nervous, scared, unfocused, and not being able to drive right, the old lady told Roxanne, "We gotta get you some clothes and take you to the hospital and report this to the police."

"No, no police," Roxanne said with authority.

Roxanne didn't wanna get the police involved 'cuz she knew Slim was a ViceLord, and she knew what ViceLords would do to her if they found out she told the police on one of their members.

"Please just take me home," Roxanne said frantically.

"You sure you don't want me to take you to my home and get you cleaned up first?" the old lady asked.

"Naw, please just take me home," Roxanne said.

"Where do you live?" the old lady asked.

Roxanne gave her her address.

The rest of the ride, all three of their minds were filled with sick satanic thoughts as each individual remained silent.

Once the old lady pulled up in front of Roxanne's house, she looked at her, feeling sorry and sad for her. "You sure you'll be okay?" the old lady asked.

"I'm going to be all right," Roxanne said with tears running down her face.

Roxanne got out the car with her hands over her breasts, running to her doorstep. She rang the doorbell twice, then her grandmother let her in as she fell to floor crying out, "He raped me!"

The old lady and her daughter rode home, crying and mentally thanking God that they'd never been attacked or raped before.

Roxanne's grandmother and the rest of the family pleaded with her to tell the cops, but she never did. Roxanne didn't want to jeopardize the safety of herself and her family. A couple of days later, Roxanne's family sent her to live in Atlanta with her aunt Rachel.

A few days later, Phill pulled up to Slim and Double J's joint, parked in the middle of the street, and bailed outta the car.

"You's a stupid motherfucker. You done went and raped that girl. Do you know how much time rapes carry? Nigga, ain't no ViceLord gotta rape no hos. Shiit, we got hos throwing us the pussy," Phill said as he ran back to his car and smashed off, burning rubber.

Double J looked at Slim with a frown on his face, with curiosity running through his head.

"Man, what the fuck is Phill talking about?" Double J asked.

"I don't know what that nigga tripping about," Slim said.

"What the fuck he talking about somebody got raped?" Double J said.

"I told you, I don't know what the fuck that nigga talking about," Slim said.

Later on that day, Phill came through and politely closed Double J and Slim down. He took their joint and gave it to one of the universal elites. Phill was tired of Double J and Slim's bullshit. They weren't paying him his g a week. They were leaving their workers in jail, weren't bonding them out. Nor were they standing on nation business. Then this nigga Slim went and raped a ho.

Phill found out about the rape through Roxanne's little cousins who were Renegade ViceLords. Roxanne's cousins were shorties. They weren't experienced in gunslinging yet, so they hollered at Phill to see if Phill would violate Slim. Phill lied and told them he'd violate them if they made sure she didn't press charges. Roxanne never pressed charges.

Now Slim and Double J didn't have a joint to sell their dope from. Slim was mad at Double J for the money he fucked up in the past. Double J was mad at Slim for committing that rape. Both of them were mad at Phill for taking their joint. Slim and Double J didn't talk to each other for almost a week.

Slim ended up going over Double J's crib to get back some of his belongings. Double J and Slim ended up making back up. They went to this dope spot on the low end that was supposed to have some good dope.

For the first time in life, Slim shot dope into his veins. The rush felt better than sex, snorting dope, smoking lace joints, or any other thing he'd experienced in life. From that day forth, Slim felt the true meaning of "High 'til I die," because Slim knew he'd forever be a dope fiend.

Chapter 5

Months later, January 1972

Slim and Double J had become straight up dope fiends. The majority of their cars was confiscated by the repo man. All their jewelry, leathers, and almost everything else they owned were either sold or pawned.

They had been accustomed to making fast money and spending it fast. They had an expensive cost of living. But by them steadily spending fast and not making it fast anymore, the money they did possess started to become extinct.

They had resorted to doing whatever it took to get high. They was on some straight dope fiend shit.

Slim had begun doing a little pimping to get money to buy dope. Double J was against soliciting women. Although Double J was true dope fiend, he still respected women.

One night, Double J and Slim had finished doing some petty hustling. Double J decided to spend a night at Slim's crib. Double

J usually didn't spend nights out—he'd go home to his wife each night—but not this night.

The next morning, Double J woke up outta his sleep as the sun shone on his face.

Double J went into the bathroom to take a piss and then went to Slim's room with one thing on his mind: getting some dope. As he walked to Slim's bedroom, he noticed that the bedroom door was partially opened. He didn't want to knock just in case they were asleep. So he looked in to see if they were awake, and yes, they were wide awake.

To Double J's surprise, there were Slim; Slim's white chick, Angie; and two black women, Reese and Tricey.

There Slim stood with his shirt off, face and head looking like he ain't shaved in years, nodding and shooting dope into his veins.

The three women were on the bed, doing the nasty. Angie was on all fours while Reese tortured her pussy from the back with this big black strap-on dildo as Tricey was on her knees holding Angie's head to her pussy. It was as if she was forcing her to eat her pussy.

"Bitch, stop acting like you ain't up with it and perform for the customers," Slim said.

Slim had turned innocent Angie into a drug fiend and a prostitute.

Double J burst into the room.

"Lord, what the fuck is you on? You done turned your main girl into a ho," Double J said.

"She's my bottom bitch," Slim said.

"But that damn girl is four months pregnant and you got her selling pussy to other women," Double J said.

The three ladies kept doing what they were doing as if Slim or Double J wasn't even there.

"Nigga, do you want to fuck her?" Slim asked.

"Naw, man! You know I'm married, but let me get some of that dope," Double J said.

Slim gave Double J the needle. As he watched the girls sexing, he shot dope into his veins.

Chapter 6

Slim started robbing solo. Sometimes Slim would stick people up by himself 'cuz he didn't want to share the profit with Double J or anybody else.

Slim was from the west side, so he'd go to the south side and rob 'cuz nobody really knew him out south. Late at night, he'd catch women walking by themselves on streets where there wasn't very much traffic and rob them for everything.

One time, he robbed this young Mexican lady who didn't speak very much English on a dark street at the back of a high school. After robbing her, she began cursing him out in Spanish. He didn't speak any Spanish but he could tell that she was saying some foul shit 'cuz of her body language.

In rage, he forced her into his car at gunpoint and pulled her into the nearest alley. He began punching her in her face like they were in a heavyweight professional boxers' match until she was knocked unconscious. He undressed her slowly with ease as if she were his actual girlfriend and as if he was getting ready for lovemaking.

Once undressed, while she was sprawled out over the front seats unconscious, he paused for a second, checking out her flawless body, which made his dick get hard as a brick. Violently, sexually crazed, with a frustrated, erotic craving, he took the pussy.

After nutting in the pussy, he turned her over and took her booty. Afterward, he dressed her and easily laid her in the alley, behind a big garbage can.

Six o'clock the next morning, she awoke from the barking of dogs. Slowly she stood up, feeling the pain of her battered face and the tissues in her pussy and ass that were torn. As she slowly began limping up the alley, she saw this man pulling out his garage. He was a police officer on his way to work.

She flagged him down, and after seeing her bloody face, he immediately put the car in park, got out and helped her get into the passenger seat of his car. Once she was in, he showed her his badge. She let out a great sigh of relief.

He then drove her to the county hospital to be examined by a doctor. On the way there, she told him the horrifying story about what had happened to her last night. Well, at least the part she'd remember before actually going unconscious. The officer was so pissed off that he said if he ever caught the individual who did that to her, the criminal wouldn't have to worry about going to jail. He'd probably shoot and kill the guy on sight.

The doctor's examination showed that she'd been beaten and raped in her vagina and anus. The doctor gave her twelve stitches in three different parts of her face.

The officer then took her to the police station to file a report. Once they made it within the police station, all the other officers stared at her in silence. The officer wound up filing a police report and taking pictures of her bruises.

She told the truth in the report. The report stated that she'd been robbed, abducted into a red Chevy Impala, taken into an alley, beaten unconscious, and left within that alley. All these things were done by a masked gunman.

Slim wasn't a dummy. The same night, he burned up that red Chevy Impala. He didn't give a fuck about that car. It was stolen steamer.

After that night, over the course of a month, Slim had committed four more rapes—three masked and one unmasked. So now the authorities had a sketch of what he looked like. But a sketch wasn't the same as an actual picture. As a matter of fact, the individual who did the sketching didn't do a good job of making it look like Slim.

Slim continued hanging out with Double J, robbing, thieving, pimping Angie, and doing whatever else it took to support his dope habit. Slim lived a double life that no one knew of. No one ever knew that Slim had secretly turned into a rapist.

Slim started to go up to the University of Chicago late at night to prey on the women coming from night school. At first, Slim couldn't rob or rape any of the women because the university's security cops would patrol the university frequently. Before long, Slim studied and learned the time the university security cops would patrol certain areas of the university.

One night after the students exited the first entrance of the school (which was on a side street), Slim saw her. A redhead stood almost six feet, makeup was flawless, and she walked like she was auditioning for a beauty pageant that she would definitely win.

Slim couldn't do anything to her because there were too many other students around.

He ended up stalking her for a few days until, one night, he caught her walking up the street by herself. He walked up to her unmasked. She saw him coming toward her. She thought he was getting ready to strike up a conversation in order to get a date or something. She was interested, because Slim wasn't a bad-looking guy although he was a dope fiend.

As Slim made it to her, he upped a chrome .44. "Bitch, you bet not say a word or I'ma kill your ass," he said fiercely and sincerely.

"Oh my gosh, oh my gosh, take whatever you want," she said as she handed him her purse. "Just please don't hurt me."

"Bitch, shut up and follow me. I ain't gone hurt you," Slim said. Slim walked her to his car at gunpoint and forced her in.

Once they got into the car and he drove off, she pleaded for him not to hurt her.

"I told you I ain't gone hurt you," he said.

In the back of her mind, she knew he was lying. What else would an individual abduct someone at gunpoint for in the nighttime? *I hope the police pulls on the side of us or pull us over for a traffic violation,* she thought.

Once they were far away from the campus, he pulled over and duct-taped her mouth, handcuffed her hands together at the back the same exact way the police do it, and blindfolded her.

He drove her to the other side of town, to his grandfather's home. Once he made it to his grandfather's home, he pulled up in the garage, which was in the back of the house. He escorted her from the garage and took her to the basement. The neighbors couldn't see what was going on because of the wooden fences that surrounded the garage and the back of the house.

In her heart and mind, she cried out for him to let her free.

Once he got her in the basement, he made her get on her knees as he uncuffed her hands then tied up her hands and feet with cords, leaving the blindfold on her eyes and the duct tape around her mouth. She'd never been so scared in her life.

Slim then went upstairs to the second floor to check on his grandfather who was sound asleep.

His grandfather was eighty-eight years old. He caught a disease when he was eighty that made him blind. His grandfather didn't have very much company besides the nurses who would come to check on him each morning, bathe him, feed him, and do other things of that nature. He'd even bribe a few nurses into having sex with him. His grandfather lived in and owned a two-flat building.

Slim figured that his grandfather's basement would be a good place to keep the female he kidnapped. Slim knew that he was the only one who had keys to the basement, that his grandfather didn't have company besides the nurses, and that his grandfather couldn't get up and move around on his own, so therefore nobody would be coming into the basement.

Even if Slim's grandfather did have lots of company, his grandmother wouldn't let nobody in the basement, 'cuz his grandfather used to be a gangster back in his younger days and kept a lot of guns he had from back in the day in the basement.

For years, his grandfather stopped renting out the first floor to tenants, because some tenants didn't pay their rent on time.

After Slim saw that his grandfather was sound asleep, he went back into the basement and stared at this hot pretty young white lady he kidnapped. He couldn't stop staring at her. Although she was tied up, blindfolded, and her mouth was duct-taped he still enjoyed watching her beautiful features.

Slim began to slowly undress his victim.

She began crying. As tears ran down her face, she was thinking like, *Damn, he finna rape me.*

She tried to move her body, struggling for him not to rape her, but it was like a mission impossible.

As he slowly undressed her, his dick got hard at the sight of her freshly shaved pussy. As he upped his dick and entered her pussy with force, it was like heaven on earth for him. To her it was like a living hell. As he began taking the pussy from her, he started slapping on her ass cheeks, calling her every disrespectful name in the book. In a sick, sexual, perverted way, he was really enjoying himself.

All night, he did almost every sexual act known to man, from fingering her pussy and ass and sucking her titties to sticking his dick in her pussy and ass. And for the first time in life, he stuck his tongue up a woman's ass.

A couple of days later, on a cold winter's night, Slim and Double J was sitting in a car in Garfield Park, finishing shooting and snorting dope and smoking lace joints, wondering to themselves what they could do to make some more money to get high.

"Lord, what we gone do to get some more dope?" Slim asked Double J.

"I don't know. That's a good question," Double J said.

Both men remained silent for a brief moment, enjoying their highs and trying to figure out how they was gonna get some more dope.

"Let's steal some cars," Double J said.

"Hell naw, man, that's a headache. First we gotta find some cars to steal, then we gotta find somebody to buy the parts off it," Slim said.

"Well, when you come up with something better, then let me know," Double J said.

"I'm tired of stealing cars, boosting clothes, and pimping. All that shit takes too long. I be needing instant money. I love to get high," Slim said.

"Yeah, I feel you, 'cuz I'm tired of the same shit. I like robbing dope spots 'cuz you get money and dope right then and there. But we done robbed damn near every spot out west. And the ones we didn't rob was because they had guns on it or they was patting us down," Double J said.

"Let's order a pizza," Slim said.

Double J turned his head, directly facing Slim, looking at him like he was crazy. "Damn, you went from trying to figure out how to get some money to ordering a pizza," Double J said sarcastically.

"I'm talking about robbing the pizza man," Slim said.

"Robbing the pizza man is burned up. Everybody's been doing it. Majority of the pizza men don't even have that much money on them, just in case they do get robbed," Double J said.

"They gone have some money on them. Whatever he have, it'll be enough to get some dope, and we gone get something to eat, all for free," Slim said.

Double J began laughing and thinking *This nigga Slim is silly.*

"The average pizza man ain't gone come to certain hoods," Double J said.

"Yeah, I know. We gone go to one of them nice-ass hoods and call him and give him one of the addresses. Once he makes it to the address, before he even gets a chance to knock on the door, here comes me to take his shit," Slim said.

"Sounds like a good plan to me, so, uhhh, what we waiting on?" Double J said.

Slim pulled off and rode for about twenty minutes to a hood that wasn't ghetto.

He pulled on a super-quiet block and got the address from the house that was on the corner. They then went to the pay phone and ordered two large cheese pizzas with most of the toppings.

As they went back, they parked in front of the house with the address they gave. It was as if both of them could actually taste and smell the pizza. They couldn't wait to get paid and wrap their lips around them pizzas.

In no time flat, the pizza man was pulling up and parking right behind them. They saw a Hispanic-looking dude get out the car with two big pizzas in his hands.

Slim jumped out the driver's side of the car with gun in hand. "Bitch, give me them motherfucking pizzas and empty your pockets," Slim said.

The pizza man did exactly what Slim said with no hesitation, scared to death.

"Bitch, get in the car and drive off," Slim said after robbing him.

The pizza man got in his car and pulled off, damn near causing a car collision once he made it to the intersection.

Slim got into the car and pulled off, going in the opposite direction from the pizza man.

Once they made it back to the hood, they parked and began eating pizza and counting the money.

"Damn, Lord, this pizza is a bomb," Double J said.

"It came from Home Run Inn," Slim said. Slim continued counting the money. "We got two hundred and eighty dollars," Slim said.

"Give me my half," Double J said.

Slim counted out a hundred and forty and passed it to Double J. What Double J didn't know was that Slim only pulled out some of the money outta his pocket. He played for the rest.

They continued eating pizza on their way to the dope spot. They spent majority of that two-eighty getting high that night.

Two days later, while Slim was asleep, he had a dream that two midget women—one was black, one was white—were taking turns sucking on his dick. When he was about to unleash a load of nut, he awoke to the reality of his girl Angie lying there asshole-naked, sucking on his dick, and it felt so good to him. As he unleashed his nut down Angie's throat, he began rubbing on her titties and pregnant belly.

Afterward they both stood up as he looked her straight in the eyes and told her, "See, that's why I love you so." Then he kissed her on her left cheek and hugged her tightly.

They ended up getting high then getting dressed and going to a breakfast joint. While they sat at the table eating breakfast, a glimpse of the woman's face he had tied up in his grandfather's basement flashed in his mind.

Damn, I done left that lady tied up in the basement for two days with nothing to eat, Slim thought.

Slim and Angie ate, and then Slim immediately dropped her off at home. On his way to his grandfather's home, he stopped at McDonalds to buy the lady he'd kidnapped something to eat.

Once he made it to his grandfather's basement, his victim could hear his footsteps and began yelling and crying, but no one could hear her cries because of the duct tape around her mouth. She surely thought that eventually he'd kill her.

For the last two days, she'd been living a nonfiction horror story. She'd tried to get loose, to escape, but always came up unsuccessful.

Slim took the blindfold off and said, "How are you doing sleeping beauty?"

Her eyes got wide as she became more scared than ever by this maniac.

"I'm going to take this tape off your mouth to feed you. If you start to make any noise, I'm putting the tape back on your mouth and you won't eat," he said.

She nodded her head up and down in agreement. He put the blindfold back on. As soon as he took the tape off her mouth, she began yelling at the top of her lungs, "Somebody, please help me! Somebody, please!"

Before she could finish yelling, he put the tape back around her mouth. "I guess you don't wanna eat," he said sinisterly.

He pulled off his pants, got on his knees, and began rubbing her clitoris with his left hand and fondling his own dick with his right hand. As Slim began to get erect and the moisture of her pussy started to be felt on his hand, he got behind her and shoved his dick in her pussy. The tightness combined with the moisture and him being high felt great. He slammed his dick in and out her pussy showing no remorse for it.

Afterward he went up to the second floor and checked on his grandfather. His grandfather was doing okay.

He went back to the basement.

He began whispering in his victims ear, "I'm going to ask you one more time, do you want to eat something?"

She began shaking her head up and down.

"If I take this tape off your mouth and you start hollering and shit, I'ma make sure you don't eat for a long-ass time," he said.

He took the tape off her mouth. She didn't say a word. She was starving, and she knew that no matter how loud she'd holler, no one would probably hear her.

As she opened her mouth wide, all Slim could do was visualize his dick going in and out her mouth.

With a split-second decision, he decided to use some type of tool to feed her 'cuz if he used his hands, she might try to bite off some of his fingers. He looked over at the barbecue grill, walked over, and opened it up. There sat a tool used to grip and flip meat. He went to the sink, rinsed the tool, and went back over and began feeding her the cold McDonalds.

She ate the food like she was a starving little kid from one of them third-world countries.

After she finished eating, she began to cry out to him, "Please, please let me go. I'll give you anything. My family is rich. They'll make sure you get compensated for letting me free."

He put the tape back over her mouth, thinking about the compensation money. *If I let this ho go and try to get compensated, my ass gone be in jail forever,* he thought.

He forced her to the floor, lying flat on her stomach, and dived into her pussy full force, slamming his dope fiend dick in and out of her tight pussy as hard as he possibly could while admiring the view of the way her ass cheeks would jiggle each time he'd bounce up and down on her.

Slim and Double J's dope habits had started as a monkey on their back and turned into a real live silverback gorilla.

They began robbing any- and everybody, from cab drivers, pizza men, corner stores, hood restaurants, and dope dealers to old people and all. Every single day, they'd rob many different people, just to get high.

A month after the robbing spree began, Chicago police were on the hunt for Double J and Slim 'cuz they'd robbed so many people. Some of the corner stores and hood restaurants, they'd robbed more than once, and witnesses had positively indentified Double J and Slim.

Now Double J and Slim were on the run.

Double J's wife had filed for a divorce. She didn't wanna be with no dope fiend–ass nigga. So Double J was living from house to house. A majority of the people he lived with was some of his dope fiend buddies.

Slim, on the other hand, had told Angie to move in with one of her friends, and he himself stayed in his grandfather's building. Slim assumed that no one from the hood knew where his grandfather lived, so he figured his grandfather's home would be a good place to hide out in.

A couple of weeks went by. Slim had just finished shooting up some dope and went back to his grandfather's basement. He fed his victim. After she finished eating, he put the tape back over her mouth. He got naked and took off her blindfold to finally let her see his full body naked.

He laid her flat on her stomach and went off in her ass for the first time. She yelled, screamed, and cried tears. Slim couldn't hear her yells, screams, or cries because of the tape around her mouth.

In the midst of Slim having his way with her ass, the basement door flew open.

"Freeze! Police!" Almost thirty police officers flooded the room. The police immediately snatched Slim off his victim, handcuffed him, and told him that he was being charged with twenty separate counts of armed robbery.

They untied the kidnapped woman. To the police, she seemed to be almost lifeless, with her booty bleeding as if she were stabbed in it. Once they took the duct tape off her mouth, she jumped up, crying, "Oh my gosh, thank you for rescuing me," she said.

They wrapped a blanket around her as she told her nonfiction horror story.

As the police searched the basement, they found all seven of the old guns his grandfather had and put them on Slim. Now Slim had twenty counts of robbery, a kidnapping, a sexual assault, and seven unlawful use of weapons. He was never getting outta jail. And when and if he did, he'd be an old man.

They came to find out that the lady he'd kidnapped and raped repeatedly was Suzan Armstrong, a twenty-seven-year-old English teacher.

On the ride to the police station, the police beat his ass. They gave him two black eyes, a busted nose, and knocked out two of his teeth.

Once he made it to the police station, they ended up putting him in a lineup. Five more business owners picked him out of the lineup for robbing their businesses. One other woman picked him out of a lineup for raping her. She was the one he raped with no mask on.

Once he made it to the Cook County jail, he felt the full effect of being dope sick. He sat in the bull pen, crying out to Allah, Father of the Universe, as he threw up his guts. It was as if twenty maniacs were all poking away at his stomach with small sharp objects. He'd never felt so much pain in his life.

Once he finally made it to the dec the guys screened him to see if he was gang affiliated. Once they found out he was a ViceLord, they checked to see if he had any status. Once they found out he wasn't a universal elite, they showed him the ropes and introduced him to all the brothers.

They next day, they gave him a knife and put him on the ViceLords' security.

A few days later, Slim got in touch with his grandfather and Angie. His grandfather started sending money, and Angie began visiting on his visiting days.

After a few weeks of being in the county jail, Slim began to notice the ViceLords and everybody else on the dec start straying away from him.

One morning Slim didn't wake for breakfast. He overslept. While asleep, three big dudes came into his dark cell and began beating the shit out of him with man-made weapons. Slim didn't stand a chance of fighting back.

One man took his pants off and took his booty. Slim's screams were like horrifying echoes as the tissue in his booty hole got torn.

The ViceLords and all other gangs under the fin were against homosexuality; therefore, a ViceLord or any other gang under the fin wouldn't rape another man or women. But other gangs didn't give a fuck about homosexuality, especially if a man let another man rape him. The other gangs that weren't fin ball looked at it as, if a nigga let another nigga rape him, then he needed to be raped. A majority—if not all—gangs in Chicago was against raping women. That's why they raped him—so he could see how it felt to be raped.

Afterward Slim ran to the ViceLords, body filled with pain, barely able to see because of his eyes being covered with blood, crying out for the ViceLords' assistance.

The ViceLord and everybody on the dec laughed at him as if he were a comedian on stage and they were the audience.

Slim looked around, crying out for help. As they laughed, he couldn't believe what was going on. The dramatization was that of a horror flick for Slim.

One ViceLord shouted out, "We don't fuck with no raper man."

Slim then ran to the COs. The COs called 10-10 and within seconds, a gang of COs flew on the dec, whupping the inmates' asses and putting the dec on lockdown and escorted Slim to the jail's hospital.

Slim received seventeen stitches and ten staples. The staples were in his head. The stitches were in various places in his body, including his ass. He got fucked up real bad. Slim told the COs he didn't know what happen. He didn't know who did that to him. Slim didn't believe in telling the police shit.

Slim was escorted back to the dec, which was still on lockdown, to get his things. Slim went to the cells of a few of the ViceLords who were universal elites. "Lord, ya'll gone let them niggas get down on me like that," Slim said.

"You know we don't get down like that," one of the universal elites said through the cell door.

"Like what?" Slim asked.

"We heard you was locked up for raping hos. We against that, Lord. We ain't ever honoring you as no ViceLord no more. Shiiit, since you been raped, you're a faggot now. Wherever you go in jail, you ain't gone get no respect for letting them niggas rape you."

Slim went to other ViceLords' cells, and they didn't even wanna talk to him, disgusted by him being a raper man and letting niggas rape him.

Once Slim made it to PC, right then and there, he saw two of his homies from the streets. They had fucked up some people's drugs and commissary and checked into PC 'cuz they couldn't pay them.

Slim immediately noticed there were a lot of faggots in PC. He didn't like being around the faggots.

After a couple of months in jail, Slim's grandfather died. That was so fucked up for him. His grandfather was the only family he ever really had. He never knew his real dad. His mom had been dead for many years. She was killed in a car accident when he was a kid. The rest of his family lived down south, and the little family he had that lived in Chicago was phony as hell.

He couldn't even attend his grandfather's funeral 'cuz it cost $1,500 for the county jail to escort inmates to funerals.

A couple months after Slim's grandfather's death, Double J was found in an abandon building, dead, with a needle stuck in his arm. He died of an overdose of dope.

Slim came to find out that his girl Angie was fucking around with a nigga from the hood.

It was as if Slim and his entire world were beginning to fall apart.

Chapter 7

Angie began feeling labor pains. "My water just broke. I'm going into labor," Angie told her lover, Todd.

Todd's eyes got wide. Todd immediately drove her to the hospital.

After seven hours of labor, Angie gave birth. Once the baby was released from Angie, the female doctor stated, "It's a beautiful little girl. She's beautiful enough to be a queen." The baby weighed six pounds and two ounces.

Angie had stop getting high when she was seven months pregnant so the baby wouldn't have any drugs in her system so DCFS wouldn't take the baby from her. Therefore, the baby came out healthy.

Angie looked in her beautiful little baby's eyes, and it was as if she could see the queen her daughter was destined to be, so she named her Queeny.

Queeny had gray eyes. Usually when a baby is born with gray eyes, they don't remain that color. They change to hazel, green, brown, even blue, as the baby gets older. Queeny had brown hair and high yellow skin. You could look at her and tell she was mixed with white and black.

A couple weeks after the baby was born, Angie took Queeny to the county jail to see her dad.

Slim came out to the visiting room and saw the baby in her hands. He didn't even know that she had given birth.

"Here is your daughter," Angie said through the tiny holes in the glass.

Slim instantly began smiling, looking through the glass of the visiting cage as Angie took the blanket off the baby's face. "She so cute. What is her name?" Slim asked.

"I named her Queeny because she's destined to be a queen," Angie said.

"I didn't even know you had the baby. When did you have her?" Slim asked.

"A couple weeks ago," Angie said.

"She's so cute. She looks just like you," he said.

"She looks more like you to me," Angie said.

As the baby opened her eyes, it was as if he could see the sunrise. Reality started to set in. Slim began thinking like, *Damn, I'm never getting outta jail. My child is going to be a bastard.*

The visit didn't last long 'cuz Slim couldn't stand to be around Angie and Queeny knowing he'd never see the streets again in order to actually be a part of their lives.

Angie and her boyfriend Todd began living in this studio apartment on the north side of Chicago.

Angie had stopped getting high when she was seven months pregnant, but once she had Queeny, she started right back, getting high at an all-time high. She always had regrets for letting Slim turn her into an addict 'cuz she knew drugs were her downfall, but she loved to get high.

Todd and Angie had devoted their lives to the usage of drugs.

One late night, Todd was coming back home from the twenty-four-hour liquor store.

As Todd opened the door, someone pushed him into their apartment.

Todd turned around, on the verge of laying hands on whoever pushed him, but turned around and saw that big-ass gun.

"Nigga, step back," the gunman said fiercely in a Jamaican accent.

Once Todd stepped all the way into the apartment, Angie saw the gunman step in behind Todd, and she yelled out, "We finna die."

The gunman immediately shut the door, leaving it unlocked. He then put his index finger over his mouth, shushing Angie. "Be cool and be quiet. I ain't gone hurt ya'll. I'm just gone rob ya'll and leave ya'll here tied up so ya'll can't call the police once I leave," the gunman said sincerely.

Rob us? We ain't got shit, Todd thought.

The robber took off his hoodie. He was black as hell, with Jamaican dreads in his head.

Aw shit! This is one of those crazy-ass Jamaicans, Todd thought.

Todd instantly began sizing him up. Just in case the guy slipped up, he'd try to knock the gun outta the Jamaican's hand and take it.

The gunman stood about five feet seven, and Todd could tell that he had been to the joint before 'cuz he was swole to death.

Within seconds, another man dressed in black came in. He looked as if he could be the other guy's big brother. The second man came right in and blindfolded Todd and Angie. He then made them get on their knees, duct tape their hands behind their backs, duct tape their legs together, and put duct tape around their mouths.

Angie and Todd weren't worried about what the robbers would do to them because they honestly believed that the robbers would only rob them and then leave. Todd and Angie were more worried about how they was going to get free from that duct tape.

The first robber began to notice Queeny sitting in her rocking chair asleep. As he stepped closer to her, she awoke, opening her beautiful eyes.

She's so cute, the robber thought.

Both men upped knives and began stabbing away at Todd and Angie's flesh as Queeny watched emotionlessly because she was only a baby and didn't know or understand what was going on.

Outside, it began to rain and thunder as the so-called robbers continued stabbing Todd and Angie up over thirty times apiece, leaving them for dead.

Within minutes, the killers left the two bodies there, laid out in their own puddles of blood that filled the carpet.

They left Queeny lying there in her rocking chair, smiling and listening to a Fisher-Price toy that played baby music.

As they left, they didn't bother to take anything because they weren't robbers. They were sent to kill. They ran out, leaving the door open.

A few years earlier, Todd used to buy dope from some Jamaicans up north but wound up having them front him some dope, and he fuck the money up. He thought he'd never see the Jamaicans again.

But he was wrong. One of the Jamaicans saw him coming out of their apartment building and sent killers.

The next morning, one of the neighbors had been in and out her apartment all that morning for various reasons and noticed that their door had been open all that morning.

The first time she saw the door open, it really wasn't any concern to her. But after seeing it open for hours, she knocked on it to see if everything was all right. After not getting a response from her hard knocks, she opened it and saw the bleeding dead bodies and began screaming. It was as if the screams echoed for blocks and blocks.

She ran to her apartment, scared to death, as if a killer were actually after her. She went into her apartment, locked the door, and put the chain on it. Ran to the phone and dialed 911.

After the fourth ring, the dispatcher answered. "Hello, this Chicago police dispatcher. May I help you?"

"It's two dead people. It's two dead people," she said, breathing heavy, crying, scared nervous.

"Calm down, ma'am. Now can you repeat yourself?" the dispatcher said.

"Two of my neighbors are lying in their front room, dead. Somebody killed them," the lady said.

"Ma'am, give me the address, and I'll send help over immediately," the dispatcher said.

"1170 N. Jarvis," the lady said.

"What apartment or floor?" the dispatcher asked.

"Apartment 2B," she said.

"Help will be over shortly," the dispatcher said. "Did you see who did these murders?"

"No, damnit! I don't want to talk. Send the police over here," the lady said.

Before the dispatcher could say another word, she'd hung up the phone.

This was a prominently white neighborhood; therefore, the police were there in no time.

Two rookie cops entered the apartment first and became sick to their stomachs. As all the other police entered and saw the dead bodies, it was nothing to them. They seen dead bodies many times before.

One of the rookie cops, who was a white woman in her midtwenties, began crying "Why, why, why would somebody do this?" as tears ran down her face.

They took Queeny to the hospital to see if everything was all right with her. Queeny was okay. The authorities tried to find Queeny's family and came up unsuccessful.

Angie's family mainly lived in other states and didn't even know a child existed. Those who lived in Chicago or near Chicago didn't want to have anything to do with the baby because she was partially black. They were racist as hell. They even disowned Angie when she first began fucking around with Slim. They felt like Angie had disgraced their family name.

Once Slim found out about Angie being killed, he felt like he had nothing else worth living for.

The next morning, after Slim found out about Angie, a female officer came through, doing the 11:00 a.m. count. She immediately noticed that some of the two-man cells only had one inmate in, which was fucking up her count, 'cuz she was used to counting by twos.

Slim was in the cell by himself. He had no celly. His last celly had gone home a couple of days ago.

The woman CO came to count Slim, looked through his cell door, and there Slim was, asshole-naked, hanging from a homemade rope he made from bed sheets.

The CO began instantly screaming. She started screaming so loud that she woke up everybody on the dec. All the inmates began looking outta the chuckhole of their cell doors as the other COs rushed in to see what was going on.

Once the COs made it to her, she said in a loud screeching voice, "He hung himself."

The COs instantly keyed the door open and took him down from the rope.

One CO knew how to check his pulse. The CO checked his pulse, looked at the other officers with water in his eyes, and said, "He's dead."

The other CO got on his walkie-talkie and called for doctors to come and attend to Slim's body.

One of the other COs grabbed the big piece of paper that was taped to his stomach and read it out loud: "That's one thing about life is that at the end of it, we must all die, and I chose my own time to die. I'll see you in hell where my sinful soul will dwell."

The room got silent, as his handwritten words were a reality check for the CO's. They knew that one day we must all die.

Police ended up turning Queeny over to the custody of DCFS.

Within weeks, this elderly lady, who was a landlord in one of the buildings that Angie and Slim lived in together before, attended both Angie's and Slim's funerals and found out Queeny was with DCFS. The elderly lady tried to locate Slim's and Angie's families, and she came to find out that neither Slim's nor Angie's family gave a fuck about Queeny. The elderly lady, Christine, took it upon herself to obtain custody of Queeny.

At first, DCFS didn't want to give Christine custody of Queeny 'cuz she was old and because she wasn't married. One of Christine's grandkids was lovers with the twenty-seventh ward alderman, and he helped Christine obtain custody of Queeny.

Queeny brought joy and sunshine to Christine's life. Christine had never been happier than she'd been in her entire sixty-five years of living.

Christine died at the age of seventy when Queeny was only five. When Christine died, it was as if a piece of Queeny died inside. Although she was really young, she still felt the pain of losing Christine. Queeny never knew her mom and dad or any of their family. All she knew was Christine. Christine treated her as if she was her very own daughter.

After Christine's death, none of her family members wanted to adopt Queeny. One of Christine's daughters, Roseline, ended up taking custody of Queeny. Roseline was Christine's only daughter who turned out bad. Roseline was an alcoholic and tooted raw cocaine.

Inside Roseline's home, it smelled like a dead body was there. Roseline didn't know or understand what clean meant. Roseline's house wasn't even fit for wild animals to live in.

Daily, Roseline would beat Queeny for petty reasons. Queeny cried from Roseline's beatings. They would literally haunt her in her sleep. Some nights, she couldn't sleep, constantly awaking from nightmares of Roseline's beatings. Queeny always promised herself that if she ever had kids, she'd show nothing but love and would never put her hands on them under any circumstances.

Chapter 8

A few years later, although Queeny was still experiencing difficulties with Roseline, she had no other choice because this was all the family she really had.

Queeny maintained good grades in school. She was a real smart kid. The only problem she had was that she got into many fights in school because they assumed she was white. The school she went to was all populated by blacks. Although she was mixed with white and black, she mainly looked white. The immature kids would make racial slurs and continue picking on her.

She got tired of going through bullshit at home with Roseline, and at school, with the kids bullying her, she began starting fights, becoming the bully herself. If anyone at school would create any problems, she'd instantly start a fistfight with anybody, releasing all her anger and frustration on them. In no time, she began to get respect from the kids at school.

King Phill would see Queeny walking to school some mornings. Phill would look at Queeny and feel sorry for her. Phill knew her story. He knew her mom and dad was dead, and that Roseline was a drug addict.

Queeny knew Phill as well. Ever since she could remember, within her young life, Phill always helped her out with Christmas gifts and school supplies among other things.

One day, while Queeny was walking to school alone, he decided to walk her to school. "Queeny, slow down. I'ma walk you to school," Phill said.

"Why don't you drop me off in your car?" Queeny said.

"Somebody in my car. I'm just gone walk you to school," he said.

Phill began to pour his heart out to her and give her a little game. "I like seeing you go to school, go to college and do something with your life. You're destined for fortune and fame. Never settle for anything less than the best. Don't never let a man rule or ruin your life. Live your life like the queen of all queens," Phill said.

___

When Queeny was twelve, Roseline became a prostitute.

One night, Roseline went out on the ho stroll to sell some pussy and never came back. People in the neighborhood assumed she was killed by a trick, but her dead body was never found and no one witnessed her being killed. There were only assumptions.

King Phill had his sister Rachel get custody of Queeny.

Rachel was an alcoholic, but she didn't use drugs and she took care of her business, doing the best she could to raise her own kids. Rachel had five kids of her own. Rachel's two teenage boys were eighteen and seventeen years old, and her other three kids' (who were girls) ages were fifteen, thirteen, and eleven.

Queeny began smoking weed with Tom and Paul, Rachel's two sons, and hanging on the streets a little, seeing the actions and transactions of the ViceLords. She began being infatuated with the ViceLord nation. The ViceLords showed out as far as selling dope and getting money. Most women are attracted to money. She was intrigued by the mass amount of men who was representing VL. They wore their hats to the left and dressed in the slickest gear. There were many other gangs in Chicago, but the ViceLords were mostly adored by the women.

Queeny didn't need any finances because Phill and Rochelle made sure she was straight financially. But with her being young and dumb, she began to get involved in criminal activities, not only for the extra money, but for the excitement as well.

At age fourteen, Queeny and some of the niggas she went to high school with would go to clothing stores and steal. They'd do the thieving while Queeny would be talking to the store workers for long periods as a distraction method. They'd take the clothing and sell them to dope dealers. The money was cool, but Queeny was full of greed and wanted more. She became victim to the fast life and fast money.

Before long, she began selling dope with Tom and Paul. Tom, Paul, and Queeny knew that if Phill found out, they'd be in deep shit. King Phill didn't want any of his family members using or selling drugs, but he didn't attempt to stop the men in his family from using or selling drugs, although he didn't like it. As far as the women were concerned, he'd go crazy if he'd found out they were selling or using dope.

One day, Phill noticed that Queeny was hanging on one of the spots in the hood during school hours. Phill began snapping at

Queeny. He told her that every time school hours were in process, she'd better be in school. And when she got outta school, she still couldn't hang out at any dope spots.

The same week, he caught her hanging at one of the hood's dope spots—this time, after school hours.

She made up an excuse, claiming that she was passing by and began talking to a nigga she went to school with. Phill told her that if she didn't get her act together, he'd stop giving her money. That was his way and other street niggas' way of punishing people— ceasing to provide them with finances—but that didn't work. She continued to hang at the dope spots and continued selling dope.

At this time, within Chicago, a majority of the dope spots were behind closed doors. But Tom and Paul's dope house continued to get raided by the police; therefore, they decided to start selling their dope on the corners. Therefore, they wanted Queeny to work, because the police wouldn't suspect her as the one selling the dope. The only problem is that she was a candidate for a stickup. She got robbed twice in one week.

Tom and Paul came to the realization that she was still a little girl, and there was no need for her to be out there. Tom and Paul knew that she could get shot by the stickup man, catch a juvenile case, and a lot of other bad shit could happen.

Tom and Paul started telling her that she didn't have to sell dope, because they'd give her money and Phill would too, only if she behaved herself.

She'd told them that she enjoyed selling dope, which was the truth. She was selling dope partially for the money and partially for the thrill and art of it. The boys told her that the streets were cold and unfair. She then told them that if they didn't want her to work for them, there'll be others who would let her work.

The boys knew in the back of their minds that she was right. They both became upset that they even introduced her to this aspect of the street life.

So she wouldn't be on the spot, they then started letting her go to the table to bag up dope. Sometimes they'd be at the table with her. Sometimes she'd do it by herself. The pay was greater for her, and there was less risk of her getting robbed or catching a case. And Phill would never find out about her going to the table.

One day, Queeny was walking home from school through a dope spot that wasn't indoors. It was out on the corner, and she saw a member of the ViceLords shooting at a rival gang. This was her first time seeing a gun being shot. She liked the excitement.

The night before, at a party, the ViceLords and GDs got into a fight over one guy who felt a female's ass. The two men ended up fighting. One man was a ViceLord and the other one was a GD. It led to a mass amount of both gangs fighting in the club.

The club had metal detectors; therefore, they couldn't get in with their guns or any other weapons. Once the crowd dispersed out of the club and went to their cars, one of the ViceLords opened fire and wounded one of the GDs. He didn't die, but he was seriously injured, which led to a street war against the ViceLords and GDs.

During this war, she heard so much gunfire it became like music to her ears.

During this particular war, she started carrying guns, not for her personal use, but to only transport them for Tom and Paul or other members of the ViceLords. By her being a female, it was less chance for the police to harass her than they would a man.

She liked carrying guns, she craved for the day she'd be able to squeeze the trigger of one.

One time, one of the guys who worked for her brothers purchased a fully loaded .32 revolver from a dope fiend for forty dollars. Normally when an individual from the streets buys a gun, they immediately shot it to see if it'll shoot with no defects, but he didn't. He wanted to wait until nightfall.

Queeny was there when he bought the gun. She wanted to hear how it would sound. She adored the sound of gunfire. He told her to wait to tonight, and he'd let her shoot it.

Her eyes opened with amazement, thinking *I can't wait until tonight.*

Later on that night, he let her shoot it. She thought it would be difficult to shoot. All along, it was like chewing bubble gum.

The first shot felt and sounded so good to her that she unloaded all six shots into the sky.

Chapter 9

A fter months progressed along, the ViceLords and the GDs'
war had long ceased. Now the ViceLords were into it with
each other. The Insanes were into it with the Renegade ViceLords.
This was unusual because all branches of ViceLords worked
together. But one of the Insanes robbed one of the Renegades for
ten thousand in drugs.

Queeny wanted to be involved and do some shootings, but they
wouldn't let her because she was a female, and so young. In reality,
they didn't take her seriously as far as doing any shootings. More
and more, Queeny would gaze at the skies viciously, lusting for
the day she could unload a gun. Not in the skies like she once did
before but in a human being this time.

Although Queeny was so young, still in her own heart and
mind, she felt as a queen over all. Queeny knew the meaning of
power, and she wanted it in abundance.

Once Queeny initially started bagging up dope for Tom and
Paul, she stopped hustling directly on the dope spot for a little
while.

One day, Queeny started back hustling on Tom and Paul's joint just to get a little extra money and was robbed for the third time.

Once her brothers Tom and Paul found out about it, they told her once again to stay away from the dope spots. She didn't listen.

Tom and Paul got tired of their dope spots getting robbed, so they started paying a man two hundred each day to stand on security with a gun just in case the stickup man came by. The security man shift would consist of twelve hours.

By this time, Tom and Paul had all sorts of people in play to run their dope spot. Tom and Paul basically didn't do shit but collect money.

One day, Queeny decided to get up with Tom and Paul's workers to take the security position of holding the gun just in case the stickup man came by.

She took this position for two reasons: To be in possession of the gun so she could bust it if the stickup man ever came by—she could shoot the shit outta him or them. Also, so she could show the guys that she had more heart than them. While standing on security, she prayed that the stickup man would come by.

She took this security position on a saturday. She knew that if Phill caught her on the spot on a saturday she'd think of some lame excuse of why she was hanging on the spot and knew she'd have less problems from Phill, being that it wasn't a school day.

The security hours revolved around her curfew. The security hours were twelve hours a day. Usually 8:00 a.m. to 8:00 p.m. then 8:00 p.m. to 8:00 a.m. Her curfew was at 10:00 p.m., so she'd work the shift from 8:00 a.m. to 8:00 p.m.

She ended up working security on saturday and sunday.

Sunday morning, a stickup a man robbed the workers. With her being on security, she was supposed to make sure the stickup man didn't even get a chance to rob the workers, but he did.

As the stickup man ran to his car after robbing the workers, she saw him running with his gun in hand as the workers yelled, "He just robbed me!"

She unloaded a .38 into the back window of his car. She didn't hit him although she was really trying.

When this incident occurred, it was broad daylight. Everyone saw it.

She immediately went to a house in the hood to stash the weapon and went home.

Although she didn't hit the stickup man, she didn't find this out 'til later on.

She sat at home, traumatized, thinking that she'd shot and killed him and that she'd be going to jail for a long-ass time.

The entire day, it was the talk of the hood, how Queeny's young ass popped that pistol.

In this day and age, in the 1990s, you didn't have too many females shooting guns like the females in the 1980s. The women in the 1990s were more caught up in being pretty girls, mainly dressing fresh, partying, and having fun.

Once Tom and Paul heard about it, they went home snapping on her.

"Girl, we give you money and momma and Phill give you money and we let you go to the table for us. What the fuck was you even doing out there on security for a funky two hundred dollars?" Tom said.

"I wasn't doing it for the money. I was out there just in case the stickup man came through," Queeny said.

"Why the fuck is you worried about the stickup man for?" Paul asked.

"Because I'ma queen, and I got my own ways of doing things," Queeny said.

"Girl, you done lost your motherfucking mind. A queen, my ass! You betta hope that guy ain't get shot or killed. If he did, your ass gone be the queen of jail," Paul said.

The next morning, King Phill heard what she'd done. Phill knew it was Tom and Paul's dope spot; therefore, King Phill was intelligent enough to know that the Tom and Paul had something to do with it, one way or the other.

Phill confronted Tom and Paul and didn't even give them a chance to explain. Phill had both Tom and Paul violated by other members of the ViceLord nation.

Phill wanted to beat Queeny's ass, but he didn't because she was a girl. He was against putting his hands on females, especially a little girl whom he considered to be a part of his family.

The next day, Phill told Queeny to pack her shit—she was moving. He took her to the house of one of his other sisters who lived on the south side of town.

After several weeks, Queeny ran away from the crib of Phill's sister Sheila. Sheila was rude and disrespectful at the mouth and too controlling. She knew if she didn't leave from Phill's sister Sheila's crib they would end up fighting.

Queeny went back to the West Side to live with one of the girls she went to school with, Susan.

Queeny didn't have too many girlfriends because she was the true essence of a tomboy and mainly hung around with the guys. But she and Susan were real cool. She knew her since grammar school. In grammar school, she spent a lot of time with Susan and her family. Once she got to high school, she didn't hang out with her a lot. She'd mostly kicked it with her in school.

She knew she couldn't stay with Susan's family for too long. It'd only be temporarily—maybe for a few weeks or a couple months at the most.

It was cool for Queeny to live with Susan because Susan lived close to the school and they had some of the same classes together.

Once King Phill found out that Queeny was missing, the first thing that came to his mind was that something bad had happen to her. Not once did it cross his mind that she'd run away from home.

King Phill began looking for Queeny relentlessly. He also told everyone he knew that if someone had any information of her whereabouts, he'd pay heavily for that information.

A couple of days later, one of Phill's tightest homies saw her going to school and went and told Phill. Phill sat in his car outside of Queeny's high school, waiting for her to depart.

Once school was over, he saw Queeny exit the door among a gang of other students. When he first saw her, he couldn't believe it.

Queeny began walking past his car and didn't even notice it. Phill lowered his window. "Queeny, get your ass in this car," Phill said.

She jumped right in the passenger seat.

"Girl, where the fuck you been? I've been worried about you, thinking something bad happened to you," Phill said.

"I've been over my friend Susan's house. Me and your sister weren't getting along. Your sister don't know how to treat people," Queeny said.

Phill wanted to curse her out, but he knew that it'd only make matters worse. Phill drove her around for hours, talking to her on a civilized level, telling her that she was a queen and a beautiful human being and that she deserved better than being some hood rat or some low-life drug addict.

Phill knew that on the route she was going, she was destined for self-destruction.

"Your momma and daddy's demise came from them running the streets and using drugs, and I know you ain't ready to die. And I ain't ready to bury you in a casket. I love you as you're my very own. I always cared about you even when you were a little girl. I want for you the same things I'd want for my very own daughter if I had one," Phill said.

"I know in a few more years you're gonna be grown and you'll have to make your own decisions, but I hope that I can inspire you to be a great woman instead of a nobody. You're destined to be a queen in your own mind in time," Phill said.

She ended up moving back into Rochelle's home. She stopped selling dope and getting into trouble for the time being. Although she continued to smoke weed, she stayed away from the streets.

Chapter 10

Queeny stayed out of trouble for a couple of years. Phill would spend lots of time with Queeny because he loved her and wanted her to be a success story of being an honest working citizen and a respected businesswoman.

By the time Queeny was sixteen, Phill's prince Black was checking her out, but Black knew if he got involved with her, Phill would be pissed off. Prince was a snake in the flesh of a human, a dope-fiend killer-slash-stickup-man. King Phill made him the prince for one main reason. Phill knew that Black would run the ViceLord mob with an iron fist and wouldn't take any bullshit.

Black even started hanging out with Queeny. Phill didn't mind. He figured Queeny was like Black's goddaughter or younger sister. Although Phill knew Black was a snake, he didn't think he'd ever snake him.

When Black and Queeny would hang out together, they'd smoke weed and do average shit like going to the show, shopping, or just riding around bending blocks.

Around this time, Queeny's grades began to excel. She began to get a higher learning, with plans of being a college student.

Around the time Queeny was seventeen, she was riding in the car with Phill. Phill was going to pick up some money that a nigga owed him. He usually had someone to take care of his drug business. The reason why he went this time to take care of this transaction himself was because he was only collecting money.

The reason he took Queeny with him was because she was already in the car.

Phill had been sweating this nigga to pay him some money he owed him. He'd fronted him four and a half ounces of raw cocaine. But the nigga who owed him had been bullshitting on paying him. The nigga finally beeped him, and Phill called him as they made arrangements for Phill to come pick up the money he owed him.

Once Phill made it to his destination, he parked in front of the building the nigga gave him the address to.

As soon as he finished parking, the nigga who owed Phill the money ran up to the car in a madman rage, shooting and hitting Phill in the head three times.

At first, the triggerman was unaware that Queeny was in the car until he start shooting up Phill. After he shot Phill in the head, at the third shot, Queeny frantically tried to open the door and get out of the car but didn't make it out. The triggerman shot her twice in the neck as she fell out the door, onto the ground. He then shot her once in the back and fled the scene of the crime. In the back of his mind, he was positive that he had killed Phill and Queeny.

Silky Mac was the killer. Silky Mac was one of Phill's long-term homies. Phill knew Silky Mac almost all his life and would've never thought he'd cross him, especially not for something small as a four and a half.

Silky Mac began using more cocaine than selling and ended up fucking up Phill's money. Usually, when Silky Mac would pay Phill, he'd be short. This time, Silky Mac had fucked up more than half of the money. Silky Mac knew that if he didn't pay Phill, Phill would have his joint robbed repeatedly or possibly have him shot or killed. Silky Mac had clout for the ViceLords but not like Phill.

Silky Mac figured that if he killed Phill and no one knew about it, he would get away with the murder and paying Phill, and he wouldn't have to worry about anyone doing anything to him.

Phill had so many people attending the funeral that it was as if a celebrity had died. Silky Mac was one of the pallbearers.

After Phill got killed, Phill's followers and Silky Mac and his guys walked the streets like zombies day and night, night and day, trying to find out any information on who killed Phill.

If they'd ever found out who killed Phill, that individual or anyone else who was related or even affiliated with him would have to die. Unfortunately, the only witness was Queeny, who was in critical condition.

Silky Mac heard that Queeny survived. Silky Mac was only a little worried, although he assumed she didn't know him. He also figured that it happened so quickly that she wouldn't recognize it was him even if she did see him again.

Several days after the funeral, everyone was still sad. Although Phill was a gang chief, he did a lot of good things for people: paid people's ways through college, helped people with bills, even stopped people from getting killed or being endangered by his own ViceLord members. He even forced some people to rehab to stop their addiction. Phill had some bad ways, but he had some good ways as well.

For the next past couple weeks, Phill's followers among others including Homicide had been visiting Queeny daily anxious to know who the killer was, but she was still in critical condition.

By a twist of fate of luck, this particular day and time, Prince Black came to the hospital shortly after her recovery. Black was the first one who saw her after her recovery. This first thing that came out of Black's mouth was "Who did this to you and Phill?"

"Silky Mac," Queeny said.

"Silky Mac," Black said in disbelief, surprised. "Which Silky Mac?" Black asked.

"Conservative Silky Mac," Queeny said.

"You sure it was Silky Mac?" Black asked in disbelief.

As Queeny attempted to tell him she was sure it was Silky Mac, Black mentally blocked Queeny out and paused, thinking *I only know one Silky Mac* and *Why would he kill Phill?*

Queeny began to vividly tell Black the horrifying story, and Black was focused, listening attentively. As she talked, it was as if Black could visualize the ordeal as if he was actually there.

"Phill had got a beep, looked at his beeper, and told me to grab the cellular phone outta his glove compartment. He dialed the number off his beeper. Once the person on the other line answered, Phill asked him 'Who is this?' Then Phill was like, 'Silky Mac, what the fuck took you so long to get up with me?' I don't know what Silky Mac said. Then Phill asked him, did he have all the money he owed him? Phill then hung up and drove to where Silky

Mac was. We drove to this big brown building and parked, and then Silky Mac came outta nowhere, shooting."

Black paused as his mind went blank for a few seconds and closed his eyes, visualizing the bullets ripping through Phill's flesh, putting him to death.

Black then opened his eyes.

"You sure it was Silky Mac? How do you know Silky Mac?" Black asked.

"I know it was Silky Mac because I heard Phill say his name over the phone, and I know Silky Mac personally 'cuz he fucks with my friend Susan's mother," she said.

"Did you tell anybody about what happened?" Black asked.

"Naw, I'm just waking up after I got shot," Queeny said.

"Don't tell nobody, you hear me, girl? Don't tell nobody," Black said.

"A'ight," Queeny said.

Black immediately left the hospital, filled with rage. Once he entered his car, he remembered that he had pictures of Silky Mac from the past that they took at a club.

He went and got the pictures and went right back to the hospital.

Once he made it back to the hospital, he noticed that Rochelle and her daughters were there. Black sat down and chilled out, impatiently waiting for Rochelle and her daughters to leave in order to show Queeny the pictures to see if she could positively ID Silky Mac.

Once Rochelle and her daughters left, Black showed her the pictures and told her to pick out which individual was Silky Mac. Each picture displayed a group of niggas on it. Black had already had it on his mind that if she could pick out Silky Mac outta the groups, then she was right in knowing who exactly took Phill's life from him.

With no hesitation, she picked out Silky Mac on each and every picture. "You bet not tell nobody about Silky Mac killing Phill. If they ask who killed Phill and shot you, tell them you don't know 'cuz it happened so fast," Black told her.

"I know how this shit go. He took Phill's life. Now you'll take his—eye for an eye," Queeny said.

Black slightly smiled, thinking, *This girl got a little game under her belt.*

"I gotta go. I gotta run some errands," Black said.

As Black sat in his car outside the hospital, he tried to put all the puzzle pieces together. He remembered what Quenny said, that he owed Phill some money.

But Phill's a good nigga. He would've given him some work or fronted him some shit to get on. Aw, this nigga must've been fucking up the money and couldn't pay Phill back. So he told Phill to meet him outside the hood to collect, and once Phill came to collect, he killed him, not knowing that Queeny would be with him. This pussy-ass nigga came to the funeral, was even one of the pallbearers, and roamed the streets with us, looking for the one who killed Phill, and all along he was the one who did it. He did all this shit so he wouldn't be suspect as the killer, Black thought.

Black yelled out, "Bitch-ass nigga!"

At first, Silky Mac wasn't hiding out because he assumed Queeny didn't see him when the shooting occurred, and if she did see him during the shooting, she didn't know who he was. But now Silky Mac was hiding out. He started to get nervous about if Queeny would recognize him or not.

What Silky Mac didn't know was Queeny already knew exactly who he was.

Silky Mac was the chief of the Conservative ViceLords, which was a branch of ViceLords that didn't have a large number of members.

Black told all the IVL to kill any CVL they see and that anyone who killed Silky Mac will be granted fifty thousand. Once people heard about that fifty thousand, everybody and their momma was looking for Silky Mac. Most people didn't give a fuck about avenging Phill's death. They were only interested in that fifty thousand.

Less than an hour later, there were casualties of street wars. The Insanes went everywhere the Cs hung out at and caused bloodshed. What made this war different was that the CVLs didn't know they were in war at first. Therefore, they'd be somewhere chilling. Seeing members of the Insanes walk up, the Cs would assume that they were just coming to kick it or buy some drugs. All along, they were coming to commit bloody murder.

The streets were filled with madness. There was no peace or sleep, nothing but continuous gunfire, death, and destruction. It was like something out of a religious book. How the creator brought certain villages and towns to an end. Even the police were nervous to patrol the streets.

The next day after Black gave word to the IVL to slay Silky Mac or any other CVL they came across, the CVLs began to retaliate. The CVLs still didn't know what the war was about. The only thing they knew was that the Insanes were coming through, fucking them up, and that they must battle. The Cs didn't stand a chance. The Insanes were deeper and had more heartless killers.

Usually, when two different branches of ViceLords had a problem, they'd resolve it by putting someone in violation. It was rare that it resulted in gunfire, and when it did, it didn't last long. The chiefs would squash the problem. But this war would be a never-ending bloodshed because a king was killed. Never in the history of ViceLord existence was a king killed. Usually the worst that would happen to a king was he'd get lots of time in the state or federal prison or die of a disease or even natural causes.

At this point, Silky Mac had gone to a family reunion a day before the war kicked off.

A day after the war, he called one of his homies' house in Chicago for nothing more than to tell him that the family reunion in Memphis was fun. When he called his homey Tim's house, before he could get a chance to explain how good the reunion was, Tim began snapping out.

"Lord, we warring with the Insanes. It's like Vietnam in the streets. I ain't never heard this much gunfire," Tim said.

"What ya'll warring with the Insanes for?" Silky Mac asked.

"I don't know, man. They just been coming through, shooting motherfuckers in broad daylight as if they don't even give a fuck."

"Make sure all the brothers are secure with guns and shit. I'll investigate to see what the problem is," Silky Mac said.

Silky Mac called one of his hos from the hood and asked her why was it war in the streets between the Cs and the Insanes. He knew she'd know 'cuz she was the hoods' spy and detective. She stayed in everybody's business. Coincidentally, she knew what the war was about 'cuz her little brother was an Insane.

"They warrring 'cuz they think you is the one that killed Phill," she said.

"I ain't kill Phill," Silky Mac said.

"That's what they think. Black told the Insanes to kill any CVL they see on sight, and he got a price on your head for fifty g's," she said.

"Why would they think I killed Phill? I got love for Phill. Phill was my guy," Silky Mac said.

"I don't know, but I know that they think you were the one that killed Phill," she said.

Silky Mac immediately hung up the phone without even saying bye.

Silky Mac sat for hours, trying to figure out who told Black that, because no one was around to witness the murder. Silky Mac knew that he was in for a world of trouble and figured that he'd better stay properly placed away from Chicago, in Memphis.

Weeks passed along, and Silky Mac was still nowhere to be found.

Now not only was Black and the Insanes looking for him, Homicide was too. They came to find out that an old lady and her granddaughter had witnessed the entire murder of Phill and the attempted murder of Queeny. At first they didn't wanna tell anyone because they were too scared that Silky Mac would kill them if he found out they'd told the police on him. But both the mother's and granddaughter's consciences got the best of them. Feeling guilty, they decided to inform the authorities of what they'd witnessed. After Homicide found out Silky Mac was the killer, they went out on an all-out manhunt.

Homicide began repeatedly questioning Queeny, was Silky Mac the one who killed Phill and shot her? They'd continue to show her mugshots and other photos of Silky Mac. She continued to tell them that she didn't actually see who shot her. Homicide could get a conviction with just the old lady and her granddaughter as witnesses. But they knew that with Queeny, the old lady, and her granddaughter as witnesses, Silky Mac would get found guilty beyond reasonable doubt.

Queeny still never told anyone but Black that Silky Mac was the one who did it. Black didn't want Silky Mac to go to prison. Black wanted to take his life as he took Phill's life. Black believed in the old-school rule that under no circumstances were you to work with the police. Other people believed that if you testified on someone as far as witnessing to family member or friend being shot, then you weren't actually snitching, because they shot a loved one. But in reality, if an individual worked with the police in any shape, form, or fashion, you're still a stool pigeon.

Through it all, Queeny told no one of Silky Mac being the one. The only reason that people in the streets knew that Silky Mac was the one who killed Phill was because Black told everybody. Black never told anybody that Queeny told him that. The only reason Black told people was so that they'd avenge Phill's death. Black couldn't just tell people to shoot up the Cs without telling them that Silky Mac killed Phill.

Approximately one month after Black gave word to have all the Cs and Silky Mac whacked, Silky Mac was still nowhere to be found. The CVLs, on the other hand, were mostly dead, killed by the Insanes. And those Cs who weren't killed got fucked up so bad that they wished they were dead. The CVLs who were still alive, they were hiding out. Some even relocated to other states. During this war, many Insanes and some Cs were caught in cases of violence, such as murders, attempted murders, arsons, and gun cases, among other shit.

One day, Queeny asked Black, "Did you find Silky Mac yet?" That was her indirect way of asking Black, did he kill Silky Mac bitch ass yet? She knew that if Black ever caught Silky Mac, he'd be in the history books.

Black told her, "No, I can't seem to find him."

"Did you check on their spot out south?" Queeny said.

Black paused, looking at Queeny, clueless.

"What spot out south?" Black asked.

"The Cs got a block out south," Queeny said.

Black looked at Queeny angrily, as if he'd wanted to bite her head off.

"Why didn't you tell me about this block out south?" Black said.

"I assumed you'd find Silky on your own," she said.

"Where is this spot out south, and how do you know about it?" Black asked.

"It's around Seventy-Third and Green," she said.

"Ain't no ViceLords around there. That's all GDs and BDs," Black said.

"The Cs got one block around there. I know about this block. Years ago, Phill sent me to live with his sister out south for a little while. When I used to walk to the store, I remember seeing Silky Mac standing on Green," she said.

"How do know if it's one of the Cs' blocks? He could've knew some people around there and was, rotating, with them," Black said.

"I could tell, because everybody had their hats to the left. And Silky used to be standing around dictating things."

Black immediately left Queeny to his destination at Seventy-Third and Green. Black went by himself in an unmarked car.

All the while, driving over there, he assumed that Queeny didn't know what she was talking about, because that area was filled with GDs and BDs who hated ViceLords.

Once he finally made it to Seventy-Third and Green, he noticed that all the niggas on that block wore their hats to the left. Then he noticed two of Silky Mac's guys who were from out west on the block as well.

Damn! Queeny knew what she was talking about, Black thought.

As he drove back to the hood, he wondered how they get a block in the heart of the GD's. He then figured it out. He'd saw Silky Mac at a club one time with some guys who had their hats to the right. Black could tell that the niggas were ballers as far as getting money from the way they dressed; Silky Mac walked over to Black, introduced his cousins to him. Black shook their hands, and they went their separate ways.

Black figured out that Silky Mac's family were GDs who had juice for the GDs, and let Silky get a block in their hood.

Later on that night, Black and eleven of his guys went through Seventy-Third and Green with fully loaded semiautomatic weapons, killed ten men, and wounded seven others. This incident had the Chicago Police Department leery because they'd never seen that amount of casualties and injuries all at once in over forty years within Chicago since Al Capone's Saint Valentine's Day Massacre. After that day, the CVLs on Seventy-Third and Green were no more. Those who weren't out there to witness the mass bloodshed were glad and decided to do other things with their lives after all the killings and imprisonments of other CVLs throughout the city in this short period. Some even flipped to join other gangs. Others left the street life alone. Some even became Christians.

Approximately six months later, Homicide found Silky Mac in Memphis, Tennessee, at a family member's house. He was brought back to Chicago's Cook County Jail, eventually convicted of the murder of Phill and attempted murder of Queeny, and sentenced to fifty-five years in prison.

Queeny never testified against him in court, but the other two witnesses did. Silky Mac didn't last long in prison. He was stabbed to death by some of King Phill's loyal followers. 'Til this very day, you'll never see too many CVLs in the streets of Chicago or in the Illinois prison system due to Silky Mac's rat play and slaying of King Phill.

Chapter 11

Black started spending more time with Queeny. He'd always liked her, and every time he'd see her, it was as if he could see the loving memory of Phill. He didn't want to start fucking around with her 'cuz she was so young. He also knew that if Phill was living, he wouldn't try to fuck with her, so now he didn't want to do it since he was dead and gone.

One night, Black was drunk off dope and had smoked weed with Queeny. Black couldn't take his eyes off her. It was as if he could look into her eyes and see his future. He became hypnotized by her beauty. Before he knew it, he and Queeny were in his apartment, asshole-naked, enjoying passionate, hardcore sex as his dope dick thrust in and out of her pussy for hours.

Before long, Queeny moved into Black's apartment. Phill's sister didn't want her to live with him because she didn't want her to be involved with a man who was over twice her age and a dope fiend. But it was nothing Rochelle could do about it, because in reality, Queeny wasn't her real daughter, and Queeny was several months away from being eighteen years old, so she was almost legally an adult. Rochelle knew Queeny would have to make her own decisions in life. Queeny claimed that there was nothing going on between her and Black, but Rochelle wasn't a dummy. It was obvious they were fucking.

Black was forty years old and in love with this seventeen-year-old girl.

Black and Queeny had sex an unnumbered amount of times. But once they moved in together, their sex life got even greater.

Queeny was a virgin before Black and her got together. Once she moved in, he began turning her out, eating that pussy all the time, sticking his tongue up her ass, and everything. Sometimes all he'd do was eat her pussy.

She'd always had it in her mind that she was a queen. No matter what she'd did, she wanted to be dominant as a queen. Sometimes while Black was fucking her, she'd talk dirty to him as if she were the ruler. Sometimes she'd say things like "You pussy motherfucker, you can't fuck no harder than that. You fuck like a bitch." Most men would've snapped after such statement, even within sex, but Black loved it. Also while he'd be eating her pussy, she'd talk to him dirty, saying things like "Suck this pussy, you old dirty bastard, you."

Black loved it. It was like music to his ears. It took him a long time to convince Queeny to suck his dick. Once he finally convinced her, she'd do it all the time willingly. She even liked doing it just for him. She really liked it when they'd go down on each other at the same time.

Chapter 12

Six months after living with Black, Queeny was eighteen years old, still in high school, with plans of finishing high school and going off to college. But things didn't go as planned.

During the six months they lived together, Queeny caught Black cheating with other women many times.

Black even slapped her twice despite the domestic violence act. That really pissed her off, because she still felt as a queen, and queens don't get slapped around. Black even got her pregnant twice. The first time, she had an abortion. The second time, she had a miscarriage. She had no plans on having children until she was older, ready, and stable. As a kid, she'd always promised herself that she'd be the best parent to her children, if she'd ever have any.

She decided to stop fucking with Black and to move outta his apartment to be on her own. She wanted to move back into Rochelle's home but decided that it wouldn't be a good idea. First of all, Rochelle probably wouldn't let her move back in after she told her not to leave in the first place. She also felt that she was grown and had to live on her own, coinciding with her feeling like a queen, and claiming herself to be the ruler of her own domain would first consist of her having her own apartment. The other part of her domain would be controlling her heart, mind, and body.

She ended up finding a part-time job after school, which wasn't sufficient enough to pay the bills for an apartment although she lived in the ghetto.

She wound up convincing Tom and Paul to let her shake up dope for them so she could maintain the bills and continue to work part time and go to school. At first, Tom and Paul said no as far as her bagging up dope for them was concerned, but they changed their minds 'cuz she'd been doing good for a few years, and they knew she needed money to survive on her own. They even agreed that once she finished high school, they'd help pay her way through college.

Queeny's apartment was a few blocks over from Rochelle's home. Through it all, Queeny maintained a close relationship with Phill's family. She felt that she was compelled to be around Phill's family because they'd treated her with love and support as if she was their very own family. She made sure to show up each holiday and family event and simply spent as much time around them as possible.

After Queeny graduated high school, she wanted to go straight to college but wasn't totally financially stable. She could've gotten a student loan, and Tom and Paul told her they would help her out financially when she did go to college. She understood how the student loan went. But once she started college, she wanted enough money so she wouldn't have to work or bag up dope. She wanted to be able to focus on her schoolwork with no interruptions with a job or bagging up dope. She didn't want Tom or Paul to pay her way through college 'cuz she knew that when most people took care of another individual, they'd try to control their life. So she didn't go to college. She figured she'd go to college once she was financially stable, maybe in a year or two.

She ended up quitting her part-time job and began selling dope again. Tom and Paul pleaded with her not to go that route and to go to college, she didn't listen. She continued bagging up dope for them and running the joint. Running the joint consists of dropping the dope off to the pack workers, collecting the money, making sure the joint was secure, and basically making sure the entire dope spot was run correctly.

Chapter 13

By the time Queeny was nineteen, she was a supreme dope fiend and smoked lace joints. Until this very day, nobody knew how she'd started using drugs. She never shot dope into her veins, but she snorted lots of it.

In reality, she started snorting dope because it was as if her world had come to an end. Everyone she loved either betrayed her, mistreated her, or was dead, or a mixture of all three. And she never knew her real mom and dad or family. The old lady who took her in after her mom and dad were deceased was dead. Phill was also in the grave. Phill's family treated her like family, but to her, it wasn't the same as being loved by her very own family. She loved Black, but Black cheated on her frequently and slapped her around a few times. That's why she started using drugs to ease the pain of the harsh reality of this dilemma called life.

If you ever saw Queeny in person, you'd look at her and she'd be the definition of beauty. Beauty should've been her name. People who would see her snorting or purchasing dope would see her and be amazed that this young lady was a dope fiend.

At the point when Queeny was now twenty years old, Phill's family had stopped fucking with her because she was out there, bad as a dope fiend, and couldn't be trusted. Now she was on her own.

She began hanging with the dope-fiend stickup men. Although she was a woman, they respected her like one of the guys.

At first, they'd only use her to set up stickups and split the money evenly with her. With her being an attractive young female, people who hustled on the dope spots wouldn't even think that she'd set them up to get robbed. She and the other dope fiends robbed dope spots because they were an easy target and an easy way to maintain their dope habits. They'd send her to buy dope to case the joint. She'd buy dope, usually it'll be someone who liked her, and he'd talk to her for a short period of time. All the while while they're talking, she was casing the joint. She'd then go and tell the stickup crew how many workers were in the joint and tell them her assumption of if they had guns out there or not.

Before long, she'd wanted to do the robbing herself. She felt like a queen and wanted to be dominant over men, as usual. The guys didn't understand why she wanted to do the robbing herself, because when she cased the joints they'd split the money and dope evenly.

The guys respected her but didn't know if she'd fold under pressure. They didn't know how she'd react if the individual she was sticking up had a gun himself and reached for it, or if she'd hesitate in shooting if an individual wouldn't relinquish the money or dope. But they figured like, fuck it—if she wanted to do the sticking up, then that would be less work for them.

Her first stickup was a weed spot. A weed spot was easier to rob because they wouldn't get robbed often, so they weren't watching out for the stickup man that much. Around that particular day and age, the average stickup man was a dope fiend who preyed on dope spots to rob in order to use the dope they'd get from the robbery, and it was more money involved in robbing a dope spot, 'cuz most dope spots tip way harder than a reefer joint.

She performed like a pro in robbing the weed spot.

In the days to come, she'd want to rob all types of drug spots and whoever else possessed money or dope. It became like a second addiction to her, to rob. One thing the guys didn't like about her was that during stickups, she'd shoot for no reason. Sometimes she'd slap the guy she was robbing across the head with the gun and let go a shot in the air. Or she'd be finishing robbing and make the individual get naked and run away as she busted shots out the gun, not attempting to shoot them, but shooting near their direction to scare them and to flex power. Robbing people made her feel powerful as the queen she felt she was.

One bright Sunday morning, Queeny woke up dope sick. She needed a bag of dope to get her ill off but didn't have any money. She always traveled with her gun. She went to the dope spot that was three blocks away. She'd never robbed this spot or had any plans on ever robbing this spot. She was going to this spot to see if someone she knew was shopping for dope or working the pack, so she could borrow a bag of dope or ten dollars to buy dope.

One way or the other, she needed at least one bag of dope to get her ill off.

Once she actually got to the dope spot, she hung out on it for approximately fifteen minutes, waiting to see someone she knew. But nobody she knew came by to buy dope.

She didn't want to hang around the dope spot too long because the police would possibly come by and search her and find the gun she possessed. She'd have to run from the police and toss the gun.

She knew the guy that was selling the pack, but he wasn't in any way her homey or anything like that. So she stepped to him, trying to get some dope.

"Hey, man, give me a bag of dope. I'm ill," she said.

"A'ight, give me your money," he said.

"I ain't got no money," she said.

"So how you talking about getting a bag of dope if you ain't got no money?" he said.

"I need a bag on credit," she said.

"I can't do it. Could you step out the way so I can serve these customers?" he said.

"Damn! As much money as I spend, I can't get a bag of dope on credit?" she said.

"I told you naw. Now beat it," he said.

She became angry and frustrated and overwhelmed with being dope sick. Unconsciously, in a rage, she upped her gun and shot him in the stomach twice. The other customers who were behind her took off, running.

Then she took the dope he had in his hands, went through his pockets, took the money and ran home. Including the dope and the money, she'd robbed him for less than a hundred dollars.

Once she made it within her apartment, she frantically looked out her window, scared to death, knowing that she was in a world of trouble.

As her hands began shaking nervously, she bust down the bags of dope and snorted all of them.

She sat back on her couch, nodding and scratching, drunk off dope as reality started to set in. She knew that people witnessed the shootings; therefore, she'd have problems from the guys whose spot she robbed and the dude she'd shot if he lived—and the cops.

She stayed in her apartment for an hour and then went to Phill's sister Rochelle's house. Although Phill's family was actually done fucking with her, Rochelle wouldn't have a problem with her coming by every once in a while.

Queeny resorted into telling Rochelle what had happened and that she was scared to death. She stayed in Rochelle's house for a few days. Tom and Paul gave her enough dope to snort for those few days.

Four days after she shot that nigga, Tom and Paul told her that Homicide and the individuals whose spot she robbed were looking for her to fuck her up. The individuals' spot she robbed wasn't tripping about her robbing their spot. They was looking for her 'cuz she shot one of their workers.

"The nigga you shot pressing charges on you," Tom said.

"He's still alive?" Queeny said.

"Yeah, he didn't die," Tom said.

"Why is Homicide looking for me for, then?" Queeny asked.

"Homicide ain't looking for you for no murder. They looking for you for an attempt murder," Paul said.

"You betta find somewhere to hide," Tom said.

"But I ain't got nowhere to hide out," Queeny said.

"You betta find somewhere to hide 'cuz you know the police will be looking for you over here in a little while," Paul said.

Tom and Paul continued on preaching.

"We've been telling your ass for years that the streets is cold and unfair. Now you're getting ready to see things for yourself the hard way," Paul said.

Queeny went to one of her dope fiend stickup buddies' house, which was on the other side of town. She stayed there for a few days but knew it wouldn't last long because his girlfriend wouldn't be pleased with another woman living there for too long.

After two weeks, she decided to turn herself in to the police because she knew if the guy she'd shot homies caught her, they'd shoot her in return and it would possibly be fatal. She knew if she was in prison, no one could shoot her. Also, she had become a grade A dope fiend. She figured, by her being in prison, she could kick the habit.

By her serving a few years in the penitentiary, she'd get clean even from ever craving drug usage. Upon her release, she'd have a new life, a fresh start, and her victim would've moved on with his life.

She turned herself in to the Area 4, Harrison and Kedzie police station on the West Side of Chicago. Within a couple of days, she was placed in the Cook County Jail faced with the charge of first degree attempted murder of Robert Smith.

Queeny lay in the bullpens of the police station and the county jail feeling like a wild animal was in her stomach using claws to be set free. She was feeling the full effect of being dope sick. She'd been dope sick a few times before but only felt minor pains 'cuz she was always able to get dope one way or the other before she got totally sick.

I swear to God, I ain't never using dope no more, Queeny thought, begging God to relieve her of this pain of being dope sick.

After being in the Cook County Jail for a short period, her cell mates advised her to take a cop-out for a suitable sentence—basically, take a short number of years by pleading guilty without going through trial and letting the judge give her a lot of time in prison.

Queeny was facing six to thirty years if she went to trial and got found guilty.

In some cases, when an individual was found guilty of an attempted murder, the judge wouldn't use any discretion in sentencing the defendant to excessive time in prison to make examples outta people for getting such violent cases—so that other people in the future would be hesitant of committing the same violent acts and afraid of the lengthy prison term he or she would be facing if convicted.

Queeny wasn't ready to cop out just yet. She wanted to wait it out to weigh her options.

While in the county jail, Queeny got into a few fights over petty shit, she won each time. She would fight dirty, doing whatever it took to win. She knew how to fight because she'd had to do a lot of it in grammar school.

In the county, she gained a name for herself. They'd call her Dirty Girl. They called her Dirty Girl 'cuz she'd fight dirty.

While in county, other inmates would smuggle drugs in to sell or use or both. They'd try to give her drugs. She always turned them down. She didn't start back getting high. She had it embedded in her mind that she'd remain drug-free. She knew there were better things in life than being a drug fiend. She also knew that being a dope fiend was what got her in prison in the first place. And she knew that it was the death of her mom and dad, because they were drug addicts.

Eventually she began working a job as a porter. The pay was two dollars a day, which was cool in jail. Fourteen dollars every week for commissary was enough to get cosmetics, cigarettes, coffee, and a little food. She started smoking cigarettes and drinking coffee only to ease the pain of prison life.

At this point, she had no one helping her out financially, on a frequent basis, so two dollars a day was sufficient. Phill's family would write her and send money and pictures, but it was only every once in a while not quite often. She enjoyed the self-sufficiency. It made her feel more of a woman. In her mind, she honestly felt like a self-proclaimed queen. She knew that queens didn't depend on others for the most part. Queens were rulers, and people depended on them for many things.

Sometimes while she was alone in her cell, she'd recite certain made-up sayings, her favorite saying was, "I be the ruler of life and demise. I be the queen that opens and closes eyes. I be the queen. I be me, Queeny."

Throughout her stay in county, she took care of nation business among the ViceLords. She started keeping a box for the ViceLords on the unit. The box was for the ViceLords who needed assistance, mainly for food, squares, or cosmetics, among other things. She'd have to make sure each ViceLord on her unit would pay a one-dollar box due each week. If any ViceLord on the unit needed to borrow something from the box, they could, but they must pay it back the next commissary day and pay their regular dollar box dues. Also, so the ViceLords on the new would be able to get the things they needed to begin their stay in prison.

If someone else on the unit who wasn't a ViceLord needed anything outta the box, they could get it out from Queeny, but they'd have to pay double back, which was called a two-for-one. All these things were done to maintain merchandise in the box.

Eventually, Queeny was placed lieutenant on the unit by an elite member of the ViceLords. Her position of lieutenant was a headache. She'd have to make sure the girls were secure at all times. She'd have to make sure when one of the girls was in the shower, another girl would stand by the shower on security so that the opposition couldn't and wouldn't come in to attack. As well, when the line movement occurred—like going to gym or to church, which were outside of the unit—Queeny would make sure all the ViceLords were together.

The reason they had to move together was so if anyone decided to attack one of them, all the others would be there to assist each other—basically to make sure each one was secure and safe. Many years before she came to prison, an outstanding member of the ViceLords came up with this theory of sticking together for safety off an animal channel. Certain animals in the wilderness travel together in packs so that if one of the animals was to be attacked, all the animals in the pack could be there to keep the animals in their pack from any hurt, harm, or danger. The logic behind this reasoning was brilliant. In most cases, depending on the group of animals or people, neither the human or the animal would even be attacked while in a crowd of allies.

By Queeny being the lieutenant of the unit, she also made sure there was respect shown among the ViceLords and from the opposition. She also had to make sure the ViceLords knew their literature. Unlike many other gangs around the United States, the ViceLords possessed gang literature. This gang literature consisted of laws, concepts, and policies made up by the founders of the ViceLords. All ViceLords must abide by these laws. If they didn't abide by the law of the ViceLords, they'd be disciplined by a violation. The violations raged from paying a fine of various prices, excessive exercise, or a physical violation. The physical violation was more effective, simply because after an individual got their ass beat for the physical violation, they wouldn't want another violation.

Queeny's assignment of lieutenant became more and more of a headache. But she liked doing it because of the love and respect she had for the ViceLords. And by her being in charge of others, she felt as the queen she was destined to be.

The girls on her unit loved her because she was considerate and real smart and knew how to orchestrate things.

It was two girls from Queeny's hood who were IVLs who were on the unit with her. Once they were released, they went and told Prince Black how she was conducting ViceLord business in county. Black got up with Rochelle to get Queeny's info.

Black began to send her money every once in a while and mention to her in letters to keep doing what she was doing for VL, always stay loyal to VL, and to never put any one else before VL.

Chapter 14

After nine months in county, Queeny decided to cop out. She told her public defender to see if she could cop out for the minimum on the case, which was six years. If she'd cop out for six years, she'd only have to do fifty percent of that six years, which would be three years. The public defender went into a 402 conference with the judge and state's attorney to try to see if she could get a cop out for six or seven or even eight years. The state was a true asshole, and her first cop-out was twelve years. After another month of trying to get a cop-out of lesser time, the best the PD could get was ten years. Queeny accepted the ten years and was sent to the penitentiary to do the rest of the time. She had approximately four years left to do in prison.

Once Queeny made it to the penitentiary to do the rest of her time, she was placed in a maximum-security women's prison named Dewitte CC. Usually with her time, they'd send an inmate to a medium-security prison, then after six months, they'd be able to transfer to a minimum security prison. But for some reason, they sent her straight to a max joint.

The first day within Dewitte, the girls screened her to see if she was gang affiliated, if she had any status, and where she was from.

They then gave her hygiene and cigarettes out of the box and then they introduced her to all the other ViceLords for security purposes.

The next day, she was placed on an elite member's security. In the county jail, she didn't have to do security because in the county jail, a lieutenant of the unit wasn't required to do security. But it was different in the penitentiary. If you weren't a universal elite, you must do security almost majority of the day, one way or the other.

After several weeks, Queeny got the feel of prison life in the penitentiary. Black sent her money to purchase a TV, and then she got a assignment in Dietary as a cook. Therefore she was okay far as finances were concerned.

She began to desire a higher learning—not as far as college, but simply a higher power mentally. She started spending as much time in the library as she possibly could.

While in the library, she mainly read books of black history and books of philosophy. While reading black history books, she found out that the names of the different branches of ViceLord came from ancient African tribes, such as the Conservative tribe, the Renegade tribe, and the Shabazz tribe, which the Insane ViceLords got their nickname from.

She also found out that some of the old African tribes had females as their leader, queens. She never knew these things before—certain things society and certain public school system didn't teach.

She'd learned in history classes in school that Christopher Columbus discovered America and that the Civil War was to free the slaves, which wasn't the whole truth.

As she continued to read about the ancient African queens, she read parts that stated that the queens would lead their tribe in battles. During battles, the queens would be on the frontline. That was unique to her and ironic because she felt the same way—that if anyone was under her structure and she's the leader, she will be right there on the frontline if war ever presented itself. These historic writings made her feel more and more of the queen she was destined to be.

As the days passed along, she began to do more studying, and she came to find out that Muslim beliefs began in Africa. She'd never actually studied any Muslim beliefs before, but she'd always assumed it was founded in Arabia. All along, it was founded in Africa.

One day, she decided to try to read something new. She began to read books of psychology. She began to become more intrigued by the way the human brain functioned. She began to seek more knowledge of the thinking pattern of others.

Chapter 15

There was a universal elite from her hood in the joint named Stacey. Stacey had a natural life for a murder. Stacey would have Queeny on her security, simply because they were from the same hood and part of the exact same ViceLord tribe, the Insanes. Therefore, she wanted Queeny close by her at all times. In reality, Stacey didn't need any security. She was one of the biggest women in the joint and had more heart than most of them. But it was VL law for a universal elite to have security.

One day, while everyone was out in the yard, Queeny was sent back because her shirt accidentally got caught on a fence and was torn a little. She couldn't be on the yard with a torn shirt because it would reveal body parts. She went to her cell to get another shirt then decided to go to Stacey's cell to get some squares because she was out. She caught Stacey standing up naked while another ViceLord sister was naked on her knees and eating Stacey's pussy.

Elite members weren't suppose to be without security. Therefore, Stacey used Olivia for her security, sometimes simply to have sex.

This particular day, Stacey told everybody that she and Olivia was staying back to sharpen up some knives. All along, they were having sex.

Once Stacey saw Queeny watching them having sex, she panicked.

"Girl, come in this cell. Please don't tell nobody," Stacey said.

Stacey knew that if Queeny told somebody, both she and Olivia would be violated or stabbed and wouldn't be considered ViceLords. That's one thing the ViceLords didn't condone, homosexuality. That was one of their main laws they'd enforce: no homosexual activities.

"Girl, ya'll bogus," Queeny said as she spent off and went to her own cell, which was five cells away.

Stacey and Olivia both dressed and ran down to Queeny's cell with a carton of Newports in hand, which was worth fifty dollars, trying to bribe her into not telling anybody.

"I ain't thirsty. You don't gotta give me those squares. I ain't gonna tell nobody. I really wanna bring both of ya'll asses up on charges and get ya'll violated, but I ain't, ain't gone tell nobody. But let me borrow a pack of those squares 'til store day," Queeny said.

Stacey eagerly handed her a pack of squares.

"What's ya'll business is ya'll business," Queeny said.

The following day, Stacey and Olivia hung out with Queeny, explaining their situation. "Girl, I got natural life. I ain't never getting outta jail, so I ain't got no problem with a letting a bitch suck on this pussy," Stacey said.

"I got thirty-five years to do, and I ain't got no problem with letting any one of these bitches lick this pussy," Olivia said.

"But ya'll ViceLords, and we don't get down like that," Queeny said.

"Majority of these other hos get down like that. They just ain't got caught in the act," Stacey said.

"I ain't no snake. Ya'll ain't gotta worry about me telling nobody. Nor do ya'll gotta give me any special treatment. Keep treating me the same way ya'll been treating me. Treat me like I never saw ya'll lovemaking," Queeny said.

Both Stacey and Olivia began to like Queeny even more, because the average individual would've told the ViceLords or blackmailed them for everything they owned.

At this point in time, Queeny remained peaceful, maintaining her job in Dietary and going to the library as much as possible, which was a good thing.

After a short period being in the joint, she began to take part-time college—only academic classes. She couldn't take full-time college because she'd have to quit her assignment in Dietary to do so. She needed her assignment in Dietary to assist her financially.

Her first academic class was psychology. She chose to take that class because she'd been reading psychology books in the library, and she liked psychology. After psychology, she ended up taking American history and British literature.

Chapter 16

Throughout her life, she'd only been to Christian services with the old lady Christine. She'd never been to any other services but Christian services. And she'd always been taught that God and his son Jesus were white men. While in her cell one day, she decided to read the Bible as a way to find inner peace and tranquility. She read a verse in the Bible that made an indirect statement that Jesus was black. She began to read more parts of the Bible that coincided with Jesus as well as others in the Bible who were black. Every once in a while, while alone in her cell, she got on her knees to pray. When she prayed, she prayed to Black Jesus. To her, by Jesus being black, he could feel her pain.

As she prayed, she talked to Black Jesus as if he was there in the cell with her. She seriously believed in Black Jesus.

She decided to began attending Al-Islam, Muslim services. Through it all, she learned how to slightly speak Arabic and she learned how to perform Muslim prayers. She also learned about false holidays.

She came to find out that much of ViceLord literature was from the concept of the holy Bible and the Koran.

After being in county for ten months and the penitentiary for six months, she had a few fights and got into a little trouble here and there, but never in her wildest dreams had she ever thought she was getting ready to turn into the true essence of a beast.

One day, after coming from her assigned job in Dietary, she noticed that damn near all the ViceLords in the cell house were on her gallery. She became nervous, thinking it was a scenario where the lady Lords were on the verge of creating a riot against the opposition or possibly even against the administration. She came to find out that a ViceLord called Nigeria had came to the gallery next cell over from Queeny.

She had the nickname Nigeria because she was actually from Nigeria. Nigeria was one of the main suppliers of heroin in the Chicago land area, among other places within the Midwest.

Nigeria moved to Chicago with her family approximately ten years prior to that very day. Through some way, her family and she was able to obtain green cards, therefore they weren't illegal aliens.

Nigeria would travel back to Nigeria frequently to get dope and have people smuggle it into the United States. The dope Nigeria sold was a bomb, and she sold it for cheap prices.

Nigeria was twenty years old. Her money exceeded being rich. She was rich to the third power. That's why all the inmates huddled around her. They respected her for the money and the power. Queeny had heard about Nigeria in the free world and in jail. Prince Black and everybody else were buying dope from Nigeria.

That day, Queeny met Nigeria for the first time. Nigeria was a universal elite; therefore, they placed Queeny on her security, because she was right in the cell next from hers. All the other girls wanted to be on her security simply to be at the side of this lady with all that money.

The next day, Queeny and Nigeria conversed about many different things. They hit it off instantly. Unlike the other girls, Queeny wasn't an ass-kisser. She'd treat Nigeria like she'd treat all the other girls. Nigeria liked Queeny for that. Queeny mentioned to Nigeria that she knew Black. She came to find out that Nigeria and Black were friends, ex-lovers, and business partners through dope transactions. Nigeria would even talk to Black over the phone while she was in jail, but only every once in a while. Each time Nigeria would talk to Black, she'd put Queeny on the phone to talk to him as well.

In no time, Nigeria began having problems with inmates and staff members. Some were jealous. Others were just on bullshit. Nigeria wasn't a violent woman. She only had power because of her money. Some of the ViceLords thought that her status as a universal elite was bogus, but they couldn't verify it because the individual she got it from was deceased.

One day in Dietary, at lunch, one of the other ViceLords' sisters bumped hard into Nigeria intentionally and knowingly and didn't say "Excuse me." After she bumped into Nigeria, she then told her, "Bitch, watch where you're going."

Queeny immediately jumped at this female with rage and fucked her up in 0.3 seconds. The police didn't see it; therefore, nobody went to seg.

Later on that day, Queeny was violated for her actions. She broke the law. She knew better than to act the way she did. Nigeria was pleased with Queeny's courage. The next day, Nigeria talked to Black over the phone and told him how Queeny performed. Black was pleased and disappointed. He was pleased that she stood up to that lady but disappointed that she bore arms against another ViceLord. Black then told Queeny over the phone to think first before she put her hands on one of the ViceLord sisters.

Queeny adored the power that Nigeria had because of the excessive amount of money she possessed. Nigeria was younger than the average inmate and didn't have a lot of heart. Queeny wanted this power that Nigeria had and would do anything to get it.

Queeny knew that if she'd be Nigeria's backbone as far as she had any trouble, she'd have access to Nigeria's money one way or the other, which meant power. Queeny got into two more fights for Nigeria—one female was an opposition member, the other female was not gang affiliated.

The female who was not gang affiliated, Queeny stabbed her real bad. In that day and age, in the Illinois prison system, inmates who stabbed other inmates wouldn't catch new cases when they stabbed an inmate. They'd only get a short time in seg. The only time they would catch a case was when an inmate was killed. But they would have to worry about the inmates' allies stabbing them in revenge. By this female being non–gang affiliated, she had no allies. She even went home a few months later.

Nigeria would tell Black of all Queeny's actions. When he found out she stabbed someone, he made her a five-star universal elite of the ViceLord nation. Queeny really began to feel like a queen.

No longer would she have to do security. Now people would do her security. Before long, she was the head universal elite over all the universal elites in Dewitte. Now she was really becoming more in the likeness of a queen.

Chapter 17

A few years later, Nigeria was released. Nigeria and Queeny kept in contact because they grew an immense friendship. Nigeria told Queeny that upon her release, she'd help her get financially stable in dope sales if she wanted her to.

At the time when Nigeria was released from prison, Queeny had six months left to do before she was released. Usually, when inmates get short of time, they humbled themselves. But Queeny was still in the penitentiary causing havoc, gaining more respect for being a humanized demon.

One time, Queeny was placed in seg for arguing with a CO. Stacey made arrangements to get her outta seg early and to have her placed in the cell with her. Stacey had grown a liking for her because she was a stand-up woman with a good heart. Stacey always liked having Queeny around because they were the same hood and both Insanes.

Stacey had moved into a different cell while Queeny was in seg, a cell that was all the way at the end of the gallery. Stacey moved to this cell for more privacy.

With Stacey moving to a different cell, once the COs let Queeny outta seg and told her what cell she was moving to, she didn't know it'd be Stacey's cell.

Queeny entered the cell and saw Stacey.

"I'm going to have to beat your ass in this cell," Queeny said in a joking manner.

"I'll beat your lil ass," Stacey replied in a joking manner.

"Where your girlfriend Olivia at?" Queeny said.

"She transferred to a medium joint last week," Stacey said.

"Don't be in here on no gay shit, or I'm beating your ass," Queeny said.

Then Stacey hugged Queeny. "I ain't on that with you. I was on that with Olivia because she wanted to be on that," Stacey said. "Whatever you need, feel free to get it from me anytime. You don't even have to ask. Just get it from the bags under my bunk. I got plenty commissary. You know it's love anytime you need me, I'm here for you," Stacey said.

Queeny and Stacey became the best of cellies and even closer friends. They stayed up late nights, reminiscing about the things they'd done in their past life. Queeny would often inform Stacey of the truth of black history, and they'll even sat down and learn more ViceLord literature, which seemed endless. The forefathers of the ViceLords created unnumbered amounts of meaningful literature.

After being cellies for a month, Queeny woke up outta her sleep one night to take a piss. As she sat on the toilet, she noticed Stacey was lying on the bottom bunk, flat on her back, knees in the air, with her feet flat on the bed, asshole-naked and fucking herself with a giant-sized summer sausage.

Before Queeny even got a chance to piss, she grabbed her knife from her stash spot and upped it on Stacey.

"Bitch, I told you not to be on no gay shit in this cell," Queeny said.

Stacey was scared to death, 'cuz she knew Queeny was a fool and wouldn't have any problem stabbing her up. "Girl, I wouldn't never do nothing to disrespect you. This ain't no gay shit. Majority of the girls do this when their cellies are gone or asleep. How is this gay when I'm doing this by myself?" Stacey asked.

Queeny began thinking like, *Damn, she's right. It ain't gay unless it's with another woman.* "Next time, make sure I'm asleep first," Queeny said.

"Shiit, you was asleep. You was up there snoring," Stacey said.

Queeny then sat down and pissed, got in the top bunk and went back to sleep. Once Queeny was back asleep, Stacey continued fucking herself with the summer sausage.

As the sunlight shone across their faces the next morning, Queeny and Stacey both awoke and prepared to go to breakfast. While heavily secured by the ViceLord sisters, Queeny remained silent, visualizing the ordeal she saw last night of Stacey fucking herself with that summer sausage.

When they made it back from breakfast and went to their cell, Queeny began asking questions about the feeling of being fucked with a summer sausage. Stacey knew in the back of her mind that Queeny was lusting for sex, not specifically with another woman, just in general.

Stacey began to tell Queeny that the best sex is with another woman, because a woman knows how to treat the pussy because she has one herself. Queeny acted like she wasn't trying to hear nothing about being with another woman, but all along, she was bi-curious.

Stacey began to tell Queeny that if she even decided to fuck herself with a summer sausage, it'll be a bomb because she'd be in control.

A few days passed, and Queeny was in the cell by herself, yearning for sexual intercourse. She remembered what Stacey told her about the summer sausage. She kept numerous summer sausages in her personal property. She liked to eat chopped summer sausage with her meals.

She grabbed a summer sausage outta her bag, then unwrapped it, and began sucking on it like it was actual dick. Then she pulled down her pants to her knees and firmly placed the summer sausage in her pussy. She began pushing it in and out her pussy swiftly. This was the best sex she'd ever had. Probably 'cuz she hadn't had sex in years. From that day forth, each time she was alone or when Stacey was asleep, she'd fuck herself with a summer sausage.

Before long, Queeny began to ask Stacey indirectly about homosexuality. Stacey was intelligent and advanced enough to know that Queeny wanted her pussy eaten, and Stacey was willing and interested in doing so.

Each day, Stacey would tell Queeny of her homosexual stories. Queeny would interestedly listen. Stacey admitted that before she even came to jail she was a bustdown, a woman whom performed sexual acts with more than one man simultaneously. "A lot of women be interested on taking a walk on the wildside in bed but is too afraid of what others may say or think. We only got one life to live and we must live it," Stacey said.

A few nights passed, and Stacey and Queeny stayed up all night this particular night, smoking squares and drinking coffee, when Queeny began to talk more and more about woman-to-woman lesbian sex.

"Why are you steady asking about woman-to-woman sex?" Stacey asked, looking dead into Queeny's beautiful brown eyes, already knowing the answer to her question but just trying to see what she'd say.

"I'm just curious," Queeny said.

"If you wanna talk to me about something, go ahead and tell me, girl. You know I got nothing but love for you. What's talked about between me and you is our secret," Stacey said.

"I wanna see what it's like to get my pussy ate by another woman," Queeny said.

Stacey paused, amazed and shocked that she made such a statement outta her mouth. With no hesitation, Stacey and Queeny undressed. Stacey began giving Queeny the best oral sex she'd ever had. All the while, while Stacey was eating her pussy, Queeny gently massaged her own titty nipples, feeling the best pleasure ever. Now Queeny knew why certain women turned gay.

As time progressed along, Stacey and Queeny's sex life was at its all-time high. Each time they were alone, they'd either be kissing or fingering each other or performing some other sexual acts.

Queeny felt as the dominant one in sex. She'd talk to Stacey while in the midst of lovemaking, asking questions such as "Slut, who your chief is?"

Stacey would answer, "You're my chief and my queen." It was hilarious to Stacey when Queeny would talk dirty to her in the act of sex. Stacey kind of liked the dirty talk.

The rest of Queeny's stay in prison was more peaceful. She'd fallen in love with Stacey, which made her days more tranquil. She continued to stand for the ViceLord nation's business but on a more diplomatic level.

Most of her time was spent lovemaking with Stacey and reading various books from the library.

Right before her release, she gave herself the title of the queen of all ViceLords. There had been a couple of different queens of two different particular branches of ViceLords, but never in history was it a queen over all ViceLords.

Chapter 18

Upon Queeny's release, Black made sure she had a place to stay, gave her five hundred to go shopping, and told her he could assist her in obtaining a job. The last thing she had on her mind was finding a job. She wanted lots of money, and the best way she knew how to get it was slanging dope to fiends.

She tried to get up with Nigeria when she first got out, but Nigeria was on a three-week vacation in the Bahamas.

After she had been out for three weeks, she was established in an apartment outside the ghetto and she had purchased a large wardrobe, so she was good.

Not only did Black give her money to go shopping. Many of the ViceLords hit her with money too and were trying to get some of that "fresh out of jail" pussy. She took the money but was no longer interested in dicks. She loved pussy more than men did.

A lot of people she never saw or even met before came to meet her. They'd been hearing about her past lifestyle and wanted to meet the self-proclaimed queen.

Phill's family showed her a lot of love when she got out. They were happy that she was finally free. They hoped she'd make the right decisions with her life.

Once Nigeria was back from the Bahamas, she and Queeny met up. They rode through the downtown area, reminiscing of jailhouse stories as well as future plans—places they wanted to go, things they wanted to see and do.

"Black told me he could find you a job," Nigeria said.

Queeny gave Nigeria a look of disgust. "How much dope can you front me?" Queeny asked.

"You just got out, and you already trying to sell some dope," Nigeria said.

"You know I ain't going to be the one selling it. I'ma pay workers for that," Queeny said.

"Yeah, you got a point. I'll see what I can do for you," Nigeria said.

They continued to ride off into the sunset like something out of a movie. After they finished kicking it that day, Queeny ended up spending a night at Nigeria's home in Hyde Park.

The next day, Queeny awoke to the strong smell of weed smoke mixed with cigar smoke.

"Damn, that shit smell good," Queeny said.

Nigeria tried to pass Queeny the blunt.

"Naw, I don't smoke weed. I didn't know you smoked weed. You wasn't smoking when we was in jail," Queeny said.

"I just started a few months ago. Some of my homies turned me out," Nigeria said.

Nigeria then upped a big bag filled with twenty-five grams of heroin. Queeny smiled as if she'd hit the jackpot. "I'll front you this twenty-five grams of dope, and you must bring me back twenty-five hundred. Usually I sell twenty-five grams for thirty-seven fifty, I sell them for one fifty a gram, but for you—only for you—bring me back twenty-five hundred. You saving twelve fifty," Nigeria said.

"My dope is good enough to sell for two hundred a gram, but I sell them for one fifty to outdo the competitors. It'll be a smart choice for you if you sell grams and bags. You can sell grams for two hundred and make good profit. And you can sell one mack for ten dollars. I got a remedy to put on dope, which I ain't told nobody about it," Nigeria said.

"What's the remedy?" Queeny asked.

"I put Sleepinal pills mixed with dorms on the dope. Sleepinal pills help dope fiends to get their nod on. It's a bomb," Nigeria said.

Queeny, being an ex–dope fiend, knew that Nigeria knew exactly what she was talking about, 'cuz dope fiends loved to nod while enjoying the bomb on the dope. Queeny used to go to the table, bagging up dope for Tom and Paul back in the day, so she knew that people put all type of shit on dope. But she'd never heard of anyone using Sleepinal to put on dope.

"I got a block where the Ebony ViceLords sell their rocks at. You can put your dope out there if you want to," Nigeria said. Nigeria was the chief of the Ebony ViceLords, so she could lay down licks wherever Ebony ViceLords were.

"If I let you sell dope on that joint, you gotta make sure the joint don't sell more than a stack a day on the dope. Nor can you work twenty-four hours a day. You can only work in the daytime," Nigeria said.

"Why must I only let the joint sell a stack a day and work only in the daytime?" Queeny asked.

"'Cuz the joint is up north. We can't sell dope flamboyantly like ya'll do out west," Nigeria said.

"How can I control how much a dope spot sells in a day? You know when somebody got good dope, people come from all over to buy good dope," Queeny said.

"You gone have to put a lot of mix on the dope," Nigeria said.

"But if I put a lot of mix on it, it's not gone be good dope no mo," Queeny said.

"If you put a lotta mix on the dope, that won't make it no bad dope, but it won't be as good either. It'll just be average. And you'll make a lot of profit. Like, if your dope sells a stack a day, you'll be making about five or six hundred a day in profit, then add five or six hundred times seven. At the end of the week, you'd been done checked a few stacks. Not including the money you'll be getting off selling grams for two hundred or better. Then once you get on your feet a little, you'll be able to open up dope spots everywhere," Nigeria said.

"So what if the dope still sells more than a stack after I put a lot of mix on it?" Queeny asked.

"Once you sell a stack in a day, you must shut it down 'til the next day. That way, you'll have less problems from the police," Nigeria said. "See, out west, you can sell forty or fifty thousand a day on the dope because it's ghetto. Up north ain't got no ghetto parts."

Queeny instantly tried going through Tom and Paul to pop off some of her dope. What she didn't know was that Tom and Paul had recently stopped selling dope and running the streets. Tom and Paul had gotten tired of the death and destruction in the streets and decided to live a honest life. Both Tom and Paul had regular jobs. Tom had, had a son while Queeny was away and was planning on getting married. Paul had two daughters while Queeny was a way.

Rochelle, Tom, Paul, and the rest of Rochelle's family were planning on moving down south for a change and better living.

Approximately five days later, Queeny began selling dope up north. She began making more money than she'd expected because a lot of people wanted to buy grams of dope for various prices. Sometimes she'd sell them for two hundred. Other times, she'd sell them for two hundred and fifty. On the block where she sold dope at, the EVLs sold rock cocaine; therefore, she always had workers to work her dope. Those who would sell their own rock packs would also sell her dope.

Chapter 19

After Queeny had been out of prison for four months, Rochelle, Tom, Paul, and the rest of the family decided to pack it up and move down south. Once again, Queeny knew she had to be on her own. She was used to it.

Rochelle threw a party celebrating their departure. Everybody was there. Many men were at Queeny, trying to get some of that pussy she wasn't going.

After the party that night, Black tried to fuck Queeny, and she didn't let him.

Some people wondered why Queeny did all that time in jail, got out, and wasn't fucking around sexually with anyone—well, at least that they knew of.

With her being an elite member of the ViceLords, Black would use her to conduct ViceLord nation affairs. Although Black and Queeny were IVLs, they still had say-so over every different branch of ViceLords because they were universal elites. Within the ViceLords, there are different kind of elites. Supreme elites who were the kings, queens, and princes, and those who controlled the entire mob. Regular universal elites would either be a five-star or three-star universal elite, who were elites of all ViceLords and controlled ViceLords as well but weren't the heads of the entire ViceLords like the supreme elites, but they could enforce law within VL. Then they had the branch elites who could only dictate things in their branch of ViceLords, like an Insane could only dictate things to the Insanes or a branch elite of the CVLs could only dictate things within the CVLs' branch.

Black would use Queeny to enforce law, like orchestrate meetings for various locations where ViceLords dwelled, in order for members to be present to enforce the laws, policies, and well-being of VL.

One time, Black, Queeny, and a few of the other universal elites were going to this area where the Lords were getting a lotta money off dope but was treating the ViceLords bogus. The nigga would have Lord nam working for him and would pay them a little of nothing. The nigga wouldn't even bound his guys out who caught cases for him that had petty bounds. And when other members of ViceLords in his area got into street wars with the opposition he wouldn't assist them in any shape, form, or fashion. Black and his team were going to this guy's spot to tell him that if he didn't get into compliance with ViceLords, he couldn't sell dope on VL land.

As they made it to the guy's dope spot, they tried talking to him on a civilized level, but it turned into an argument. While they were arguing, Queeny walked across the street to Black's car to get a light for his cigarette. While lighting the cigarette, she heard gunshots. She looked up, and the guy they'd come to tell that he had to shut his dope spot down had opened fire, shot two of the other universal elites who came with Black, and Queeny, Ant, and Milton. Black was lucky to be able to run away, but while he ran, the guy began shooting at him but didn't hit him.

Black kept a .45 automatic in a stash spot in his car that Queeny knew about. Sometimes, when Black left his car he'd leave the keys in the ignition. Black was a gang chief. He wasn't worried about anyone pulling off with his car. He was well-known and well-respected.

Coincidentally, he left the keys in the ignition this particular time. After Queeny heard the gunshots, she looked up at Ant, and Milton was laid out on the ground. She immediately grabbed the gun and started up the car and chased Alvin down, ran him over, got out the car, and unloaded the four fimp within his body. She then drove a few blocks looking for Black and found him.

Black jumped into the passenger side of the car, breathing heavy.

"I done caught a murder. I done killed that stud," Queeny said.

"Fuck that nigga. That nigga deserve to die," Black said.

"Drive back to pick up Ant and Milton. We gotta hurry up and get them to the hospital. That pussy-ass nigga shot them," Black said.

"I just committed a murder. I'm not finna go back there. Don't worry. The ambulance will be there shortly to get them," Queeny said.

"We gotta go back and pick up Ant and Milton," Black said.

"Nigga, I can you let you out. You can go back and get them yourself. I'm not finna go right back to where I done killed a nigga at," Queeny said.

Black stayed in the car with Queeny as they fled from that area.

Within thirty minutes, Black and Queeny were at one of Black's low-key apartments. Black and Queeny were both confused, not knowing what to do.

Black sat down and thought for a little while. Black came up with the proper procedure after committing a murder, which was to get rid of the murder weapon. He waited to later on that night and threw the gun in the sewer.

Black knew that this murder happened in broad daylight, and most likely, Queeny and he would have to await trial for the murder of Alvin. And maybe a double murder or even a triple murder depending on if Ant and Milton were killed. Sometimes, Homicide would twist murders up and charge people with all three murders, especially if witnesses would testify against them.

Black prayed that none of the three men were killed. Black didn't give a fuck about Alvin. He didn't want to catch that murder on Alvin.

For a couple of days, Black hoped and prayed that he and Queeny wouldn't be codefendants on a murder.

After a couple of days, he received a beep from Ant's wife. He immediately called her back. He thought she was going to ask of Ant's whereabouts, but she was beeping him because Ant wondered if Black and Queeny were okay.

Black told her that he and Queeny were safe. Ant's wife told Black that Ant, Milton, and Alvin were good because they were still living. Black felt a great sign of relief when she told him that no one was killed.

Black asked Ant's wife how she knew about Alvin. She told him that Alvin was dating one of her best friends from work. Her friend

Ann was in love with him. Black then asked her, was she sure Alvin wasn't dead? She said she was positive Alvin wasn't dead.

Black began wiping the sweat off his head, relieved of the burden of wondering if one—if not all—of them was killed.

Black ended up finding out what hospital Alvin was in. He sent someone up there to investigate to see if Alvin would be a real nigga or a stool pigeon and tell the police what really happen, that Queeny shot him. The individual he sent couldn't get in to see him because Alvin was in the part of the Cook County Hospital for those who were being investigated of a crime. When the police and the ambulance showed up to the scene of the crime, they noticed that Alvin still had his unloaded gun in his hand; therefore, obviously, they linked him to the shootings of Ant and Milton. Ant and Milton told the police they didn't know who shot them.

After a week, Black was still worried that Queeny would have to await trial for the attempted murder on Alvin.

Black found a way to get in touch with one of Alvin's sisters to see if he was going to work with the police or not.

Alvin then sent word through others to tell Black he wasn't going to tell the police and he'd pay thousands for Ant and Milton not to tell the police on him. Black sent word back to him that Ant or Milton or anybody else he fucked with was no stool penguin. "But still, send us ten thousand. We will squash the whole ordeal. After you send that ten thousand, we better not see you again, or you must die."

Alvin wasn't a coward, but he didn't want any trouble out of Black because he knew if he'd killed Black, every ViceLord in the city would be looking for him because Black was a prince. And if he went to jail for doing anything to Black, he wouldn't be safe. The ViceLords would stab him up and take his life from him.

Within approximately two weeks Alvin sent ten thousand to Black through a female friend. Within three weeks, Alvin was healed enough to move around on his own. He was sent to the Cook County Jail, and charged with a UUW and his bond set at only 2,500. He bonded out and immediately fled the to Atlanta, Georgia. Black never saw Alvin again.

Ant, and Milton wanted to kill Alvin for shooting them up. That's why Black took the ten thousand and told him to never show his face in the Chicagoland area again, because he knew that Ant and Milton would want to kill him and would definitely do so with the probability of catching a murder. Even if they'd did the killing in an orderly fashion, they'd still be suspect.

Black figured with Alvin nowhere to be found, they gained 10,000, get his dope spot, bring structure to the ViceLords within his area, and Ant and Milton wouldn't catch a murder case. He split the 10,000 up in four ways, 2,500 apiece. It wasn't very much money to any of them, but it was an extra 2,500.

Approximately seven weeks after the shooting occurred with Alvin, Ant, Milton, Black, and Queeny began hanging in the area that Alvin once ran to enhance structure and unity and to enforce VL law in that area.

Before long, Queeny began to sell dope and cocaine on Alvin's old dope spot. She brought cocaine from Black and dope from Nigeria.

Overnight, Queeny had Alvin's old dope spot selling anywhere from thirty to forty thousand on a good day. In no time flat, Queeny had stacked well in six figures.

Chapter 20

Black began to attempt to rekindle an old relationship with Queeny. Queeny was not interested. It wasn't because she didn't want to be lovers with Black. It was because she was a full-fledged lesbian. Her only interest was to become lovers with other women.

Being a lesbian coincided with her notion of being dominant over men as a queen. Within sexual relationships with men, she would attempt to be dominant, but in reality, the men were dominant over her one way or the other. By her being a lesbian, she'd be the dominant one over her lovers as the queen she'd dreamed to be.

Impending her release, she'd only had sex with rubber dicks. She did wanna have sex, but it wasn't easy to find a lesbian just walking down the street. She actually wanted to fuck Nigeria but didn't want to come at her like that to ruin their friendship and business venture if she wasn't up with it.

Queeny being a lady, she knew that money brought bitches. Specifically, women were infatuated with cash flow. Over time, she'd began meeting many females. Most of them were hood rats. She'd buy them nice things in exchange for sex. Nothing expensive. It'd be something cheap like a leather jacket or a pair of tennis shoes. She'd be shocked of the things women would do for a little money.

Queeny began to open up dope spots everywhere. Majority of them would put up numbers, double-digit thousand stacks each day.

As her finance constantly grew, she'd find herself getting with classier chicks. Once again, this was shocking to her that she'd influence all these heterosexual women to indulge in homosexual acts. The way she'd get them was through showing off one of her cars, jewelry, etc. Sometimes, she'd take them through one of her dope spots to show them that she had clout.

Queeny had more money and power than many men. And women were infatuated with that. A majority of the women she dated had heard of her name and fame prior to them even meeting her. Now she was really the queen of all queens.

At first, while interacting with women and other people, she'd keep her homosexuality in the closet. But before long, she'd reveal who she actually was. In some events, while hanging with women, if they didn't know she was gay, she'd tell them. All the women she'd hang out with weren't interested in her money or loving it was that she was cool to be around. Her lifestyle was that of the rich and famous.

Queeny had become a major player on the hos. She had an advantage over men, which was she was a woman and knew how to touch the heart, mind, and body of a woman.

Queeny rented out and apartment on the north side of Chicago, down the street from the lakefront. She'd have numerous women walking around in it in the nude at the same time daily. This was her player's pad.

She began to take some of her favorable lovers to places they'd never been before, like to the Grand Canyon, Cancun, and various spots in Florida. She was like a savior and a mentor to her girlfriends.

Through it all, she'd maintained her friendship with Stacey. She'd write Stacey and always sent her money and pictures and made sure she'd always be able to call her to utilize three ways or whatever else she needed. Queeny also communicated with other women in prison—some she'd met while she was in prison and some of her homies she met after her release who were placed in prison.

Chapter 21

The ViceLord nation became more dependent on Queeny's leadership. She stood on VL business with an iron fist. Her heart was that of a lion.

The average individual who went to prison for an attempted murder and was involved with the incident with Alvin would have been more diplomatic with their actions. She became worse with time. Every time you'd turn around, she was having shootouts with someone and committing senseless murders. Some of her shootings were in broad daylight, where people were shot and lived, but a few of them were killed. She'd became power-struck. No one or nothing could control her. Black used to attempt to talk to her, but it was like talking to a brick wall. She knew that now she didn't have to worry about catching too many cases, because people didn't want to testify against the queen of the ViceLords. And if they did, she could easily have them whacked or she would simply pay off a witness large sums of money to not work with the police.

More and more her followers began to grow. The ViceLords would follow her, and people who weren't VL wanted to join to be a part of her team. Queeny began to formulate a mob within the mob of VL that consist of murderers, torturers, and villains—those who would do anything for the upliftment of the very VL nation and anything for her.

Queeny began to overrule some of Black's decisions. Like if Black told an individual who was VL that he could sell dope on VL land, Queeny might come through and shut him down.

Queeny began to ride on other outstanding members and dictate their pace in the ViceLords. They'd honor it because most of the time she'd be righteous and within the guidelines of VL. Other times, she'd be doing things her way, but they'd still honor her rulings due to fear of what she'd do if they crossed her.

Queeny began to get more respect, not just from the ViceLords but from street thugs in general. Queeny became a cold-blooded killer, and she enjoyed it.

In due time, Black ended up catching a murder and was found guilty and sentenced to natural life in prison, which left Queeny in charge of the ViceLords.

Queeny ended up catching a UUW, which carried two to five years in prison. By her being on parole, she couldn't bond out. At this time, an individual on parole in Illinois couldn't bond out on parole if he or she had caught a UUW or a violent case.

She sat in the county for a little while and eventually was found guilty of UUW and sentenced to four years in prison, which she only had to serve eighteen months after receiving her six months good time.

They sent her to a minimum-security facility. She immediately became aware that the minimum joint was different from the max joints. It was more movement and more peaceful, not really any gangbanging going on, dorms instead of cells.

She had things better this bide because she was a queen of a gang and had lots of money. Although she didn't wanna be in prison, eighteen months wasn't a lot of time for her to do. She had many people in play to take care of her drug business while she was in prison.

Shortly after being in the penitentiary, she began to focus more on her inner self by reading. She began to read books of the judicial system. It was a lot of things about the legal system she didn't know about. She also started to read urban novels, books of witchcraft, and she even started back reading the Koran as she did on her first bide. She wasn't confused in her readings. She simply found a way to be free by reading diverse reading material.

Through it all, she did what it took to enhance knowledge. One way she enhanced her knowledge was by listening to certain staff members who would tell her about different ways to invest her money.

One of the female COs took a genuine liking for Queeny and would talk to her about more ways to invest money and things she should be doing to make her future prosperous. This CO taught Queeny about small-cap, midcap, and large-cap investments and how to invest in stocks and bonds.

This CO gave her the game about investing in real estate. She told her that if she invested in property and once she got insurance on her property, no matter what, she'd always make some sort of profit.

This particular CO taught her lots of knowledge about ways to enhance finance and how to help others get financially stable without simply giving them money—like, for instance, if someone she knew had a talent who wanted to go to college but couldn't leave their day job to pursue their goals, she should spend her money to help that individual.

As time progressed along, this CO, Ms. Styles, continued on giving her game about great investments.

Ms. Styles told Queeny that if she helped someone obtain a career as a musician or sent them to college, in most cases, she could depend on them for financial assistance. Also that same person she'd help to be a success could eventually help the next man or woman to become a success. Queeny never looked at things in that manner. She was too caught up in the street life.

Now Queeny had greater ambitions and goals to accomplish. She figured out ways to clean up her dirty money legally upon her release.

While in prison, Queeny continued to attempt to maintain control over the ViceLords in the free world through orders over the phone, which was extremely difficult. The prison phones were tapped, and it wasn't the same as being there in person.

Prior to her incarceration, the ViceLord structure was beginning to depart a little. Mainly because a majority of the heads had retired or was locked up in the feds and the state, and even a couple had gotten killed. But when she was out, she was able to maintain structure somewhat, though not to its fullest extent like before. Now that she was gone, a large portion of the ViceLords weren't honoring the law.

A lot of old-school ViceLords who did believe in the concept of ViceLords. A lot of young ignorant ViceLords were only interested in foolishly gangbanging and getting money, not even rotating with the mass amount of ViceLords, only fucking with their own click.

Without lawmen to enforce VL law, the streets where VLs dwelled were filled with anarchy.

Not only was the ViceLords—other organizations were beginning to crumble. Killings of their own gang members were popular. There was no peace or sleep in the streets.

Queeny was amazed at how fast things turned over for the worse. After five months of being imprisoned—three in the county and two in the joint—she began hearing about this guy named Bushwick who was creating madness in the streets.

They called him Bushwick because he resembled this rapper who used to rap with the Geto Boys back in the day.

Queeny remembered Bushwick from when he was a lil boy. Bushwick was one of the shorty Lords who used to sell dope packs for people in the hood and fight dogs. Bushwick got locked up for an attempted murder for shooting his very own brother twice for slapping their mother.

Prior to Bushwick going to prison, he was basically a nobody. But while in prison, Bushwick turned into a gorilla. He'd create problems. He stayed in the middle of bullshit.

Bushwick and Black were in the same prison. Black took a liking for Bushwick 'cuz he was a stand-up nigga. Although Bushwick was a little dude, he carried himself as a giant.

Bushwick was an IVL, from the same hood Black and Queeny were from. While in jail together, Black made Bushwick a three-star universal elite. Upon Bushwick's release, Black gave him permission to have a dope spot in the hood.

Once Bushwick got out, he immediately opened up that dope spot, selling dime bags of raw cocaine. Around this time, there weren't too many people selling raw powder cocaine. The average cocaine spot would be selling rocked cocaine.

Bushwick conquered the cocaine market in his area and in surrounding areas. He got majority of the customers for various reasons: there weren't too many people selling raw cocaine and his bags were big as hell; therefore, he'd get customers who snorted and those who smoked cocaine. Those who smoked it would buy his bags of raw cocaine to cook it up to smoke.

Overnight, Bushwick began making so much money because he had a big family that sold his cocaine in various areas, all through Chicagoland, Rockford, Springfield, and even in other states. He eventually started selling rock cocaine, dope, and weed.

Bushwick started getting so much money that he started his own small clothing line called Bush Wear.

Like many other dope dealers who started getting lots of money and had manpower, he started getting power-struck. Bushwick began an unnumbered murdering spree, most of the time by his damn self.

His very first murder was a cat who owed him several hundred dollars. Several hundred dollars weren't shit to him. It was just the principle of someone owing him.

It was one late night, and Bushwick was riding alone outside of the hood, high off leaf, and saw this nigga Julius who owed him money. Bushwick rode up to him and asked him, "Where's the money you owe me?" Julius made up some lame ass excuse. Before second-guessing it, Bushwick shot him two times in the face, leaving him for dead.

Bushwick was never questioned for that murder-homicide because there were no witnesses.

Bushwick fell in love with the shedding of blood. This would begin a string of terror through the city streets. Anytime Bushwick had a problem, he'd go by himself to handle the business.

His second homicide occurred when an individual from another hood where he was selling dope at kept driving down on his workers, telling them that Bushwick couldn't sell shit in his hood.

One of Bushwick's workers showed the guy to Bushwick. The nigga was standing on his dope joint as Bushwick and his worker drove by in an unmarked car. The nigga's joint was close to Bushwick's joint.

While driving past, Bushwick wanted to jump out and kill the nigga right then and there. But he didn't do it because there would be too many witnesses.

After that day, Bushwick started looking for this guy to be away from his dope spot, which was difficult. So then he'd try to follow him once he left his dope spot, but Bushwick's timing was bad 'cuz every time he came around, the nigga wouldn't never leave his dope spot.

One day, Bushwick noticed that he did leave his joint and go into a house on the end of the same block and wouldn't come out for days. The nigga had a girlfriend who lived in that house.

Bushwick conjured up a plan to catch him coming outta that house one late night and take his life away, but he knew he had to do it by concealing his identity if he didn't wanna catch a case.

One afternoon, Bushwick went to a female clothing store and bought a skirt, high heels, panties, bra, a purse, and a wig. Bushwick felt uncomfortable buying all those female items, but in reality, that wasn't strange for Bushwick, being a man, to purchase such items, because men would come into this particular women's clothing store to buy women's clothes for their wives, fiancées, and girlfriends all the time.

Later that night, Bushwick shaved off his facial hair, put on all of the women's clothing he'd bought from the women's clothing store earlier that day. He even put on the bra and the panties, as well as the wig too. He stuffed tissue in the bra.

He looked in the mirror and began laughing and thinking, *Damn, I look good as a girl.* He then filled his purse with a screwdriver, a clothes hanger, two guns (a .380, and a .38), five hundred dollars in small bills, and other miscellaneous items. He needed the screwdriver and the clothes hanger to steal a car. He needed the five hundred just in case he'd have to evade authorities or anyone else—he'd have money for a cab or to do whatever else he needed to do to be safe and get away.

He left his apartment and began walking for thirty minutes in search of a car to steal. The reason he walked for thirty minutes in search of a car to steal is because he didn't want to steal a car close to his apartment that authorities could use to link him to the murder if someone was actually killed. Also, he wanted to walk for thirty minutes to get the feel of walking properly in high heels.

While walking for thirty minutes, he was shocked at all the cars filled with men offering a lift and trying to exchange phone numbers. Not in any shape, form, or fashion was he gay. He was just amazed of how much action women actually get. One of the reasons he got so much action was because it was late night and all the men could really see was an ass in a skirt. If they'd gotten close to him, they'd notice that he was a man.

Bushwick came to a block that was peaceful and quiet. No thugs hanging out or dope-selling.

He saw a car, an old '80s Iroc, and decided to steal it because it was a sports car, extremely fast. This sports car would be essential to him getting away from anyone who would be possibly be chasing him—either the police or the homies of the man he'd possibly kill in the future.

He used the clothes hanger to unlock the door and the screwdriver to peel the neck of the car behind the steering wheel. Once he peeled the neck, he started the car up, turned the radio on to a dusties station that was playing an Al Green song, "Let's Stay Together," and smashed off with the intent to cause great bodily harm.

Once he made it to the nigga's dope spot, he parked at the end of the block and impatiently waited for an hour to see this guy and take his life away with gunfire.

After an hour passed, he left the spot, because he knew that eventually the police would harass him for sitting near a dope spot. And they'd find out that he was in a stolen motor vehicle and in possession of two firearms. He figured he'd better continue circling blocks around the dope spot. That way he'd have less problems from the police because he was dressed as a woman and he wasn't just sitting on the dope spot.

All night, he couldn't find the guy, but he continued searching.

The next morning, while riding up this nigga's dope spot, he saw him coming out his girlfriend's house. Spontaneously, he rolled down the window and said, disguising his voice like a woman, "Boy, you don't know how to call nobody back."

The nigga smiled, thinking it was one of the hos he'd met in the past.

The nigga told Bushwick to pull up to the next block. The reason he told Bushwick to pull up to the next block was because he didn't want his girlfriend to see him talking to another woman, which in turn worked out for Bushwick.

The block he pulled up on was not a dope spot. As the nigga walked up to the car, Bushwick got out of the car, holding his head down, with his hand in his purse.

The nigga got to thinking like *Damn, I don't remember her, but she's a cutie.* As Bushwick got closer, the nigga began to smile even more.

When Bushwick got close to him, he lifted his head up and smiled, upping a chrone .380 and shooting the man three times in the face. Bushwick immediately left the scene of the crime.

As time progressed along, Homicide did their investigation. The only thing one witness saw was an Iroc smashing off after hearing gunfire.

After that day, Bushwick became a self-proclaimed demon. It was as if he were the rebirth of Lucifer. He even gave himself the title King of Chicago.

Every time you'd turn around, Bushwick would be fucking niggas up. Niggas and bitches in the streets respected him. He didn't have too many problems. The main problems he had were the ones he created.

Secretly, he'd killed three of the ViceLords' head lawmen. Bushwick secretly murdered them because they were trying to enforce VL law upon him. Bushwick was rebellious against the ViceLords and everyone and anyone who was against him. He was even rebellious against anyone who had more power than him. One time, he even had a shootout with the police. The police never linked him to the shootings, because they never saw his face and had no witnesses, no fingerprints, and basically, not enough evidence.

Bushwick even told all his followers that he felt like, fuck King Phill, Prince Black, and Queen Queeny—he was the chief of IVL and the King of Chicago.

One week, Bushwick started to really get beside himself. He closed the dope spot one of the old-school ViceLords named Kane. Kane's spot was right up the street from his.

Bushwick and a few of his guys drove down on Kane and told him that he had to shut his joint down. Kane instantly started snapping out.

"Fuck you, bitch-ass niggas. If it wasn't for the shit I was doing in the eighties, you bitches wouldn't be able to work in the hood right now today. I been in the streets probably before you bitches was even born, doing shootings in the name of ViceLords. I'm one of the niggas who helped start a foundation for ViceLords in the hood and in a lot of other motherfucking hoods," Kane said.

Although Kane was right, Bushwick wasn't trying to hear that shit.

"Ya'll better get ya'll pussy ass away from me 'fore I fuck around and kill you bitches. You bitches ain't on shit," Kane said.

To Bushwick and his guys, this was like music to their ears. Bushwick and his team left impatiently, waiting for night to fall. The same night, Bushwick and twenty of his guys—some with two guns apiece—went back to Kane's spot.

When they came back, they noticed that there were five men on the spot—including Kane, which was amazing to them. Usually, when someone knew that somebody else was trying to take over their dope spot, they'd have as much men power and guns on their joint as possible.

Two of the dudes were sitting in the car. The other three, including Kane, were standing on the dope spot. It being nighttime, Bushwick and his guys crept up on Kane and his guys through the bushes.

Bushwick and his guys rushed out the bushes with guns in hand, surrounding Kane and his guys so they wouldn't be able to run.

Kane and his guys had guns, but they had them put up outdoors. It was dangerous for them to be standing on a dope spot with guns, 'cuz the police were always coming through, searching people.

Bushwick noticed two of Kane's guys sitting in the car in a vacant lot. They never noticed Bushwick and his guys 'cuz they were facing a different direction from them and they were too busy smoking weed and listening to Pac.

Bushwick and two of his guys went and grabbed them out of the car by gunpoint. He walked them over to Kane, where Kane and the other niggas were standing, already under gunpoint by Bushwick guys in the middle of a vacant lot, in the middle of the block.

Three of Bushwick's men held Kane down while Bushwick pistol-whipped the man, while Kane's workers watched under heavy gunpoint. He wanted them to watch to set an example.

Afterward, Kane was hospitalized and had to get a metal plate in his head. After leaving the hospital, Kane was never seen again. The rumor was he left the city and moved to the suburbs.

Some of Kane's guys start working for Bushwick. They liked his gruesome, heartless style and wanted to be on his team.

Within the same week, Bushwick and his guys drove down to one of Queeny's joints and told them that they'd have to close down. Queeny's workers were already equipped for situations of that nature. They'd upped various guns at Bushwick and his guys which included a Tec-22, a Glock four fimp, and a Ruger.

"You bitches betta get the fuck out my face 'fore we fuck you bitches up," one of Queeny shorties said.

Bushwick and his men immediately got the fuck outta their face, got into their cars, and burned rubber, trying to get the fuck away from all those big-ass guns. Bushwick and his men were shocked that Queeny's workers were equipped with so much artillery. Bushwick knew that he'd have problems with taking Queeny's joint although she was in prison.

Bushwick start to get nervous that Queeny's guys would try to take his joint, so he put extra artillery on it just in case.

Immediately after Bushwick and his guys left, Queeny's people went and told one of the ViceLords lawmen what had happened. Queeny's guys wanted to go to Bushwick's joint and fuck them up but decided to go by law first. To Queeny's guys, she really was the queen of all queens. For her they lived and would die for.

There weren't many lawmen who existed at this point in time. But the one they went and told went over and talked to Bushwick to squash the whole ordeal.

"I'ma squash it this time 'cuz I don't want my niggas to catch nobodies. But for the record, fuck King Phill, fuck Prince Black, and fuck that dike-ass bitch Queeny. I'm the king of the streets," Bushwick told the law man.

Chapter 22

It was one of them "tired of being locked up" days for Queeny. Tired of being around the mass amount of phony-ass individuals in prison. Tired of not being able to have sex—she couldn't have sex 'cuz the joint she was in was all dorms. She was tired of no privacy. Tired of being in prison, away from her extravagant life in society.

She chose to get on the phone to call some of her homies in the world in hopes of being cheered up one way or the other. Some of her homies told her about the stunt Bushwick pulled, trying to close her dope spot down, and that he pistol-whipped Kane and took his joint, and that he was saying fuck King Phill, Prince Black, and her.

All that shit pissed her off. *I'm the queen of all queens,* she thought before hanging up the phone.

She went and lay on her bunk. *Who the fuck do this bitch think he is telling me I can't work? And saying fuck King Phill and Prince Black. If it wasn't for us, he wouldn't be able to even think of selling dope in the hood. How could he say fuck King Phill when Phill is the one who laid down the foundation for ViceLords everywhere. That's in ViceLord literature and laws that ViceLords must always give praise to their elites and supreme elites that's dead and sacrificed their life for the upliftment of this ViceLord nation. This stud gotta die,* Queeny thought.

She got out her bunk and went and made a few more calls, questioning people of why they didn't slay Bushwick and his guys. They told her they were trying to rationalize the situation so that there wouldn't be casualties in the ViceLords and in order for them to not catch murder cases. But if he tried it again, they'd take away lives without any hesitations.

As angry as she was, she thought, *Yeah, they was right to squash it instead of reacting foolishly.*

She hung up the phone and went to the yard to exercise to relieve some stress.

Queeny began to study more of different religious. Semiconfused, she studied Al-Islam, and Christianity. She started getting more into religions because she felt she needed God in her life in every way. She began to think of the heartache created by killing people and selling dope to people. She began to think of some of the ViceLord literature that consisted of uplifting black people, not killing them or selling dope to them.

Over time, Queeny began to exercise more to relieve stress. Majority of the rest of her stay in prison was served doing some type of exercising—running laps, push-ups, or lifting iron.

Queeny was beginning to grow up mentally. She knew that upon her release, she'd have to own up to her self-proclaimed title of the queen of queens.

At times, while alone, she'd sit back and focus more on becoming a better person. As well, she'd sit back and think of ways she could mold and help others to become better individuals.

She started to take heed of the COs advice of helping others to become successful legitimately.

She enrolled in the prison's college.

Some days in school, she conjured up plans to sponsor people who wanted to go to college but couldn't afford to do so due to lack of finances. On the same note, she decided to sponsor people who rapped or sang or had any other talent. She wanted to assist people to find jobs instead of selling dope. In reality, she had the power to do all these things, but it would only come to light once she was free.

The rest of her stay in prison she stayed, besides having the ViceLords representatives on her security.

She continued to study different religions, took classes, and stayed reading books to enhance her knowledge of the concept of life within people, places, and things. Unlike her last time in jail, she wasn't involved in any chaos. She chilled out and worked on the powers of the brain. She knew that the way to survival in life came from utilizing the brain.

Chapter 23

U pon her release from prison she became more useful to the ViceLords and the community. She immediately made a rule that if a ViceLord from the hood under eighteen wasn't in school between the hours of 8:00 a.m. through 2:30 p.m., they'd get violated. That plan worked a little. Then she'd help ViceLords get jobs, especially those who were coming home from prison.

Coincidentally, she'd gotten cool with one of Chicago's black aldermen. Queeny had lots of clout. For those who had talent, like ball players, singers, rappers, and those who wanted to attend college, she'd do her best to help them.

She even had a designer to design her a clothing line, called KP Wear. She named it that outta respect for King Phill.

The clothing line consist of expensive leathers, clothing for kids, adult women and men, clothes for people in the urban community and clothing for people in the cooperate field.

She had the money for this laundered through one of her homies, Reginald. She knew Reginald since she was a kid. Reginald was one of the few niggas from the hood who wasn't gang affiliated, never sold dope or used dope, and some of his family were doctors and small business owners. So she figured she could use him to launder her money.

The first day the clothing line came out, she had a fashion show at the McCormick Place, Downtown Chicago. Everyone was there—from top designers, models, a few celebrities and athletes, and everybody from the hood.

The models came out, prancing up and down the stage like *Rip the Runway* on TV while listening to Beyoncé's song "Déjà Vu."

For hours, the models walked up and down the stage, modeling Queeny's clothing line. Queeny sat in the front row, amazed at what she had achieved. At that very moment, it was as if she couldn't hear anything or anyone in the room as she gazed at the models, amazed, as if she'd just saw something from another planet.

In days to follow, Queeny's clothing line was in stores across America as it instantly began selling to consumers. As Queeny money grew, she'd launder it through others to buy abandoned buildings to fix them up and rent them out for section 8.

Majority of her money laundering was done through the alderman and Reginald and some of his family members. She knew better to try to put things under her own name. The feds would be all over her in no time. Pending her release, she became a better individual. She became more of a peacemaker and a lawwoman for the ViceLords by utilizing her intelligence.

She'd see Bushwick often 'cuz they was from the same hood. She really wanted to put him inside a casket, but she didn't, because of her love of the ViceLords and because she was a changed woman, trying to maintain peace. She knew killings or any other type of shootings would cause problems for those she was trying to help to prosper.

This world she briefly lived in and how she was devoted to downgrade to lesser crimes and enhance prosperity would soon come to an end because of others' bullshit.

First, one of her workers who sold weight for her—dope and cocaine—was robbed for four and a half ounces of cocaine by a nigga whom she knew very well. What really pissed her off about that situation was that the nigga didn't even wear any mask or attempt to rat play by having someone else do it—he did it himself. Then one of her workers ran off with five stacks in cash. Then one of her cars was stolen by one of her old high school classmates, Big Famous, dope fiend ass.

Big Famous was a career car thief. Big Famous went in and out of jail for auto theft. Every time he was freed, cars would mysteriously come up missing from the hood.

Somebody told Queeny that they saw Big Famous steal her car.

When Queeny first got out she brought a little structure to ViceLord, but it wasn't unified like back in the day. One of the old-school ViceLords' universal elites, Stats, had gotten out of jail after doing time for a murder and started robbing, kidnapping, and extorting ViceLords from everywhere.

All these things were happening in a chronological order, and she knew she had to deal with all these matters.

Now Queeny and a band of ViceLords who were villains rode around, five cars deep, four people in each car loaded with semiautomatic weapons and handguns.

Queeny and her band of villains' first victim was Big Famous. They saw Big Famous one night, simply driving down the street, and told him to meet them in Garfield Park. Big Famous had no idea that Queeny knew he stole one of her cars.

"Why do you want me to meet you in Garfield Park?" Big Famous asked.

"Because I need to discuss some business with you. I need you to steal me some cars. I'll pay you for them," Queeny said.

The first thing came to Big Famous mind was *I'm finna get paid.*

Big Famous pulled off first as Queeny trailed him. When they made it to the middle of Garfield Park, which was called the Circle, Queeny literally blew half of Big Famous's head off with a .44.

It felt so good to her to be back to her old self again.

She had many things that had transpired and she'd let go that built up, and she released all those problems out on Big Famous.

No one besides Queeny's guys witnessed the murder 'cuz it was nighttime and no one hung in the Circle in the night time.

The next morning, Queeny and her villains start going to various spots out west, telling ViceLords that they had to abide by VL structure. That didn't work. It backfired. It became a war in the streets—ViceLords against ViceLords.

Within weeks, due to Queeny's warring with various sets of VLs in Chicago, the murder rate rose by 25 percent. That year, Chicago became the murder capital in the United States.

In no time, parts of Queeny's mob had been murdered, investigated, and locked up for committing murder.

Around that day and age, on the West Side of Chicago, when street wars occurred, they'd only last for a little while until the gangs' lawmen squashed them. This particular war would be on for life. Each time any of Queeny's people would be seen by ViceLords they were feuding with, there would be shootouts. Queeny's mob was marked for death. There were more people against law than with law, unlike back in the day.

In reality, Queeny was the good, one not the villain. She tried to keep peace and enforce law within the ViceLords. It's just that the new young generation who claimed being VL but didn't give a fuck about her nor the VL's law. They had their own way of governing and doing things, which was a system of anarchy that they'd grown to love and adore.

Before long, Stats was on Queeny's team. Stats never knew that before he was on her team she was on the verge of fucking him up for robbing and kidnapping the brothers.

What made Queeny put Stats on her team was because she was trying to enforce the law of VL. Stats was on the same thing. That's the reason why he began kidnapping, robbing, and extorting them: They were not real ViceLords. They were using the VL name in vain.

Bushwick teamed up with various ViceLords from outside the hood to get at Queeny. The main reason they wanted Queeny gone was because she had too much power and heart. She had more heart than most men. They knew that once she was gone, they'd be able to do the things they wanted to do within VL and in general. Basically, everyone who had their own joints or any amount of power wanted to be their own chiefs, and that would only come to light when Queeny was six feet deep.

They didn't wanna do the ViceLords. They just wanted to do them.

Bushwick wanted to take over at least one, if not all, of Queeny's dope spots. He mainly wanted to take the one that was in the hood. He wanted that spot so he could take over the hood. He knew that wouldn't be easy, so he devised a plan. The plan was to kill as many of Queeny's men as possible, and try to get her on the low. Then he could take over her spot and really be the king of the streets.

Bushwick began murdering Queeny's people on the low, but they couldn't locate Queeny. He'd send unmarked faces to do his dirty work killings. He did it this way in order for him to be a part of the war but not a target. Bushwick was definitely part of the war, but Queeny didn't know this at that point.

This particular war had nonstop casualties. Both sides would go round for round, no backing down. Because of this war, the Chicago Police Department hired many more officers.

The war was so intense and brutal that squad cars would park on the blocks where ViceLords dwelled. On several occasions, the ViceLords would wait to nightfall and shoot at the police because the police was stopping them from warring and selling drugs.

Once Queeny found out through truthful, reliable sources that Bushwick had teamed up with the outlaw ViceLords and was linked to many of shootings against her guys, it pissed her off.

I should've been killed that pussy-ass stud Bushwick. I knew that nigga was gonna be a problem from the beginning. But I tried to reason things out and be more civil, and look what it got me, Queeny thought.

Now she spread the word to her followers to begin fucking Bushwick and his guys up on sight.

They immediately went to his dope spot, which was in the same hood, and through gunfire, they caused bloodshed. Three were wounded, but no deaths.

Now Bushwick and his guys were on point because the nigga who wasn't shot recognized some of Queeny's guys shooting. Bushwick knew now that Queeny knew he was on the bullshit with the outlaw ViceLords, because why else would Queeny's guys come through his joint shooting?

After that, he really didn't give a fuck if she knew or not, because some of her guys shot his guys, so it was on.

The war became even more intense, because now Queeny knew Bushwick was involved.

With Queeny's and Bushwick's joints being only a few blocks away, neither one could sell dope from their joints in the hood. That would make anyone standing out there an easy target for an early death.

Twice in one week, Queeny saw Bushwick in the hood. They exchanged rapid gunfire, but neither one was shot.

Queeny began to feel depressed, knowing that she was one of the leading causes of death currently on the streets of Chicago. She began to go to this church on the south side of town. She chose to go to church on the south side of town because no one knew her in most areas out south. A majority of areas on the south side was filled with GDs, BDs, and Black P. Stones. There were ViceLords out south but not that many like out west. She went to this church called the Church of God. It was a big church that had a white pastor and a mostly black congregation.

While in prison, Queeny heard from some of her cell mates that this pastor conveyed powerful messages from God, and that his teachings of the Bible was as if God shined a light upon your world as he preached. They also told her he wasn't a hypocrite, only interested in offerings. Queeny knew he had to be on something because he was white despite a majority of his congregation being black.

She went to this church on a Sunday morning. All through service, it was as if God had shined a light upon her.

Coincidentally, the pastor began preaching about gangs being nonprofit organizations. "Every time I surf the Internet or turn my TV to the news, all I see is the devil working his evil magic. You got these little kids—babies, I call 'em—and adults that worship the devil. It's called being gang-affiliated—a ViceLord, a GD, or a Black Stone—when in reality all it is, is devil-worshipping. Within gangs, that's all you hear and see, bad things. From fights to selling drugs to killings. In the Bible, one of the Ten Commandments says 'Thou shall not kill,' but these gang members do, with no respect for God or anybody," the pastor said.

"Then you got some people who call gangs organizations. I agree with them on that, because gangs are nonprofit organizations. When you have worked at a certain job for many years, you get a pension. Gang members get old and retire. Retiring from a gang doesn't make sense to me. When you retire from a gang there's no pension, no benefits," the pastor said.

The pastor paused for a minute, reaching for his napkin and slowly wiping the sweat off his forehead. "Gang members, politicians, and even the police—those who are supposed to serve and protect, Muslims, and even our own Christian brothers have all got caught up in doing evil things for money. Money is the root of all evil. Follow the Lord and his ways. Never get caught up in greed. I'm a pastor of this big congregation, and you rarely see me collecting offerings or even donations. God will provide for me.

Always remember that all things you need in life, God will be a provider," the pastor said.

The pastor continued on, talking about a lot of topics that Queeny could relate to.

After the service, Queeny went over to shake the pastor's hand and to strike up a conversation with him.

"This is my first time hearing you preach. Keep doing what you're doing and the pearly gates of heaven await you," Queeny said.

"Thank you for the compliments, but you should be thanking God. Through God, all things exist. Through him, life is given through kids being born. Through him, he gave us air to breathe, vision to see, and all praises shall be unto thee," the pastor said.

The pastor looked into Queeny's beautiful hazel-brown eyes and began to admire her beauty.

"You're a beautiful young lady. What church do you normally attend?" the pastor asked.

"I'm not actually a church member. It's just that I've been going through some things and decided to visit your church for some upliftment," Queeny said.

"Sweetheart, what's wrong with you? What seems to be the problem?" the preacher asked.

"I have been having problems with many men. I've been the cause of death, destruction, and hate instead of loving," Queeny said.

The first thing that came to the pastor's mind was that she was involved in many bad relationships with men and that she was expressing words of death, destruction, and hate instead of loving because of bad relationships, not actually meaning those words literally.

"Sometimes you gotta let people be themselves. God has a plan for all of us. If something or someone is no good for you in some cases, God will take that individual away from you. Sometimes God puts us through troublesome times to appreciate and value the good things in life. All the bad things you've been experiencing with many men will soon come to an end, but only if you believe in the Heavenly Father. Give your life to him and pray for all bad things to turn good. Only he has the power to change your life for the better," the pastor said as Queeny genuinely hugged him.

Queeny slowly exited the church, thinking of all the things the pastor had said in service and after service.

Although it was war in the streets, Queeny found time to be alone and find tranquility. She'd go to the surburbs and take long walks in the park or rent a room in the Holiday Inn, alone.

At this point, she was seeking inner peace. All through her life, she'd had no peace. As a kid, she'd had problems that always resulted in violence. She had been around so much gunfire it was like music to her ears. She'd been in jail, stabbing and whupping hos. In the streets, she'd robbed, stolen, and killed. She'd become a cold-blooded, coldhearted killer. She wanted to change, but it was too late for that. She was in too deep.

Over time, the war between her, the outlaw ViceLords, and Bushwick didn't cease, but there was less gunfire. The reason there was less gunfire was because everybody had stopped simply having shootouts. They'd sit back and plot on murdering. The reason being that both sides had to bury their very own family members and friends; therefore, they wanted their revenge in its entirety.

Queeny and her loyal followers would now devise a way to kill the outlaw ViceLords. They'd find out where the outlaw ViceLords were lying or catch them creeping off to a ho's house or whatever and kill them. Basically, they'd catch them off their squares in areas outside their hoods as unmarked faces took their lives from them.

Queeny continued to go to the Church of God out south each Sunday. More and more, the pastor would talk directly to her, sincerely, trying to convince her to become a member.

One Sunday, she began to tell the pastor how she was feeling inside. "I been feeling real stressed out," Queeny said.

"Maybe you should get more into the Word of God. Practice meditation procedures or take some art classes," the pastor said.

"What does art classes gotta do with me being stressed out?" Queeny asked.

"Painting helps relieves stress. It requires a lot of quietness and concentration. While painting, you're only focused on painting your artwork, which results in a lot of peace. Try it. It works," the pastor said.

The pastor has a point. Maybe I should take art classes, Queeny thought.

The next day, she signed up to a college course at Kennedy King College to take an art class, among other classes. This was all ironic to her, because she was currently in a street war and started going to church and college in the midst of this bloody war. Her going to church and college was the safe haven for her to be away from the violence.

Chapter 24

Her first day of college, Queeny noticed that her art teacher and a few of her classmates were rocking KP wear.

Although Queeny was warring heavily in the streets, she was still getting money from clothing lines, rent from buildings, and dope money. It was hard for her to sell dope in certain hoods where ViceLords dwelled because of the warring. But she had all type of gangs selling dope for her, but under their names and buying weight from her guys; therefore, through it all, she kept getting money.

A few weeks after she began attending college, she met these two cousins, Regina and Stephanie.

Regina and Stephanie could see right through Queeny. They knew she wasn't this nerdy schoolgirl as she perpetrated her image to be. While at church and school, Queeny would fool people into thinking she was this quiet, innocent girl. But Regina and Stephanie weren't fooled.

Regina and Stephanie were from the streets, so they could recognize another individual from the streets. They could tell by some of the things she'd say out her mouth and by some of the things she'd do and from the expensive clothes she'd wear.

When Regina and Stephanie first met Queeny, it was a genuine interest in friendship. As time progressed, along their genuine friendship became a quest for financial growth and development.

In no time flat, Regina, Stephanie, and Queeny began hanging out a little. Queeny couldn't do too much hanging out and kicking it, because she had too much other shit going on with the ViceLords.

Regina and Stephanie began questioning Queeny about how she made her cash flow. They wondered if she'd sold drugs or what. Queeny read between the lines and knew that the girls wanted to start getting money with her one way or the other.

Eventually Regina and Stephanie began to be honest with their interest.

They started to explain to Queeny that in the area they were from, women couldn't sell dope for themselves, only for the men in the hood. Also, that money wasn't plentiful because the GDs and BDs would be warring too much to stand out and sell dope.

Regina and Stephanie wanted to see some major figures; not small-time nickel and dimes. They wanted to see five or six figures or better, not all at once, but overall.

The girls told Queeny that they didn't wanna sell dope for her. They wanted to be put in play some type of way to sell dope for themselves, or either sell some weight for her.

They also told Queeny that they had two male cousins who were stickup men. That if she could set up people to rob, their male cousins would stick them up, and they'd all split the money up evenly.

Regina and Stephanie let Queeny know that they weren't snakes, nor were their cousins snakes either.

Queeny got a lightbulb over her head, thinking like, *Damn, I could send Regina and Stephanie to become lovers with the outlaw members of ViceLord in order to set them up to be robbed and killed.*

For some reason, she figured she could trust Regina and Stephanie for the robbery part but not for the killing part. Queeny knew of too many scenarios where people were questioned for murders and turned states or, and told on who sent them to do it, which could have her locked up for a long-ass time for conspiracy to commit murder.

She figured out a way to test the girls' skills. She'd set Regina and Stephanie up for a fake task to see how they'd perform.

She purchased a car from a used car lot. It had dark tint on it. She did that because a majority of her cars were hot. A lot of people from the streets knew her cars. The dark tint was to conceal their identity. She took the girls to her own spot up north and pointed at the guy who was running the shift on her dope that day.

The girls had no idea that this was her spot and her workers.

"That's the guy right there. He the one running the joint. I just don't know where they holding the shit. I need ya'll to find out for me. The same day ya'll find out, I'll send my goons in there to rob 'em for everything they own," Queeny said.

The girls were hungry to get money. "You can drop us off around the corner," Regina said.

"Ya'll ready right now?" Queeny asked.

"Hell yeah," the girls said simultaneously.

Queeny pulled around the corner and parked. "His name is Stanley. When ya'll get finished, just call me, and I'll come back and get ya'll," Queeny said.

"Naw, we straight. We'll catch a cab or the bus," they said.

"It's a'ight. I'll come back and get ya'll," Queeny said.

"Naw, we straight. We'll holla at you later on," Gina said.

As Queeny drove off, her cell phone began ringing. "Hello," Queeny said.

"Homicide just grabbed Randell," Mike said.

"Who is this?" Queeny asked.

"This Mike."

"Damn that's fucked up. What's up with you? Are you good?" Queeny said.

"Yeah, I'm good. I gotta go. I'll holla at you later," Mike said.

"If you find out anything about Randell, let me know," Queeny said.

"Okay, I'll holla," Mike said.

"A'ight," Queeny said. Queeny nervously pushed End to conclude the call, hoping Randell wouldn't tell the police that she sent him to do those murders.

She decided to go over to the house of one of her girlfriends who lived up north. That night, her girlfriend sucked her pussy for hours then fucked her with a rubber dick, which gave her a momentary sense of relief from everything that she had going on in her life.

After sex, she sat down at a desk in her girlfriend's house and wrote both Stacey and Black letters. Through it all, she stayed in contact with Stacey and Black. After being incarcerated, she'd understand the importance of mail and support. Queeny would indirectly mention to Stacey and Black about the chaos that was going on in the streets. She couldn't actually tell them what was going on directly, because the staff in IDOC would read all incoming and outgoing mail. But Stacey and Black would understand once finished reading it.

The next day, Queeny wanted to go back to the hood but was afraid that Homicide would be looking for her because they grabbed one of her followers, Randell, and it was possible that they'd be looking for her. Queeny decided to drive to the suburbs to take a long walk in the park, alone. On her drive to the suburbs she got a call on her cell phone from Regina.

"Hello," Queeny said.

Regina, overly excited, said, "Girl, we found out the place where he is hiding the shit. He hiding it close by the joint, in a red-and-white house. The address is 7048 North Howard."

"Be cool, girl. Say no more. I'll be over there immediately," Queeny said.

On the way over to the girl's apartment, Queeny stopped at one of her safe houses where she held large sums of money and grabbed a thousand dollars.

Once Queeny made it to Regina and Stephanie's place, they both ran out and bailed in her car before she could even finish parking.

"We already talked to our cousins. They're ready to run in that crib as soon as possible," Regina said.

Once Queeny parked correctly, she reached into her pocket and tried handing the girls five hundred apiece. "Here go five hundred apiece for the both of ya'll. Dude I sent ya'll to check out was one of my workers. I just wanted to see if ya'll could perform," Queeny said.

Regina and Stephanie got quiet in disbelief.

"Girl, stop playing. We don't want no five hundred. We want the gs that's in that crib. Five hundred ain't shit. You trying to short-change us," Stephanie said.

"I knew ya'll would say that, but I'll take ya'll over there to show you I'm not lying," Queeny said.

"You just trying to keep the money that was in that house for yourself," Regina said.

"Be cool. I'm going to take you over there to show ya'll I'm telling the truth," Queeny said.

During the entire ride over there, they still didn't believe her but had to give her the benefit of the doubt.

As they rode over there, Queeny was pleased that the girls pulled it off but pissed off that her worker Stanley even gave them the opportunity to even find out where the dope and money were, especially in a short period of time such as one day or less.

Queeny now knew that Stanley was a candidate to get robbed. She considered firing Stanley, but didn't want to because he was a loyal worker and had been with her since she first started out when her money was low.

Queeny had her dope spot run similar to a regular business, like a regular job. There would be workers to do various task. She also had shifts, which consisted of people working only specific hours. Stanley worked two days out of a week, back to back. Therefore, he worked the shift the day before, and on this particular day.

As they made it a few blocks away from the joint, Queeny told Regina and Stephanie never to tell Stanley or anyone else of the whole ordeal. They both agreed. Once they made it to the joint, Queeny rode up to Stanley. "Stanley, give me a hundred dollars off that money," Queeny said.

Queeny didn't need that hundred dollars. She only did that as a quick way to prove to Regina and Stephanie that she was telling the truth. Once Stanley handed Queeny the hundred, he looked in the car and noticed Regina and Stephanie in there.

"I didn't know you knew Stephanie and Regina," Stanley said.

"I didn't know you knew them. Where do you know them from?" Queeny asked.

"I met them yesterday, walking down the street. I thought ya'll said ya'll was going to call me," Stanley said.

"Stan, we gotta go. We'll holla at you later on, man," Queeny said before the girls even got a chance to answer him.

Queeny then drove to the white-and-red house.

"Do ya'll want to see the inside of the house? I own it. I got the keys right here in my pocket," Queeny said.

"Naw, it's cool. We believe you," the girls said.

"Tell me vividly, how did you find out where he was holding the shit at?" Queeny asked.

"The shit was simple. It came naturally. Once me and Gina started walking up the block toward him, we swiftly devised a plan. The plan was to first see if he smoked weed. If he did, we'd ask him where they had some weed at. We'd go buy some weed, come back and smoke with him, and get around to tricking him into thinking he was going to fuck us. Now if he didn't smoke, we'd just sit around and kick it and eventually trick him into thinking we both wanted him to fuck us at the same damn time under the threesome act. It's not too many men that would refuse having sex with two good-looking girls at the same time," Stephanie said.

"You hos ain't all that good-looking," Queeny said as they all began laughing.

"So we walked up to him and told him that we recently moved in the hood and that we moved from outta town. Then we asked him, where do they sell weed at? He directed us to a spot around the corner. So we went around the corner bought a few sacks and went to the liquor store and bought some blunts and drinks," Stephanie said.

"We went back to the joint and asked him to roll the blunts for us because we didn't know how to roll and that we wanted to smoke the weed with him. He immediately began rolling the weed up. Outta nowhere, Gina asked him, did he have a girlfriend? That opened up the door for conversation," Stephanie said.

"Do he got a girlfriend?" Queeny asked.

"Naw," Stephanie said.

"Once we started smoking and joking, he told us that we can't hang around the joint to long 'cuz it was hot. We told him we knew how to maintain ourselves in a dope spot, and that he should be happy we standing on the spot with him 'cuz he'd have less problems outta the police with two women standing beside him," Stephanie said.

"So while we continued to smoke and drink, this ho Gina told him we'd like to have a threesome with him," Stephanie said.

"You should've seen how he looked when we began to talk about a threesome," Regina said.

"So ya'll just walked up just asking to fuck?" Queeny said.

"Naw, girl, we worked our way into it. We learned that game from the niggas we use to fuck with in the past. They wouldn't just walk up and ask to fuck. They'd talk about a lot of other different shit that led up to fucking," Regina said.

"But we ain't never did no threesome before. Well, at least I ain't," Stephanie said.

"After we got him high and drunk and had him thinking he was gonna fuck both of us, everything fell into play," Stephanie said.

"We sat back and did our observation. Every time this one dude finished selling the pack, he'd bring him the money. After dude finished selling two packs, Stanley would take the money and tell us to stay on the joint, he'll be right back. So the third time he left us on the joint, we followed him without him even knowing it. We followed him to this red-and-white house. So when he went into the house, we'd rush back to the joint, and stayed there, waiting on him, chilling. Then the fourth time he left, we followed him again, just to make sure it was the right house," Stephanie said.

"Once we finished kicking it with him, we gave him a fake phone number and spent off. We went to the red-and-white house to get the exact address and walked around the corner to the cab stand and caught a cab home," Stephanie said.

"I gotta watch you hos. You hos too slick for me," Queeny said. "Listen to me."

"We listening," the girls said.

"I got a few real licks I can send ya'll on, but ya'll can't tell nobody," Queeny said.

"We know how this shit go. We ain't gone tell nobody," Regina said.

"I don't need ya'll cousins either. I got my own team to run in the houses. I just need ya'll to find out where the houses are at," Queeny said.

"A'ight, we got you," the girls said.

"We ready now," Regina said.

"Give me a little more time. I gotta find some niggas to sick ya'll on," Queeny said.

I thought you said you already had a few licks set up, Gina thought.

"You said that you owned that red-and-white house. You must be holding," Gina said.

"Naw, I got that from one of my family members that died. Before she died, she put the deed in my name, because she had been having heart troubles and knew she wasn't going to live long," Queeny said. She was lying. She owned that building and a lot of more other shit from selling dope to fiends.

Days overlapped, and Queeny wanted to give the girls a shot at the title, but she was still afraid of getting them involved with many murders. Queeny knew that once the girls found out where certain niggas lived, she wasn't interested in robbing them—she wanted to take their lives away.

Fuck it then. If this is the only way that I can get close to certain niggas, by sicking Gina and Stephanie on them, then that's what it's gone be, Queeny thought.

Queeny sat by herself, second-guessing her decision to send Stephanie and Gina to handle the business. *The girls need the money, and I need them to find out where these niggas live, but I don't wanna get them involved with the murders,* Queeny thought.

After a week passed, Queeny decided to give the girls a chance.

"I got something for ya'll to do," Queeny said.

"What is it? We're ready for whatever. We just wanna get paid," Regina said.

"I do got something for ya'll to do, but it's a problem with me sending ya'll to set up people to get robbed," Queeny said.

"What's the problem?" Gina asked.

"The people ya'll will be setting up to rob might hesitate on giving the money up when my guys go in their houses to get the shit or they might try to reach for their guns and my guys might gotta kill them," Queeny said.

"So what's the problem?" Gina asked.

"What, we give a fuck if somebody gets killed? We ain't gone be there," Stephanie said.

"But Homicide might question ya'll, and I don't know if ya'll a fold under pressure," Queeny said.

"We ain't no stool penguins. We ain't gone tell the police shit. What goes on in the streets, stays in the streets," Regina said.

Regina then lifted up her shirt.

"Damn girl what happen to your stomach?" Queeny asked.

"When I was fifteen I got shot up by this nigga whose weed spot I use to rob. It was this nigga in the hood that use to sell plenty of weed, a straight bitch. Well, at least I thought he was until he shot the shit outta of me. I robbed his joint a few times with no mask and didn't even get that much money. Maybe a couple hundred at the most and some weed. One day, I was coming out the store and he walked up in broad daylight and told me, 'Girl, I'm tired of you steady robbing my joint.' I told the nigga fuck him and spit in his face. He upped a small chrome gun and shot me twice in the stomach," Regina said.

"Girl, I done saw people get shot and have surgery, and the doctors cut them up to get the bullets out. But your stomach looks like they had a hacking fest on it, uhhhh," Queeny said.

"While I was in the hospital, I got investigated by the police, and I never told them who shot me, and never will, fuck the police," Gina said. Gina took off her shirt and showed Queeny some stab wounds that were on her back.

Queeny looked at the stab wounds in amazement. "Somebody tried to kill you," Queeny said.

"I got into a fight with a girl. I was fucking with her man. She stabbed me in the back five times. One of the stab wounds was an inch from my heart. One more inch, I'd be dead. But I never told the police," Gina said.

"That's good that you didn't work with the police on those two incidents. But it's different when Homicide is investigating you and trying to charge you with a murder. I done even saw killers turn into stool penguins and turn states on murders when them people get to talking about you spending the rest of your natural life in prison. That's different," Queeny said.

"We been investigated for murders when we were teenagers. Even though we was up with the murders, we never told or slipped up and gave them any information," Stephanie said.

"What the fuck was ya'll doing being investigated for murders?" Queeny asked.

"Well, in our younger days the GDs use to misuse us to set up the BDs to get robbed and sometimes killed. Homicide began to notice a pattern that some of the guys we was hanging out with was mysteriously getting killed, so they started to question us about murders," Stephanie said.

"We stopped setting the BDs up 'cuz Homicide was questioning us too much. And the GDs would rob the BDs for gs and only give us a couple of hundred at the most. We felt like, why should we set people up to get robbed for gs and only get chump change? If we were going to be involved with setting niggas up, it would have to be for some high stacks," Stephanie said.

"Why was ya'll involved with setting up the BDs in the first place?" Queeny asked.

"We SOS," Stephanie said.

"What the fuck is SOS?" Queeny said.

"We GD sisters," Stephanie said.

"Ah, ya'll GDs, I'm a ViceLord," Queeny said. "I didn't know you hos been through all that shit."

"Aw, like we suppose to walk up to you and tell you we money-hungry hos. We GDs, and we set people up to get robbed and killed. I don't think that's the right way to get cool with somebody," Stephanie said sarcastically.

Queeny began to smirk, thinking, *These hos is something else.*

"It's a lot of shit you ain't told us. You a damn ViceLord, you got your own dope spot, and you own a building. Is there something else you wanna bring to the table?" Regina said sarcastically.

"Yes, I'm gay," Queeny said.

"That's sounds like a personal issue. We don't give a fuck if you have sex with animals. We wanna eat. We need money," Regina said. "You must understand something about us: we ain't no snakes, and we'll never bite the hand that feeds us. We'll never cross you under no circumstances."

The same day, Queeny rode through the hood in an unmarked car behind smoke-black tint and showed Regina and Stephanie this guy named Fatty. They called him Fatty because he was fat and every time you'd see him, he'd be eating something. Queeny told them to work their magic and get close to him. "Find out where he lives, and we gonna rob him."

Gina and Stephanie, being thirsty, told Queeny to let them out around the corner, and that they'll holla at her tomorrow.

What Gina and Stephanie didn't know was that Queeny didn't wanna rob Fatty. She wanted him dead, and they would be the key to causing him his death.

Gina and Stephanie walked up to Fatty and began cracking jokes.

"I see you like to eat a lot," Gina said.

Fatty had heard of all the fat jokes before, and they didn't hurt his feelings.

They ended up talking for a little while, going to the park in the hood and enjoying continuously smoking blunts and drinking. The girls could immediately tell that Fatty was more interested in Regina.

After a couple of hours passed, Fatty began wondering where the girls were from. "Ya'll must just moved around here. I ain't never saw ya'll before," Fatty said.

"Naw, we ain't from around here. We was just walking up the block and saw you and decided to strike up a conversation with you," Gina said.

"Outta all the guys standing on the block, why ya'll chose me?" Fatty asked.

"Because you're the cutest," Gina said.

Right then and there, Fatty began thinking, *These hos kinda slick. They gonna be wanting some money to fuck.*

Regina and Fatty ended up exchanging numbers, and they all went their separate ways. The same night, Fatty called Gina, and they had a long and meaningful conversation.

"Let me come through, pick you up so we can go a few rounds," Fatty said.

"Hell naw, I don't get down like that on the first date," Gina said.

"Naw, I was just joking. I'll come through tomorrow to pick you up. Where you live at?" Fatty asked.

"No, you can't come over here to pick me up," Gina said.

"Why not?" Fatty asked.

"My ex lives right next door to me and he's caught up in some fatal attraction shit. But still, call me tomorrow and I'll meet you in your hood or wherever you want me to meet you. I hope I ain't going to have problems outta none of your crazy-ass girlfriends," Gina said.

"No, I don't have one of them. I'll call you tomorrow," Fatty said before hanging up.

The next day, Queeny called Gina and Stephanie. They lived together out south. Gina answered the phone.

"Did ya'll become successful on finding out where he lives?" Queeny asked.

"Naw, we ain't found out where he lives just yet. You know, the last task was easy 'cuz the nigga was hustling on a dope spot.

This task might take a while 'cuz you know niggas ain't quick to let nobody know where they live. I might gotta fuck this fat motherfucker to find out where he lives," Gina said.

"Let me holla at Stephanie," Queeny said.

"She sleep. Fatty ain't interested in her. He interested in me," Gina said.

"Just keep pursuing him, and I'll see ya'll in a few days in school," Queeny said.

"Why won't I see you tomorrow in school?" Gina asked.

"You know I didn't take up that many classes, I only go to school on Mondays and Thursdays," Queeny said.

"Aww, that's right! I don't see you all during the week at school," Gina said.

"A'ight, I'll holla at you in a few days," Queeny said.

Chapter 25

Queeny went home ran herself a hot bubble bath to soak her body and to collect her thoughts. Queeny began to visualize all the bad things she'd done. She began to envision gunfire and sparks flying.

While soaking in the tub, she decided to shave her pubic hairs. She grabbed a razor and began shaving.

After shaving, she put a small mirror between her legs to enjoy the view. The baldness of her pussy looked so good to her.

She rubbed some Vaseline on the outer lips of her pussy. Before long, she began fingering herself. Her fingers wasn't satisfying enough, so she went into her room to grab her rubber dick. She went back into the washroom to finish what she'd started. She began to force the huge rubber dick in and out her pussy swiftly until she reached her orgasm. She then placed the rubber dick in her mouth and began sucking it like it was a real actual dick. At that very moment, she remembered what someone had told her in the past: that you only have one life to live and should enjoy it sexually. She wanted to get fucked by a man, which she hadn't done in a long time.

She had too many things going on to be getting involved with a man as a lover, but she promised herself that once she had the time, she would start back fucking with a man.

Queeny finished bathing, got dressed, and began to drive to this place in downtown Chicago that sold popcorn. They sold all sorts of heated, melted popcorn. On her way to the popcorn place, she got a call on her cell phone.

"Hello," Queeny said.

Before she could find out who the individual was, he began saying, "Homicide looking for you for murders."

"Who this is?" Queeny asked.

"This is Reese."

"Reese, how many times have I told you not to talk about criminal activities over the phone?" Queeny said.

Reese didn't answer. He remained silent, because Queeny had told him many times not to discuss criminal shit on the phone many times before.

"I'll meet you somewhere later on, and you can tell me all about what Homicide was talking about. Don't call me. I'll call you," Queeny said.

As Queeny continued to drive to the popcorn place, she got two more calls on her cell phone from different people indirectly talking in codes, mentioning Homicide was looking for her.

She told the last individual, Reginald, that she was going to eat popcorn.

Reginald knew that when she said she was going to eat popcorn, that was an indirect way to tell him to meet her at the popcorn place downtown.

Reginald was one of the only individuals she really trusted with her money and in general.

Once she made it to the popcorn place, Reginald was already there. First thing he did was hug her tightly. "Homicide is looking for you for many murders," Reginald said.

"How do you know they're looking for me for many murders instead of one?" Queeny asked.

"Because they told me that they was looking for you for many murders when they questioned me," Reginald said.

"Why did they question you about me?" Queeny asked.

"They've been questioning everybody about you. You need to go outta town and stay the fuck away from Chicago," Reginald said.

"How much money do you got of mines?" Queeny asked Reginald.

"Seven hundred thousand," Reginald said.

"Damn! Seven hundred thousand. I didn't know you had that much of my money," Queeny said.

"You don't keep count of the money you have people holding for you," Reginald said.

"I keep count of everyone else's money but yours. You're one of the few people I trust," Queeny said.

"You shouldn't trust no one, not even me. The same one you trust will be the one to stab you in your back," Reginald said.

Queeny looked him straight in his eyes. "See, that's why I trust you," she said.

"I don't know how much money my family got of yours, but I'm pretty sure it's more than I got," Reginald said. "Why don't you leave Chicago?"

"Don't worry. I will in due time," Queeny said.

As they sat down eating their popcorn, Reginald began checking Queeny out because she was looking good as ever. "Damn, girl, you looking all ladylike. You got on a skirt, high heels, featherweight glasses. I never saw you like this before. Usually, you be thugged out like one of the guys," Reginald said.

"I'm dressed like this to stay under the radar with the police," she said.

They ate their popcorn, Reginald hugged Queeny tightly. "I love you, and be more careful," Reginald said.

"I will," Queeny said.

They both went their separate ways.

As Reginald drove off in his car, a tear slid from his right eye, down his cheek. The tear slid from his eye because he knew that once Homicide finally caught up with Queeny, she'd never see the streets again. She might even get the death penalty. Reginald had been around Queeny since he was a little boy. Through it all, she showed him nothing but love. He really did love Queeny, and she could trust him.

As Queeny left the popcorn place worried and confused, she wondered what would be her next move. While riding down a seemingly lonely highway, her cell phone began to ring. She was hesitant to answer but went on and answered anyway. She answered it to find out it was Nigeria.

"Meet me over my house in Glendale Heights," Nigeria said.

"I didn't know you had a house in Glendale Heights," Queeny said.

"It's a low-key house that don't nobody knows about but me, but now you do. Write down my address and come over as soon as possible," Nigeria said.

"Just tell me, and I'll remember it," Queeny said.

Nigeria told Queeny the address, and Queeny drove straight over there.

Since Queeny and Nigeria first met, they always kept in contact. And ever since Queeny started selling dope on her own the first time she was released from prison, she always bought her weight of the heroin from Nigeria. For a long time, Nigeria lived in Miami. She moved from Chicago, but she never sold her buildings in Chicago. She'd come to the Chi often, and sometimes stayed for months at a time.

Nigeria still had people in play in Chicago and in various other places that would sell weight on the heroin for her. Through it all, Queeny continued to buy large quantities of heroin from Nigeria's workers.

Once Queeny made it to the address Nigeria gave her, before she could even ring the doorbell, Nigeria opened the door and snatched her in.

"Girl, what the fuck have you gotten yourself into? I only been in Chicago for two days to make sure my business was getting taken care of, and Homicide done question me twice for your whereabouts. They say that you killed more people than John Wayne Gacy. First they questioned me at my beauty shop, then they questioned me again at my liquor store," Nigeria said.

"How do they know that I even fuck with you?" Queeny asked.

"I don't know. I just know they looking for your ass, and a lot of more other people that fucks with you. You betta leave the country. I can find you somewhere to live in Nigeria. Are you financially stable? Do you need cash to hide out?" Nigeria asked.

"Girl, I got money to the ceiling," Queeny said.

"You need to start hiding out ASAP. Fuck trying to leave the city or state. Leave the country. I saw too many people on the run from the police in different states or cities always end up getting caught. With all the murder-homicide claims you're wanted for, even if you beat the majority of them, you still going to get booked on at least one of them and forced to spend the rest of your life in jail. You're an intelligent young lady. How did you get yourself in so much trouble?" Nigeria said.

"I'm being loyal to the game," Queeny said.

"'Loyal to the game,'" Nigeria said.

"I'm loyal to the ViceLords," Queeny said.

"Being loyal to the ViceLords will get you killed or stuck in the penitentiary for the rest of your life. Don't get me wrong, it's good to stand on nation business, but only to a certain extent. I used to be Ebony ViceLord–crazy. Now if any one asks me, I'm done with that. I'm non–gang affiliated. I'm focused on my dope operation, my businesses, my family, and my future," Nigeria said.

"Well, I'm going to be a ViceLord 'til I die, and I ain't ready to die. And I ain't running from the police. Fuck the police. If push comes to shove, they can get it just like any other motherfucker that cross me. To me, the police ain't no different from us. We're all human beings that can die by the hands of another. Fuck the police," Queeny said.

"Girl, you done lost your damn mind," Nigeria said.

"I'm the queen of queens of the ViceLords. I'm going to be that until the pallbearers carry me away," Queeny said.

Then both of them instantly got quiet as she looked Nigeria in her eyes. Nigeria could see the seriousness written all over Queeny's face.

Queeny ended up spending the night with Nigeria. All night, Nigeria pleaded with Queeny to leave the country. Her pleading didn't work.

The next morning, before Queeny left her home, Nigeria told her that if she ever needed some help to let her know. That was what she was there for.

Nigeria hugged Queeny, thinking, *I might not never see this girl in the free world again or even alive. That's fucked up that this girl turned out to be this way. How could she be so heartless?*

Queeny owned many buildings, but ever since the war got heated in the streets, she began to live in rented apartments. The reason being that people knew where some of her buildings were. If they didn't know, she didn't want them to know through finding out by seeing her come in and out of them. She used Reginald and his family to maintain a large portion of her property.

Queeny went to this apartment she rented on the lower part of the south side, the low end. She went there to bathe, change clothes, and get some tranquility. While bathing, she found herself getting all hot and bothered and craving for a man's dick to go in and out of her pussy vigorously, which she hadn't had in years.

Once she finished bathing, she walked to the kitchen to fix herself a cold glass of Kool-Aid as her cell phone rang. She answered it to find out it was Reginald.

"Hey, Reginald. What's going on, man?" she said.

"Nothing, just chilling. I decided to call you to see if you were safe," Reginald said.

"You don't have to worry about me. I'm a big girl and know how to take care of myself," Queeny said.

"I wanna see you. I wanna spend the day with you," Reginald said.

"Why all of a sudden you wanna see me and spend the day with me? You ain't been wanted to spend time with me. It's been times when I ain't heard from you in months," Queeny said.

"I miss you. Spend the day with me," he said.

"Boy, you know I can't be hanging out because people are looking for me," she said.

"We can spend time in my apartment. I'll fix you dinner, and we can watch some old black-and-white gangster movies," Reginald said.

"But you live in the hood," she said.

"No, I don't. I been moved from the hood. I stay way out in the hundreds," he said.

Queeny paused for a minute before saying yes, thinking that this might be a set up. *He could be setting me up for the police or to get robbed or killed,* she thought. "Yeah, I'll come over there. What time do you want me to come?" she asked.

"Right now," he said.

She really wasn't interested in going over to his house, 'cuz it could've been a set up. She just said yes to spin him.

He then gave her his address, right before they hung up the phone.

Why would Reginald set me up for the police or even to get killed or robbed? I know he don't fuck with the police or niggas from the streets. He don't need to rob me, 'cuz he got access to a large sum of my money. If I can't trust nobody, I can trust Reginald, she thought.

Queeny left her apartment and drove straight to Reginald's place. As she made it to the address Reginald gave her, she noticed it was a condominium building. She realized that he didn't even give her the apartment number. She called him.

"I'm in front of the building you gave me the address to, but you didn't give me the damn apartment number," she said.

"The apartment number is 3B. Come on up," Reginald said.

Once she made it in, she noticed that it was real clean and the living room was covered with pictures of her.

"Damn, why do you have all them pictures of me everywhere? What, you in love with me or something?" she said.

"Yes, of course I love you as I love my sister or my mother. I got all them pictures all around the house because if it wasn't for you, I wouldn't have the things I got. Without you, my life would have no meaning. Thanks to you I'm always able to shine," he said.

They went into the kitchen. Queeny became pleased with the smell of the food. "What's that you cooked?" she asked.

"I cooked some steak, and Rice-A-Roni," he said.

"Rice-A-Roni, a San Fransisco treat," she said as they both began laughing.

"I got some aged wine too," he said.

"You're a player. If I didn't know better, I'd say you was trying to fuck me," she said.

"Girl, stop playing," he said.

Reginald dimmed the kitchen light, placed candles on the table, and lit them.

"Reginald, you must really wanna fuck," she said.

"Girl, stop playing, and let's eat," he said.

As they began eating and sipping wine, Reginald began to talk to Queeny about her future. "Queeny, you need to leave the streets alone and go far away from Chicago. Change your identity and even your thug lifestyle and start all over again—a new life, a new beginning. You're a good woman. Maybe you need to get married and have kids someday. You need to leave Chicago as soon as possible, because you know as well as I do that when the police catch your ass, you ain't never getting out of jail. I know and heard of people like you that got a lotta money pay off witnesses and hire top-flight lawyers to beat their cases, but your ass got to many bodies to beat. You done killed more motherfuckers than Charles Manson and Jeffrey Dahmer put together," he said.

"I know you're one of the few people who care about me, but I got my own life to live. Like I told one of my old friends, I'm going to be a ViceLord until I die," she said.

"Girl, you done lost your damn mind," Reginald said.

"I'm going to continue to stand on ViceLord business until ViceLord is unified and is abiding by law," she said.

"Girl, now you know that will never happen," he said.

"Well, I'm going to be working on it 'til I die. I'd love to see ViceLords unified all together, doing good," she said.

"Well, why you steady killing ViceLords?" he asked.

"I'm only killing those ViceLords that say they're ViceLords but really ain't ViceLords. The new-age ViceLords just claiming it but ain't abiding by the concept of ViceLords. That's like me saying I'm a Christian, but daily, I'm committing sins. You feel me, baby? Although it's a new generation of ViceLords, the concept and laws of ViceLords will never change. If King Phill could see what ViceLord has come to, he'd be rolling in his grave. I'm not doing what I'm doing for me. I'm doing it for the love of 22, 12," she said.

"But, Queeny, sometimes you gotta let go of certain people, places, and things that's no good for you. You need to leave town 'fore the police catch your ass," he said.

"You do got a valid point outta all the things you just said, but I must, I will, and I am willing to sacrifice everything I own—even my very own life—for the upliftment of this very ViceLord nation," she said.

Queeny then smiled with a devilish grin on her face and said, "Like the rappers Bone say, 'This is the thug I be me. As long as you live, you'll never meet another bad girl like me, the queen of all queens.'"

As they continued to eat several servings of steaks and Rice-A-Roni, Reginald began to admire Queeny's outer beauty.

"Girl, you too cute to be a killer," Reginald said.

"How do killers suppose to look?" she asked.

"Not like you. You're cute, like a supermodel or one of them chicks off them Maybelline commercials," he said. Reginald put a smile on her face. "Not to be all in your personal business, but what made you turn gay?" he asked.

"I turned gay when I was in jail because it was only women around and because I always wanted to be dominant over my lovers while fucking. But I could never do that over a man, only a woman. It's funny that you brought that up, 'cuz lately I've been going through a confusing stage. I really been wanting to get fucked by a man. I haven't been fucked by a man in a long-ass time," she said.

Spontaneously they both started kissing.

Within minutes, Queeny and Reginald were asshole-naked on Reginald's couch, fucking. Queeny was on all fours as Reginald tore the pussy up from the back. Reginald fucked like he never fucked before.

"You can't fuck me no harder than that? You fuck like a bitch," Queeny said as Reginald began fucking her harder and faster.

I should've been hitting this pussy. This shit is a bomb, Reginald began thinking.

As he began to nut, he took his dick out her pussy and released his nut all over her pretty yellow ass.

He then looked up and saw his cousin Rico on the other side of the living room, asshole-naked and jagging off, watching them fuck.

"What the fuck is you doing?" Reginald said as Queeny got alarmed, looked up, saw Rico, and began covering her body.

Rico remained speechless with his dick in his hand, not knowing what to say or do.

"Who the fuck is dude?" Queeny asked.

"This is my cousin," he said.

"How did the fuck he get in here?" she asked.

"He been in here. He was in the room, asleep. Man, I should beat your pussy ass," Reginald said.

Queeny grabbed Reginald, who was on the verge of rushing toward Rico. "Naw, man, don't get him," she said. Queeny paused for a few seconds, remembering what someone had told her in the past: we only got one life to live, and we might as well enjoy it sexually. "If that nigga that thirsty to sit and watch us fuck jagging off, he might as well join in," she said.

Both Reginald and Rico looked at each other in disbelief.

Queeny ceased covering up her body, lay back on the couch flat on her stomach, and said, "Which one of you girls is gonna go first?"

Rico got on top of her and began showing her what her pussy was made for. Within a couple of minutes, Reginald was ready for his turn.

"Hurry up, man. When you nut, it's my turn, and then when I nut, it's your turn again," Reginald said.

They took turns fucking her. Each time one of them would nut, then it would be the other one's turn. They took turns fucking her for a long time. After being fucked thoroughly, Queeny sat on the couch, feeling good.

"Come closer," Queeny told Reginald.

Once he got close, she began sucking on his dick. She'd engulf his dick as if she'd been craving and dreaming of sucking his dick. Once Reginald let his nut loose in her face, she then began sucking Rico's dick. Afterward Rico went into his bedroom and came out with blunts already rolled. He gave one to Queeny to fire up, and he fired up one himself.

"Two hits and pass," Rico said.

Rico wanted them to take two hits and pass so that majority of the time, they'd always be smoking instead of impatiently waiting to hit the blunt. As the blunts rotated several times, Queeny began to feel better than she did in a long time. The weed was a bomb. Queeny hadn't smoked weed or used any other drugs in years.

As they continued to smoke, Queeny began to visualize how those two men just fucked her brains out.

After continuous inhaling and exhaling of smoke, she began to answer one of her unanswered questions: What could she do to relieve stress? The answer wasn't art or any one of those other things. It was smoking weed.

As they finished smoking the weed, the guys were anxious to continue fucking. She told them to wait as she walked into the kitchen to get the wine.

She drunk a half bottle of wine nonstop.

Once she finished drinking the half bottle of wine, Reginald bent her over on the kitchen table and began fucking her from the back.

Through the night, with breaks, the guys fucked Queeny and loved every minute of it.

In the morning, before she left the guys' condo, she asked Rico if he could take her to get some weed and if he could roll it up for her.

"Girl, you smoke and you don't know where to get weed from or how to roll it?" Rico said.

"I ain't got high in a long-ass time," she said.

"How long is a long time?" he asked.

"A long-ass time," she said.

"I got some blunts in my room already rolled up. I'll give you a few to take with you," he said.

"I'll pay you for them," she said.

"Girl, stop playing. You ain't gotta pay me for no few blunts," he said. Rico then tried to make arrangements to fuck again.

She told him, "I'll let you know when."

As she departed the condo, Rico hugged her first. Then Reginald hugged her and whispered in her ear, "Be more careful."

Queeny went to her rented apartment to cleanse herself. Usually she'd bathe in the tub. This time she chose to take a shower. The shower felt so hot and good. For some strange reason, it was a reminder of last night.

After showering, she went into the kitchen and fixed her some beef bacon and eggs. She was a true ViceLord and felt that she was forbidden to eat swine. After eating, she went into the bedroom, fired up a blunt and turned the TV on. It was around 10:00 a.m. She cut off her cell phone. She didn't feel like being bothered. As she surfed through the channels, she saw this movie called *Juice* beginning to come on BET. *Juice* was a street movie starring the deceased rapper Tupac. As she began to watch it, she became aware that this time, she'd watched the movie, it was better than all the other times she'd watched it. The movie was better because she was getting high while watching it.

Although she'd seen this movie many times before, throughout watching the movie this time, she became reminded of herself through the rapper Tupac who wanted power, juice.

All throughout her life, she wanted to have the juice, which would, in turn, possibly cost her her life as it did the rapper Tupac in the movie. The only difference with her and the movie was her situation was reality. The movie was only a set of actors playing roles.

Once she finished watching *Juice* she turned to the WGN *News at Noon*. It was showing the top story of the day: more gun violence. It showed faces of six men who were killed, all at the same incident.

"Authorities say someone kicked in the door of the house in which the six men were, killing all six men execution-style, leaving no witnesses, no fingerprints, no evidence. At this time, authorities had no leads on who the gunman or gunmen were," the news man said.

Queeny knew four outta the six who were killed. She didn't know all four personally. She knew only one personally. He was from another hood. He was one of the ViceLords who were against Queeny, and he was one of the rival ViceLords' main triggermen. The other three she knew only from seeing them around in other areas when ViceLords had structure. She used to be able to rotate with ViceLords freely.

Good. Them bitches dead, she thought.

She didn't know exactly who did the killings, but it was obvious to her that some of her guys were the cause of those six men's deaths, which was all a good thing. They killed six people and got away from the scene of the crime with no witness to point a finger at them. To her, the only fucked-up part about it was that they were all ViceLords, and ViceLords were supposed to stick together instead of warring against one another.

Once they took down the pictures of the six men who were killed and finished their report on the incident, the mayor of Chicago popped up on the screen. The mayor of Chicago began talking about how the gang violence must stop. Queeny began thinking that certain politicians—like the mayor, for example—commit more crimes than street thugs. They just did it on different levels.

The mayor of Chicago was Italian. He was being investigated by the feds for being part of the Italians' organized mob. He was also being investigated for taking numerous bribes, among other shit.

She began to think of how many times she'd seen on the news that an off-duty cop shot a man after a bar fight with no probable cause. *Chances are that he'll beat the case,* she thought.

She'd saw too many times where the police did shit under criminal elements, even got caught on tape, and still never get convicted for their crimes.

Her heart began to cry out to those on death row. She felt that the people who put other people to death by law—whether it's lethal injection or whatever—were the same as killers in the streets. The only difference was they got laws and proper procedures to justify their killings. Illinois had sent many people to death row who didn't actually commit the murders they were convicted of.

In reality, some (but not all) law officials and those who work in the judicial system to uphold the law were some of the biggest crooks.

She fired up another blunt and turned to BET to watch some music videos. A rerun of *106 & Park* was on and the new joint of the day was an upcoming artist named Keyshia Cole. Queeny had never heard of Keyshia Cole, but she sat and listened to it anyway.

The song was "Sent from Heaven." As she continued to puff on the blunt, it was as if the best melodies reached her ears.

For that brief moment in time, it was as if she was actually sent to heaven. She began reminiscing about the fun times she had in life, such as sexual intercourse with men and women, traveling to different places, getting money, and simply enjoying herself.

After the Keyshia Cole song went off, she cut the TV off and fell into a peaceful sleep.

Later on that night, she awoke to the harsh reality of being wanted by the cops and being involved with killings that would never stop, even once her own casket drops.

She set fire to another blunt and went into the kitchen to heat up a frozen cheese pizza.

While the pizza was heating up, she went into the bedroom to admire her artillery. In that apartment, she had a Tec-22, a 9-millimeter Ruger, and a .25 automatic.

While admiring her guns, she continued to puff on the blunt, thinking what she would do if the police were to kick the door in at that very moment and what she would do when and if the police caught up with her, period.

She placed the blunt in her mouth, leaving it there with no hands; grabbed the Tec-22; cocked back the hammer, putting one in the chamber; and began to smirk. In her own mind, she knew beyond reasonable doubt that if Homicide ever caught up with her, they'd never take her alive.

After she finished smoking the blunt, she went to the kitchen to check on the pizza. It was almost ready. Once it was ready, she sat down, ate it, and drank a few beers and then brushed her teeth and showered again.

After showering, she stayed up, contemplating for a few hours, and then went back to sleep.

Chapter 26

As the sunlight beamed upon Queeny's face, she awoke to see yet another day still living, free from prison. Once she brushed her teeth and showered, she debated if she should go to see Reginald and Rico—she wanted them to fuck her again.

She decided not to go see Reginald and Rico 'cuz she had other things to attend to this day. She had to go to school, and she had to check on Regina and Stephanie to see if they had accomplished the goal of finding out where Fatty lived. She grabbed the Ruger, put it in the inside of her jacket pocket, and left the apartment on her way to school.

Once she got in her car, she began to worry about homicide finding her at school. She then assumed they wouldn't find her at school, because no one knew she was enrolled in school, and Homicide won't be searching the Internet, looking online for her name in college enrollment programs.

On her way to school, she stopped at this breakfast joint. She'd ridden past this breakfast joint many times but never stopped and ate there. She decided to get a bite to eat before school. She went in and ordered egg omelets and hash browns. After eating, she had it set in her mind that she'd be back to eat there again. She even left the waitress a fifty-dollar tip.

As she made it to school, she noticed that Regina and Stephanie were standing in front of the school.

She pulled directly in front of the school and rolled down the window.

"Why ya'll standing in front of the school?" Queeny asked Regina and Stephanie.

They didn't answer, but instead, they frantically jumped in the car.

"Drive off, drive far away from here as possible," the girls said.

"We gotta go to class," Queeny said.

"Girl, just drive. We got something to tell you," Gina said.

Queeny immediately pulled off.

"Where the fuck were you at all yesterday? We've been calling your phone all day yesterday," Gina said.

"I cut my phone off. I needed a day to myself alone," Queeny said.

"Thank you very much for not telling us that you're a gang chief, a killer, and that half the ViceLords out west are looking for you to kill you. Girl, do you know Homicide is looking for you for unnumbered murders?" Regina said.

Queeny paused for a second, remaining silent. "How do you know all these things?" Queeny asked.

"Yesterday, me and Stephanie was riding with Fatty. Homicide pulled us over, asking about you. Showing us your picture, saying you was number one on Chicago's most wanted list, and that you were linked to unnumbered murders. And that you was queen of ViceLords and that they wanted you off the streets for good," Regina said.

"All three of us—Fatty, me, and Stephanie—claimed we didn't know you. Little did Homicide and Fatty know we know you real good," Gina said.

"After we pulled off from Homicide, Fatty began snapping out, saying 'I'm tired of this bitch Queeny.' Me and Stephanie played like we didn't know you even existed. So I asked Fatty, 'Who is Queeny?' He told us you were their queen. So I asked him, 'Why would you call your queen a bitch?'

"He said, 'She's our queen, true enough, but this bitch is worse than any nigga dead or alive. This bitch try to rule the ViceLords and run shit the way she want it to be ran. Half of these niggas you been seeing with their hats broke off to the left, them her guys. She got half of the ViceLord mob under her wing. She got dope spots everywhere out west and all outta town. This ho is a thoroughbred killer. If ya'll ever meet this ho, stay away from her. She ain't no good for you. I think the ho worship the devil,' Fatty told us," Gina said. "Right then and there, I faked like I had a stomachache, and we told him to drop us off at a fake address close to where we live."

"Why did ya'll tell him to drop ya'll off at a fake address?" Queeny asked.

"Just in case things get heated and we are suspects as far as setting him up to get robbed, we don't want him to know where we live," Gina said.

"That was smart to do," Queeny said.

"You know, if you ever need help from us hiding you out or whatever, we're here. Although we ain't known you for a long time, we still don't want nothing bad to happen to you, especially getting cracked for murders," Stephanie said.

"Don't worry. I know how to manage. I'm cool," Queeny said.

"You know we both love you," Gina said.

"Damn, where that come from? All of a sudden ya'll love me," Queeny said.

"We've loved you before we even met you," Gina said.

"That don't sound right. How can ya'll love me even before ya'll met me?" Queeny said.

"Well, we knew almost everything about you before we even met you. We just didn't know you was the actual Queeny we'd been hearing about, and yes, we do love you. Girls everywhere idolize you and love you," Gina said.

"Why do ya'll love me?" Queeny asked.

"Because you stand triumphant and dominant over men. Just think, what female you know has ever been a real queen of a gang? You have females that's been queens of gangs, but that was only because their husband or boyfriend was the king. And females that was queens had to be led by their king. Ain't no other queen has had power like you do. You got clout. You got more heart and brains than most men," Gina said.

"How do you know this?" Queeny asked.

"I told you, we know a lot of things about you but didn't know you were the actual Queeny. Girls everywhere know about you.

Our SOS sisters know this. Our aunties and grandmothers know this. Although some ain't pleased with you killing people and committing crimes, it's just the point of being the ruler of men. Like I said, we been knew about you. We just didn't know you were the actual Queeny we'd been hearing about. Your name has been ringing in the streets for years. You gonna go down in history and be in the history books. You're a living legend," Gina said.

Queeny smiled and started laughing. "Girl, you is something else," Queeny said.

"I'm serious, girl. Women from all over know of you and respect you for the queen you be," Gina said.

"So I guess the situation with Fatty is over," Stephanie said.

"Naw, it ain't over. It's just beginning. What I'm going through ain't got shit to do with ya'll setting people up to get robbed," Queeny said.

"What you need to be robbing people for? You got dope spots, buildings, and a lot of other shit, and the police looking for you," Gina said.

"Fuck the police. You know the reason why I rob people is for thrill of it. It's like an adrenaline rush. Besides, you can't never have too much money," Queeny said.

Queeny then set fire to her last blunt. Stephanie and Gina began looking at her like she was crazy.

"Girl, I didn't know you started smoking weed," Gina said.

"I just started back a couple of days ago," Queeny said.

Queeny pulled off the blunt long and hard, inhaling the smoke, and exhaling the smoke out her nose. Then Queeny passed the blunt to Stephanie.

Stephanie hit the blunt three times. "Damn, girl, this shit is a bomb! Where you get this weed from?" Stephanie said.

"One of my homies gave it to me," Queeny said.

"You need to find your homey and find out where he got this weed from," Stephanie said as she passed the blunt to Gina.

As they continued to ride, Queeny saw this guy named Scoop pull right up on the side of them. She saw him but he didn't see her 'cuz she was in an unmarked car, behind tint.

"There go one of the other niggas I wanna set up to rob. Get a good look at him," Queeny said.

The girls started looking at his car and instantly began laughing, 'cuz he drove a loud pink old-ass BMW.

Scoop was country as hell. Scoop was originally from down south. He was a chief for the ViceLords down south. He had family in Chicago who were ViceLords. He came to Chicago for financial growth and expansion. Once he started fucking around in the Chi, he paid his way in the ranks. Scoop had lots of money and was a thoroughbred killer.

From a distance, Queeny trailed Scoop to his destination. She followed him to the Evergreen Plaza Mall.

Once he got there, he parked in the parking lot. He stayed in his car for a while, talking on his cell phone.

Queeny thought that maybe he saw her car following him. Although she was in an unmarked car, that didn't matter if Scoop knew a car was following him. It could've been anybody in that car interested in doing some dirt to him.

As she was parked from a distance, she wondered if he was on the phone calling for reinforcements or what. What she didn't know was that he was on the phone talking to his daughters.

Queeny began wondering if she should stay or leave. *If Scoop don't come out that car in a little while, I'm leaving,* Queeny thought. "He been sitting in that car for a while. He could've peeped us following him and called on the phone for reinforcements," Queeny said.

"Fuck it. We can leave and catch him on a later date," Regina said.

"This what I'ma do. I'ma let ya'll out close to his car so he can see ya'll getting out but won't see me driving, so he'll be at ease seeing two women getting out the car," Queeny said.

Queeny pulled close by Scoops car and let the girls out. "Work ya'll magic," Queeny said as the girls stepped out the car.

Scoop didn't know Queeny's car was following him. And he didn't even pay attention to Regina and Stephanie getting out the car.

Queeny pulled off leaving the mall's parking lot. *I could've probably waited on him to come out the mall and followed him myself. I didn't need the girls. But fuck it, let the girls make the money,* Queeny thought.

The girls waited at the mall's entrance for Scoop for approximately fifteen minutes.

Once Scoop walked in the mall, they faked like they were reading an advertising poster on the wall.

They followed Scoop to a women's shoe store. Without any planning, Stephanie spontaneously walked up to Scoop in the store.

"Damn! You just wasn't never going to call me," Stephanie said.

Scoop paused, looking at her curiously. "Where I know you from?" Scoop asked.

"We met on Madison and Pulaski a few weeks ago," Stephanie said.

"I don't remember you. But anyway, forgive me for not calling. But what's up with you now?" Scoop said.

Scoop and Stephanie instantly hit it off. They went from store to store laughing, kicking it like they was old friends.

All the while, while they were conversing, Regina trailed behind them like she was a lost little kid. Scoop tried to kick it with Gina as well, but Gina would say a little something to him from time to time. She didn't want to talk much. She let Stephanie work her magic.

As Stephanie and Scoop continued to talk, Scoop asked her, did she have kids? She told him no, which was the truth. Men liked women with no kids. He began to tell her about his twin daughters—how much they reminded him of her and that he just got finished talking to them on the phone.

Stephanie began thinking, *That's why you was on the phone all that time in the car, talking to your daughters.*

After a couple of hours of them hanging out in the mall, they exchanged numbers.

"Make sure to call me tonight if you get time away from your girlfriend," Stephanie said.

"I don't have one of those. But you call me if you can get away from your boyfriend," Scoop said.

"Naw, I don't have one of those either," Stephanie said.

Stephanie and Regina ended up catching the bus home. Once they got home, they immediately called Queeny and told her everything was good.

"We got his number, and we're going to call him tonight," Stephanie said.

These hos is slick. These hos slicker than me, Queeny thought. "Do ya'll thing. I'll holla at ya'll in a couple of days," Queeny said.

"A'ight, we'll holla at you," Stephanie said.

Chapter 27

Within the next several weeks, the war in the streets intensified, ViceLord against ViceLord.

There were less shootings but more killings. They stopped having shootouts and simply shot people. They started straight killings, shooting motherfuckers in the face and in the head, making sure they were dead. They were fucking each other up left and right. They weren't playing any games.

Individuals who weren't killers turned into killers during this war. It was like a living nightmare on the streets. Within these several weeks, Queeny would remain alone, trying to figure out ways to evade the police and do more killings herself.

She'd been in contact with Regina and Stephanie over the phone but hadn't seen them in person since she left them at the mall to meet Scoop.

Queeny got a call from Gina. "Meet me at my crib. I found out some things about Fatty," Gina said.

Queeny flew over to her house. Once Queeny made it to their crib, Gina told her she knew exactly where Fatty lived.

"He lives on the fourteen hundred block of Austin," Gina said.

"I know where that's at. How did ya'll find out his info?" Queeny asked.

"It's a long story," Gina said.

"Well, I'd enjoy hearing the long story," Queeny said.

Gina lit up a blunt filled with loud, inhaled, and exhaled the smoke thoroughly. "This fat motherfucker Fatty was anxious to fuck me. He had been trying to fuck me since the first day we met. So one day, he tried to pay me to have sex with him and some of his homies. I snapped on him, 'I don't get down like that.' I told him I'll get down with only him for the right price. He told me he'd give me five hundred for one night of sex. I told him that if he gave me and Stephanie five hundred apiece, we'd perform for him on a threesome," Gina said.

"I thought you said you don't get down like that?" Queeny said.

"Well, I had never did a threesome before, but I did this time for the money. I won't do it with two men, but I will do it with a man and a woman if the price is right," Gina said.

"What's the difference?" Queeny asked.

"It's a big difference. Two, three, or four niggas ain't finna bust me down," Gina said.

"Don't knock it 'til you try it. You'll like it, trust me. But finish telling me the story," Queeny said.

"So anyway, I thought he was going to be tripping to give up a whole stack, but he was like, 'Hell yeah,' like a stack ain't nothing to him. I told him the rules of engagement with doing a threesome with me and Stephanie," Gina said.

"Rules? What rules?" Queeny asked.

"Rule number one is that, that fat motherfucker must give us the money upfront. Second rule was that we ain't fucking at motels, hotels, or at our homies' crib. He told me he'll give us the money up front and we'll fuck at his crib. But once we got there, we came to find out it was him and his girlfriend's crib," Gina said.

"How did ya'll know that it was his girlfriend's crib?" Queeny asked.

"'Cuz it was pictures of him and her all over the walls. And we noticed a closet full of women shoes and clothes in the bedroom," Gina said.

"How long it's gone take for us to get paid?" Stephanie asked.

"Don't worry about it. I'ma send somebody in his house in a few days," Queeny said.

"Take us to get some x-pills," Gina said.

On the ride to get the x-pills, Queeny began wondering why Gina didn't finish the part of the threesome.

"Why didn't you finish telling me all the story?" Queeny asked.

"I did tell you all the story," Gina said.

"I wanna hear the sex part of the story," Queeny said.

"Are you serious?" Gina asked.

"Yes, I am," Queeny said.

"Let us get some pills in our system and some liquor and smoke another blunt, and we'll tell you the whole story," Gina said.

After Gina bought six x-pills, she got back into the car, gave Stephanie two pills, kept two for herself, and tried to give Queeny two pills.

"Naw, I'm straight. I don't pop pills," Queeny said.

"Go ahead, pop these two pills. You need to pop these pills. As much shit as you're going through, these pills would be helpful," Gina said.

Yeah, you're right, Queeny thought as she took the two pills and pocketed them.

"Stop right here at this liquor store so I can get some drinks and some blunts," Gina said.

Gina went in the liquor store, bought blunts, a fifth of Grey Goose, three plastic cups, and a bottle of cranberry juice.

Once she made it back to the car, she handed Queeny and Stephanie a cup.

"Girl, put a little juice on that vodka, roll up a fat one, blaze it up, and pop them two pills, and bear witness to heaven on earth," Gina told Queeny.

They began to hit the highway, destination unknown. While they smoked and rode the highway, they began listening to Tupac's song, "What You Won't Do for love." Tupac's lyrics flowed through the speakers pleasantly as they continued smoking while their high intensified.

After a while, Queeny began to feel the effect of the pills and began thinking like, *Damn, I've been missing out on this shit all along.* Queeny turned the music to a low tone. "Finish telling me the rest of the story," Queeny said.

"Once we got to his place, I placed the address in my memory bank. Then once we got into the house, we went into the bedroom, me and him immediately got undressed. Stephanie was acting all shy and shit, like she wasn't up with program. It took this bitch forever to take her clothes off. Even when she did undress, she didn't get totally naked. She kept on her panties and bra," Gina said.

"I handed him a pill and told him to pop this first. He was like, 'I don't pop no pills. I wanna pop that pussy.' He went and popped the pill anyway and fired up a blunt. While he was smoking the blunt, I dropped to my knees and began sucking his dick," Gina said.

"You sucked his dick without him even asking," Queeny said.

"Girl, for five hundred, I'd do a lot of things without him asking. Once he nutted, he let it go in my mouth, which tasted horrible. Usually when a men is getting ready to nut in my mouth, I pull it out. I can always tell when a man is finna nut, because they dick get real hard. Once I got finished sucking his dick, I looked at Stephanie, and she was still sitting on the bed with her panties and bra on, looking stupid. I personally went over to her and snatched off her panties and bra and told Fatty to go head and fuck her. Fatty laid her on the bed and fucked the shit out of her. This bitch was hollering like he was killing her," Gina said.

"Girl, that motherfucker gotta dick bigger than a horse. That's the reason why I hesitated to take off my clothes. I didn't want that nigga to stick that big-ass dick in me and didn't wanna do threesome with you there. You my cousin. The only reason I did it was for the money," Stephanie said.

"After he finished fucking her, I sucked his dick again, and then he began fucking me from the back while Stephanie started playing with my titties," Gina said.

"Girl, you didn't suppose to tell her that part," Stephanie said.

"All night, we sex, and caught a cab home. He offered to take us home, but we said no," Gina said.

Queeny and the girls continued getting high and went to McDonalds to eat. Afterward, Queeny dropped the girls off at home and told them not to worry. She would send someone in there to get the money tonight.

Later that night, Queeny parked up the block from the address that the girls gave her. She was in an unmarked car with tinted windows as usual. She'd been waiting for Fatty from 9:00 p.m. to 2:30 a.m. She was just about to leave until Fatty's car pulled up.

With no hesitation, she put her hood over her head and walked up to Fatty. Fatty was so drunk that he didn't pay her any attention. Once she made it all the way to him, she looked at him with a devilish grin on her face and said, "Hey, Fatty." Fatty tried to reach for his gun, but before he could grab it, she shot him twice in the face—once in the eye and the other in the forehead. Once she got back to her car, she rode off, listening to a Kanye West song on the radio, "How Could You Be So Heartless?"

Chapter 28

In the process of the weeks of Regina and Stephanie hanging out with Fatty, Stephanie would hang out with Scoop. Stephanie had been fucking and sucking Scoop and knew exactly where he lived.

After going over Scoop's house a few times, she noticed a safe. She never told Gina or Queeny, she wanted to see how the situation with Fatty would play out first.

The next morning after she killed Fatty, she went to Stephanie and Regina's house and gave them a thousand dollars apiece.

"The two niggas I sent to rob him caught him in front of his house, walked him in it at gunpoint, tied him up, and found four thousand in cash and two guns. I let ya'll split the money up four ways, and I kept the guns," Queeny said.

"Girl, take some of this money. At least let us give you two hundred and fifty apiece. That way, you get five hundred out of the deal. Do you agree, Gina?" Stephanie said.

"Hell yeah, take two hundred and fifty apiece from us," Gina said.

"I don't need that lil money. I got dope spots everywhere tipping. Five hundred ain't shit to me. I'm disappointed that it wasn't more in it for ya'll. Hopefully, the next lick will be more plentiful for ya'll," Queeny said.

What Queeny didn't realize was they made fifteen hundred in no time doing nothing: five hundred apiece to fuck and a stack just to find out where a nigga lived at. They were happy with that. Regina and Stephanie didn't know that it was no robbery involved, all killing.

"We ready to start on the next lick," Stephanie said.

"Work on Scoop, and I'll get back with ya'll in a few days on the next lick," Queeny said.

"I've been hanging out with Scoop every day. I should have his address for you today or tomorrow," Stephanie said.

"When you get it, let me know. But you and Regina must understand something," Queeny said.

"What's that?" the girls asked.

"That after we rob these niggas, ya'll can no longer have ties at all. After we rob, them ya'll must make believe that them niggas don't exist no more," Queeny said.

"Not a problem with us. Fuck them niggas," Stephanie said.

"I'm going to be laid up over one of my girlfriends' houses for a few days. Like I said, if ya'll get the address, then give me a call. I'll holla at ya'll in a few days," Queeny said.

Chapter 29

Without being announced, she showed up to the front door of Reginald's condo. Before she could even knock on the door, Reginald was opening the door to leave to go to the corner store.

"Queeny, girl, what the fuck is you doing over here?" Reginald asked.

"I come to see you and Rico," Queeny said.

Reginald began smiling, thinking *She wanna get fucked again.*

"How did you get in the building without me buzzing you in?" Reginald asked.

"Somebody was leaving out. I caught the door and walked in," Queeny said.

"Girl, you know that you're welcomed here anytime, but call before you come, I could've been gone or having company," Reginald said.

"Where are you on your way to?" Queeny asked.

"I'm on my way to the store to get some blunts. Do you want me to bring you something back?" Reginald asked.

"I'll go with you," she said.

"Naw, girl, stay in here. You know the police looking for you," Reginald said.

"Not in this area, they ain't," Queeny said.

As they walked to the store, it was as a love story. They were holding hands and kissing.

Reginald full-heartedly told Queeny that he loved her and that he didn't know what he'd do if he'd ever lost her to gun violence or to the system.

She told him, "Don't worry. Everything is going to be all right."

Once they got back to his apartment, Queeny immediately undressed.

Reginald began looking at her body thinking like, "Damn! This ho look good as hell."

She fell to her knees, unbuttoned and unzipped his pants, and began sucking his dick.

Once she finished sucking his dick, she asked him, "Where's Rico at?"

"He's at work, but he should be here in a little while," Reginald said. "Why do a classy chick like you like having threesome?" Reginald asked.

"Yes, I'm a classy chick, but I feel like we only have one life to live and must enjoy it sexually. You know you enjoyed it just as much as I did," she said.

Sure did, Reginald thought. Reginald undressed and rolled up a blunt.

As he set fire to the blunt, Queeny began to remember the story that Gina told her of how she gave head to Fatty while he was smoking a blunt. *It must've felt good to him,* Queeny thought. She began sucking on Reginald's dick as he inhaled and exhaled the potent smoke.

In the midst of her sucking on his dick, Rico came through the door. At first, Rico thought it was some other ho he was with. As he looked closer, he realized it was Queeny.

Queeny felt the vibe of Rico's presence in the room, stopped doing what she was doing, looked at Rico, smiled, and started back sucking Reginald's dick.

Rico immediately undressed and began fucking Queeny from the back while she continued giving Reginald head.

Approximately fifteen minutes later, Queeny lay flat on her stomach and told both men that she wanted them to take turns fucking her as they did the last time. But this time, she wanted it harder. For hours, both men repeatedly fucked her as hard as they possibly could. She really enjoyed herself.

After hours of sexing, she took a shower and was on the verge of leaving. But before she could leave, Reginald stopped her in her tracks.

"Be careful, and anytime you need some assistance, just let me know," Reginald said.

While riding off from their place, she got a phone call. "Queeny, I'm tired of your shit," the individual on the other line said.

"Who is this?" Queeny asked.

"This is Candy."

"What I do now?" Queeny said.

"You been neglecting to spend time with me. You ain't been showing no love," Candy said.

"But you know I have so many things I have to do in these streets," Queeny said.

"When are you coming over here?" Candy asked.

"I'm on my way now," Queeny said.

They ended their phone conversation, and Queeny drove straight over to Candy's house.

Candy was Queeny's number one main girl she was in love with.

Both Queeny and Candy shared something in common: they both were mixed, white and black, and had come from broken homes.

Once Queeny made it to Candy's home, she noticed that she had on a see-through lingerie set.

Candy began to get real emotional. "Girl, I love you, and I miss you when you ain't around. Why can't you at least come home every night? It's times I don't even see you for weeks. Every time I call your cell phone, the line is busy or it's off," Candy said.

"No lie, I've been going through so much shit in the streets. I'm on the run from the police and everything," Queeny said.

"That still ain't no excuse for you not to be spending time with me. We can be on the run together," Candy said.

"I don't know why you're acting like that. You know I love you," Queeny said.

Queeny then kissed Candy on the mouth and began fingering her pussy.

Before long, Candy and Queeny were performing oral sex on each other simultaneously. All night long, they sexed while listening to R. Kelly.

The next morning, after Queeny awoke, she shitted and showered. Before Queeny left, she promised Candy she'd start spending more time with her.

"You promise you'll start coming through more often," Candy said.

"I promise," Queeny said.

"I don't believe you," Candy said.

"On King Phill, I'll call you tonight, even if I don't be able to come over," Queeny said.

Chapter 30

A round ten at night, Queeny got a call from Stephanie.

"I know where Scoop lives," Stephanie said.

"Straight up," Queeny said.

"Yeah, he lives in Chicago Heights," Stephanie said.

"I'm on my way over your house," Queeny said.

While riding to Stephanie and Gina's crib, she gave Candy a call. She'd promised Candy she'd call, and she stuck to her word. All during the drive from her apartment to Stephanie's house, she and Candy romanced over the phone.

Once she got a block away from their house, she told Candy she'd call her back tomorrow right before they ended their phone conversation.

As Queeny entered Stephanie and Gina's place, she noticed that their crib was smoked out. All she saw were clouds of weed smoke. "Damn, this motherfucker smoked the fuck out," Queeny said.

Stephanie immediately told Queeny the address and told her the description of the house and the block.

Queeny smoked a little weed with them and left on a mission. Queeny went and put on a disguise and drove straight to Scoop house. She parked her unmarked car three houses down from where Scoop lived. She adjusted her seat to lean back and relax. She had it set in her mind that it would be a long time before Scoop showed up—possibly even days before he'd come home.

After five minutes, he pulled up and parked right in front of his house. She couldn't believe it. As her heart started racing, her adrenaline rush came to life. She smiled, overjoyed about finally catching that bitch Scoop.

Scoop got out of his car and opened his back door, reaching for two bags. He felt a tap on his shoulder, stood up with both bags in hand, dropping them to the ground, and there she was. He panicked, not knowing what to do, and couldn't believe it was her. In 0.7 seconds, she shot him twice in the eye and twice in the head, grabbed both bags, and fled the scene.

As she drove away, her heart raced. She was scared that the police would be all over her because Scoop lived in the suburbs.

Within minutes, she was on the e-way, smoking a blunt, listening to the Kanye west song, "How Could You Be So Heartless?"

Once she made it to her secret apartment hideaway, she decided to look in the bags she got from Scoop. She saw two pairs of men's shoes in boxes, one in each bag.

What the fuck I'ma do with some men's shoes? she thought. She decided to look in the boxes to see what kind of shoes they were. To her surprise, both boxes were filled with money. She counted the money out of one box, and it was $7,500 in large bills. She counted the money in the second box—it was $4,500.

She started smiling, thinking, *Damn, I got twelve stacks for killing a nigga.*

She played with her own pussy and titties in the tub for a little while and eventually got out the tub, ate a snack, and went straight to sleep.

The next night, she went over Stephanie and Regina's house with the money. They knew she was bringing money, but she never told them how much. Once Queeny made it to their house, she told them she got twelve thousand. They couldn't believe it.

Once Gina and Stephanie counted the twelve thousand, they were so happy they began jumping and screaming as if they had won the lottery.

Spontaneously, Gina grabbed Queeny, hugged her tightly, and began tongue-kissing her. Queeny snatched her mouth away from Gina and started laughing sinisterly.

Queeny started kissing Gina back, her kisses tasting sweet, like mints.

Once they stopped kissing, Gina begged Queeny to let her eat her pussy. In no time flat, all three women were naked as Gina and Stephanie took turns eating away at Queeny's pussy and doing whatever it took to please Queeny.

After that night, all three women got real close to one another.

Gina and Stephanie were smart. They saved the money from the licks so that one day, they could find a way to invest their money to make more money.

Queeny showed them two more ViceLords she wanted to set up. The girls found out where they lived each time. Queeny gave them five thousand apiece for each lick.

More and more, Homicide was looking for Queeny. She heard that the feds were looking for her too, but she didn't believe the feds were looking for her because the feds were more high-tech than Homicide and smarter. She knew if the feds were looking for her, they'd probably found her by now.

Queeny decided to drop outta of school and stop secretly going to church but instead plot more killings.

She remembered a day and age when the ViceLords were a beautiful organization that drew as a whole, although there were always a few corrupt individuals. Now the ViceLords who were to be holy or divine were as followers of Lucifer. As she'd think of the ViceLords, she'd visualize the burning of eternal fire, drugs that would take you higher, and ancient ViceLord pioneers whom she'd always respect and admire.

Sitting alone, she blazed up a fat blunt stuffed with loud. *Damn, I don't know what to do. I try to uplift ViceLords and keep structure, but in reality, I created a neverending massacre. On King Phill, 'til I die, niggas that don't respect the ViceLords go to continue to die,* she thought.

She went through Reginald and others to check on her buildings and clothing line, and everything was good. Clothing line sales had skyrocketed.

She decided to drive through the hood in disguise in an unmarked car with tinted windows. While driving through the hood, she noticed that the hood looked like a ghost town. There was nobody outside—that was because of all the shootings and killings. She began to feel sorrow for those who were killed and weren't alive to see today or tomorrow. On almost every block in her hood, she'd see spray paint on the walls of those slain ViceLord soldiers. Some were even as young as fourteen or fifteen years old. Her heart cried out to the family members and friends of these young men, although she still felt that people had to die if they weren't going to respect the ViceLords.

On her way leaving the hood, she slowly rode past this donut shop. Inside was a homicide detective who was assigned to murders that Queeny supposedly did or even had something to do with. The homicide detective was tired of all the killings and not being able to locate Queeny. So he saw this car with tinted windows riding slowly and hoped on the inside of the car would be a ViceLord who had any leads to Queeny's whereabouts. Never in his wildest dreams would he ever imagine that Queeny was inside that vehicle.

So he ran to his car. By this time, Queeny was only a short distance away. He pulled behind her, flicking his headlights on and off, turning on his siren.

Queeny's heart began racing. She couldn't believe she let the police get behind her without her even knowing. She felt like a fool for not watching her rearview mirror.

She thought about taking off but second-guessed it because she didn't want to get in a high-speed chase, get into an accident, and wake up in cuffs. She pulled over, scared to death, and confused, not knowing what to do. *How do the police know I'm in this car?* she thought. *Aw, they don't know I'm in this car, so why would they pull me over?*

As the homicide detective stepped to the window with pictures in his hand on the verge of questioning, she lowered the window and shot the detective five times in the stomach. The detective wore his vest every single day for the last twenty years. This particular day, he didn't wear his vest and caught those five to the stomach.

Queeny smashed off and got away.

She went to get a lot of money and some clothes. She now knew she'd have to leave Chicago.

She hit the road, destination unknown. On the beginning of her journey, she began to listen to Eminem's song "Stan."

The homicide officer survived the five shots and had no idea that Queeny was the one who shot him because she was disguised.

Queeny wound up in Waukegan. She decided to go to Waukegan because she had no real ties there and it was close to Chicago. She knew her way around Waukegan because previously she used to sell a little weight on the dope there.

She rented a motel room with a fake ID so the authorities wouldn't trace her. She rented the motel room for a week.

During that week, she went shopping for casual clothing so she could look like a nerd or a church girl.

For the entire week, she kept her phone off, having no ties to anyone.

Gina, Stephanie, and Reginald, among others, were worried about Queeny. No one had heard from her in a whole week. Candy and two of her other lovers thought that she was dead or in prison.

Queeny wound up renting the second floor in this building this old couple owned. After a few weeks, the old couple started charging Queeny less rent because she was a good tenant. She was always nice and quiet and had no company.

Queeny ended up getting rid of the car she bought from Chicago, and buying two used cars from a lot in Waukegan. Both cars were fast, so she could evade the police if need be.

After a month and a half of living in Waukegan, she decided to call Reginald, Stephanie, and Gina. All three of them were relieved that she was doing all right, still living free from prison.

Gina and Stephanie had rented out a storefront and opened a twenty-four hour restaurant in the hood. They started going to school for culinary arts.

Reginald was doing good. He was still standing on Queeny's buildings and inspiring others to rock Queeny's clothing line. He told Queeny that whenever they met again, he wanted to go heads up with her sexually without Rico and that he wanted to lick on her pussy forever and a day nonstop. Hearing that brought her joy within.

About a week later, Queeny called to the Chi again to talk to some other people, and she came to find out that a lot of her guys were killed and locked up for murders, and that a lotta outlaw ViceLords were killed and locked up for bodies on her guys.

More and more, Homicide searched for Queeny, but she couldn't be found.

Ever since she moved to Waukegan, she began to live a peaceful, average life. She stayed in the house most of the time, chilling out, thinking, and plotting on shit.

I wanna go to the grocery store, but I'm feeling bad vibes. Maybe I should just stay in the house, she thought one day.

She decided to go to the grocery store because she really needed some groceries. As she was trying to enter her car, a red Buick Century drove past her really fast, almost running her over.

Damn, that bitch almost hit me, Queeny thought.

Queeny pulled off. A block away, she got caught at a red light right next to the red Buick Century. Queeny tilted her head slightly, looking into the car.

That bitch looks familiar, Queeny thought as the light turned green and she proceeded to the grocery store.

The woman in the red Buick Century picked up her cell phone and frantically started dialing numbers.

"Hello," he said.

"Bushwick, guess who I just saw?" the woman in the Buick said.

"Who is this?" he asked.

"It's me, Lisa. I'm calling you from a new number."

"Aw, okay, what's going on, Lisa?" Bushwick said.

"Shit, guess who I just saw," she said.

"Who?" he asked.

"Queeny."

"Get the fuck outta here. You ain't seen no Queeny," Bushwick said.

"Yes, I did. At first, I couldn't believe it. I seen her getting in the car and almost made a mistake and ran her over."

"Fuck making a mistake. You should've ran that bitch over on purpose," he said.

"Then after that, she pulled on the side of me at a red light, and that's when I knew for sho' that was her," she said.

"I don't believe you," he said.

"I'm telling you, that was her," she said.

"Where did you see her at?" he asked.

"I just told you, coming out of a house," she said.

"Where the house at?" he asked.

"On Saint Charles," she said.

"Saint Charles? Where the fuck is that at?" he asked.

"It's in Waukegan," she said.

"I use to fuck around in Waukegan, but I don't remember no street called Saint Charles. Did you get the address?" he asked.

"Naw, but I can go right back to get the address," she said.

"Yeah, go get it for me, and I'll call you back in a little while," he said.

"Okay, I got you, bye-bye," she said.

"Bye," he said. *This bitch don't know what the fuck she talking about,* Bushwick thought.

He decided to call his guy Tony Spade. He decided to call him because he was a thoroughbred on the killing side, and Homicide wasn't looking for him for any bodies.

"Tony, this Bushwick, Lord."

"Lord, where you been? I ain't heard from you in a while," Tony said.

"You know Homicide looking for me, so I been traveling from state to state. I need you to go with me to handle some business for me," Bushwick said.

"Where you at? I'm on my way," Tony said.

"Let me come to you," Bushwick said.

Bushwick wrote down Tony's address, called Lisa back, got Queeny's address, changed clothes, and went straight over to Tony.

Bushwick pulled up to the apartment building Tony was at, parked, and got out of the car. *Damn, it's dark as hell on this block,* Bushwick thought. He looked up, saw the streetlights out, and knew why it was dark.

He walked up to the gate of the big apartment building then walked up the walkway to the address Tony gave him. He pushed the button of the doorbell. Tony looked out the second floor window and saw Bushwick all dressed up like a girl and started laughing.

"Damn, nigga, you didn't even tell me you was gay," Tony said.

"Nigga, stop playing. I hate faggots," Bushwick said.

Tony push the buzzer to buzz Bushwick in. Once Bushwick finally made it within the apartment, he saw how clean and plush it was and became impressed.

"Who crib is this?" Bushwick asked.

"This my shit," Tony said.

Tony instantly took Bushwick to the back room, lifted up the mattress, and showed Bushwick all the guns. Bushwick smiled, knowing that trouble was soon to come and that they were getting ready to have some fun.

"What business do you need to take care of?" Tony asked.

"Well, I don't need you to take care of any business for me. I need you to go with me to get Queeny," Bushwick said.

"Queeny," Tony said.

"Yeah, Queeny," Bushwick said.

"How the fuck we gone get Queeny?" Tony asked.

"I heard she was living in Waukegan. I don't know how true it is, but I'm finna go investigate," Bushwick said.

"Who told you she was in Waukegan?" Tony asked.

"This ho I use to fuck with," Bushwick said.

"What we waiting on?" Tony asked.

They grabbed a few of the guns and was on their way out of the house. Before they could leave, Tony paused. "Lord, hold on a minute. What the fuck is you doing dressed up like a woman?" Tony asked.

"This is my disguise," Bushwick said.

"Damn, Lord, you couldn't pick no better disguise than that," Tony said.

"This is a good disguise, because women don't look like suspect like men do," Bushwick said.

"Okay, if you say so. Cut off that light, and let's ride," Tony said.

On their journey to Waukegan, both men yearned to catch Queeny and take away her life in the most brutal form imaginable to mankind.

On the way there, Bushwick convinced Tony to get in disguise. They stopped at a clothing store. Tony bought himself some clothes to disguise himself like a religious man.

They made it to the spot Lisa gave them the address to and lamped on Queeny for three days and two nights. The third night, both men were getting restless.

"Lord, this ho don't know what she talking about. Ain't nobody came out this house since we came three days ago," Tony said.

"You can't say that, 'cuz we be leaving to go to restaurants, and we be going to that motel to take showers," Bushwick said.

"But that only be for a little while," Tony said.

"But people could be coming out the building during the little while we be gone," Bushwick said.

"True that, but if this ho don't come out in a couple of days, you can take me back home," Tony said.

"I'm taking myself back home. I understand this is a big two-way street, but it's dangerous for us to be sitting here for days with all these guns, and Homicide looking for me. Although we been parked on different areas on both sides of the street, we still look suspicious," Bushwick said.

"But it'll be all worth it if we catch Queeny," Tony said.

"Yeah, you got a valid point," Bushwick said.

Nights later, Bushwick was waking out of his sleep and saw Queeny—dressed up, professional-looking like a businesswoman—coming out of that building. Bushwick couldn't believe it. Bushwick started to shake Tony, trying to wake him up.

"Lord, they she go. Wake up, Lord," Bushwick said.

Tony awoke and saw Queeny and couldn't believe it. They saw her, but she didn't see them. She got into her car and drove off. They trailed her from a distance for about two minutes.

All the time they were trailing her, she felt bad vibes. *I should've stayed in the house. I should've stayed in the house,* she thought.

She pulled to a quiet street to use a pay phone.

What the fuck this ho using a pay phone for? Don't nobody use pay phones no more.

She used various pay phones so that if the phones of the people she was calling were tapped, they still would have a problem tracing her exact whereabouts.

Outta nowhere, Queeny felt a bat strike her across her head and the electric shock of a taser gun as someone took her gun from her waist before she even got a chance to reach for it. She was lifted up and slammed into a trunk, and she heard the wheels of a car burn rubber.

She lay in the trunk, almost lifeless, crying out from the pain of her busted head. This was the worst pain she'd ever felt in life.

An hour later, the trunk opened. Though she was unable to move, she was electric-shocked again and snatched outta the trunk by two people whom she could barely see due to her not being all the way focused, as the blood ran down her face. She cried out moans of being in pain. She was dragged into a house, stripped of all her clothes as the two individuals doctored her head.

After she fell into a state of unconsciousness, she awoke to see a lady standing over, her doing something to her head. Queeny was momentarily relieved of the pain that she'd once felt.

The lady who was standing over her was Lisa, who was a registered nurse. Bushwick had Lisa shoot lots of numbing medicine for Queeny's head and put staples in it.

Queeny tried to move, but her entire nude body was tied up, and duct tape was stuck across her mouth.

Lisa left the house, as Queeny was now fully conscious. As the blood had been cleaned off her face, she was able to see Bushwick and Tony. Now everything came to light. She wondered how they got so close to her without her even seeing it and how they knew she was in Waukegan.

Bushwick lifted Queeny up, putting her on her knees, taking the tape off her mouth, as her ankles remained tied together, and her arms remained tied behind her back.

"Bitch, you betta tell me where every last one of your guys that's been doing all the shootings hiding out at," Bushwick said.

"Bend down, Lord. Let me tell you," Queeny said in a low seductive tone.

Once he bent down, she spit in his face and began laughing sinisterly.

"This bitch spit in my face," he said, as he backhand-slapped her.

Bushwick and Tony welcomed Queeny to their torture chamber. First they put they tape over her mouth and began burning her with melted plastic, hot forks, and hot butter knives. She cried out for them to stop, but her cries weren't heard.

They went from burning her to actually stabbing her with forks, to beating her with their fists and a mop stick. They took the tape off her mouth and asked her again.

She told them, "I ain't telling you bitches shit."

Buchwick was so mad, he put the tape back on her mouth and stabbed her with a knife in her neck as she began yelling and screaming at the top of her lungs. They couldn't hear her, though, because of the tape over her mouth.

Bushwick and Tony started fucking her up, beating her with almost anything they could get their hands on. But they didn't want to go all-out because they needed her conscious to tell them where her guys were. Little did they know that she didn't know where her guys were hiding out, and even if she did, she still wouldn't tell them.

Queeny felt so stupid for letting them catch her off her square. She cried out that they should just kill her because the pain was at its all-time high.

Bushwick took the tape off her mouth and stuck a broomstick far up in her pussy. As she yelled and screamed, Bushwick and Tony laughed at her. She still didn't give up any information.

"I hear someone screaming," the lady upstairs said to her husband.

"It's probably the TV. You hearing shit. You always hearing shit. I'm trying to sleep, and you talking about a motherfucker screaming," the husband said.

Tony decided to go to the washroom. As he closed the door, he lifted up the lid. He took out his dick to piss and heard a gunshot that sounded like a cannon. He got scared and pissed everywhere.

He ran out the washroom to see what was going on, and there Queeny was, laid on the floor with blood flowing from her head. Bushwick stood over her with a big-ass chrome .44 in his hand, madder than a motherfucker.

Tony came closer, smiling, glad that the bitch Queeny was dead. As Tony came closer, he examined Queeny. His back was positioned to Bushwick.

Bushwick shot Tony twice in the head, and Tony fell right on top of Queeny. Bushwick put the gun in his own mouth, pulled the trigger, and took his own life.

After the first shot that killed Queeny, the upstairs tenants called the police. After all the other shots, the tenants were so shaken up they didn't know whether to leave or what. They hid under the bed 'til the police arrived.

Once the police arrived, the upstairs tenants let them into Lisa's house with their extra key.

The police went in with guns drawn and came to see these three dead bodies sprawled out on the floor, which surprised them and scared them all at the same time.

After the police called in medical assistance, they came to find out that all three were dead.

Later that day, as they did their investigation, Homicide questioned Lisa. Lisa told them she didn't know how Bushwick and the other two got in her house. Lisa said she used to fuck around with Bushwick in the past but didn't know how he got in the house. Maybe he stole her keys and got copies made in the past when they used to fuck around. Homicide knew Lisa was lying, but there was nothing they could do because they had no witnesses. The only three witnesses were dead. That's why Bushwick killed Tony, so he wouldn't be a witness to anything. Bushwick killed himself 'cuz he knew one day, Homicide would catch up with him and he'd never get out of jail. Life in the pen wasn't for Bushwick—he'd just rather die.

Queeny, Tony, and Bushwick's deaths hit the CNN news. After everybody heard about it, they blamed it on themselves. Black and Stacey felt guilty and sad. They felt they were the ones who turned her out. In reality, she turned herself out.

Bushwick's and Tony's funerals were held out of town.

Queeny's funeral was held in the hood a week after she was killed. Area 4 Police Station sent a lot of police there to secure the premises.

Everybody was at the funeral. It was as if a celebrity had died. People from everywhere came. Many people came who didn't even know Queeny on a personal level. They came because they'd heard about her. They'd idolized her. Some even cried tears that shall shed internally over the years.

Once the pallbearers escorted Queeny outta the church, they took her to a hearse custom-made for her that had the whole top cut off. They opened her casket and drove her slowly through the West Side, mainly in areas were ViceLords dwelled. Several police cars trailed, as ViceLords—men and women—walked beside her hearse with weapons concealed from the police. They were all dressed in black and gold, with their hats broke off to left, throwing V.L. up, as crowds of people on each side of the streets spectated. Some even shed tears, paying their last respects to this self-made legendary black queen.

During the burial, some actually wished they could've died with her.

A lot of people got five-pointed stars tattooed on the left side of their face and on other parts of their bodies that had words outside of it saying "RIP five-star universal elite Queen Queeny."

'Til this very day, in many states where the ViceLords dwelled, they honor Queeny as being the Queen of all Queens.

Parts of a Book of Poetry published by Alan Hines,

Thug Poetry Volume 1

1. Board Walk

Down by the Boardwalk wars were fought.

Literature was taught.

Trumpets sounded off, gun fire sought, as blasphemy flowed fluently from mouths.

Shorties was sent off. Lives was lost.

Traps were set, rats, and snakes was caught.

As more guns was brought.

Stool penguins were put out;

Hit in their mouth and hung like the past centuries down south.

Those that won earn respect, and clout, and this came about on California, and Flournoy a place called the Boardwalk.

2. Mexican and black

I can feel your pain.

We're like one in the same.

I cried endless tears when I heard that Immigration came and took you back to Mexico's poverty range.

In Spanish speaking I'd scream blasphemy incentitys of Immigrations name in vain.

If this is a free country why they won't let you remain.

The land of liberty is all a game for personal gain.

I just hate hearing immigrations name, it feels worser than a sickening pain.

I imagine how you felt a mental torture of firely flames, for my ancestors it was the same as slave ships came, being shackled, and chained, stripped of names, whipped with whips inhumanly, like a wild animal being tamed.

Chased down like futuristic centuries war games.

In the blink of an eye circumstances change, amongst cruel, and usual conditions that's derange.

I can definitely feel your pain, because we're one in the same.

3. Blind

Eyes closed, as if I'm blind;
blind, going back and forth during this present time.

As fiends constantly in lines, rocks and blows they buying, as drug dealers money inclines.

Lost in a false state of mind.

In the life of mines I caught my fiancee cheating on Valentines with another woman, a female friend of mines, it wasn't her first or last time.

Formulated men of flesh I am.

Living to dying.

Funeral after funeral tears won't even come out to much crying.

Seeing the downfall of those childhood friends, family members, and of mankind.

Sometimes I wish I couldn't see the chaos of wordly crimes, sometimes I wish I was blind.

4. Urgent Message

S he had a urgent message which was practice safe sexing.
Partners get free H.I.V. tested.

Was a mental doctor for kids that had been molested.

Wore only pink to support breast cancer awareness.

Practice non-smoking so she wouldn't catch cancer.

She brought forth urgent messages all along she was already A.I.D.S. infected,

Wanted others to learn from her mistake as lessons.

Until death she spit urgent messages.

5. Beginning

In the beginning there were Adam & Eve;
a bitten fruit brought forth sin, a deceive, Lucifer achieved,
now comes forth lusting and greed.

Broke and starven, the rich wont feed.

And then came the ViceLords, the Breeds, and the G.D.'s Creeds.
Devilish deeds.

Feds cutting heads bodies fall no one to lead.

Trapped in time frames places don't want to leave.

Getting high as a way to be free.

No since of direction, confused as can be.

Stuck in the dark without a light to see, from the beginning to infinite.

6. Twins I Never Wanted You To See

Twins I never wanted you to see the shaded side where it's dark.

A teenage mom, once a month waiting on food stamps in the form of a Link Card.

Baby daddy vanish, ventured off somewhere in Mars.

Never wanted you to see hypes with lighters that spark selling their bodies for sums that aren't large.

That's why I preach to you reach for the stars.

Know that it's life beyond the drug dealers with fancy cars.

To me both of the twins are superstars.

I love from near or far.

Earth angels is what you are.

That's why I continuously preach to you about being in the likeness of God.

7. Split Decision

With precision he made a split second decision.

Within gunfire took away a man's existence.

Now it'll be little kids that'll grow up without their father at Christmas.

A mom that will blame herself for her sons life being diminished.

Using the devils inventions, with ill intuitions as his partner told him no he didn't listen.

In a bad split decision he caught a murder with a co-defendant.

Blew trial, natural life was his sentence.

Split decisions.

8. Unproperly Place

A place where grown men cry.
Some hung themselves they'd rather die.
Trapped in cells with Lucifer by their sides.
Overtime family and friends left them behind.
No money orders, no waiting in commissary lines, must grind.
Eyes wide open to the past of being blind, to falsehood of love from mankind.
Unproperly place doing hard times.

9. Progress

Great dreams of projects, prospects.

Disapprovals, protest.

Kept going after rejects, continuous progress.

Cold world didn't get the best.

Not too much stress, exercised was no sweat.

Loved the kids to death.

Would definitely strive for excellence until the last breath.

Life was a test that was passed through progress.

10. Ms. Season

In the Summer she'd shine like the sunlight so bright.

In the Spring is when she'd allow the wonderful joys of life to be seen.

In the fall is when she'd encourage people to stand tall through it all.

In the winter is when she'd be in the holiday spirit, spreading her wealth feeling a privilege in giving.

11. Cold World

E ven in the summertime cold minds plot on a new day and age massacre of St. Valetines.

Financial assistance hard to find.

Living to dying, death shall come in due time.

Watch you front and behind.

Criminal minds, even those that make laws commit white collar crimes.

Draw off symbols and signs.

Twins listen to dad as he tell you the truth without lying.

Love all, trust none of any kind, in this cold world the devil design.

12. Repressed

R epressed dreams wanted to live them out like a king.
Until reality came flowing like the Mississippi river of disastrous streams.

Poetry and non-fiction stories being told from the eyes of a dope fiend.

Alienated human beings, poison contaminated queens, premeditated schemes.

Fatherless, troubled teens.

The epidemic of A.I.D.S, poverty, and shattered dreams was waking up, and seen.

Replenished unfinished repressed dreams.

13. A Streets Curse

For you my brother our love never begin at birth.

For I showed love and you used me for what I was worth.

For there was no Holy Divine day, no real praises to the ones that really uplifted that got slayed;

instead you misused me to sell packs, and run your joint so you could get paid.....lead me astray.

For they didn't really abide by the Fataha, the five points of the golden star, the most gracious and merciful one Allah.

The Oath was wrote as only one piece that controlled, shaped and mold, put over eyes a blind fold of those that were in charge that possessed hearts that was so cold.

Till this day a lot of brothers still on count and won't let go.

14. Reality Formed

Once upon a time in America there were artwork, poetic love poems.

Little girls getting their dreams to have pony's and unicorns.

Until reality came in the form of a storm.

Barking dogs sirens and the sounds of burglar alarms.

Killed their own parents, children of the corn.

Behold of the pale white horse with a horn like a unicorn.

Hurricanes, floods, and thunderstorms.

Blood dripping, and pouring.

Continuous deaths, and mourning.

Tormented racist legislative candidates in closets performing.

The last days of revelation is up and forming.....

Reality in its rawest form.

15. No Social

No social, but yet and still I stay close to.
I know what you go through.

Through my pen I write poetry and nonfiction wishing it could actually be true, as citizenship forever comes through.

I'm always praying for each one of you.

Although you speak no English which is a foreign language to you, with all respect due let you have socials, and be considered Americans to.....

16. Growed Up

I growed up in the days of old, silently staring in the mirror reminiscing of my youth turned cold.

By dope fiends, pipe smokers it's was stole, and sold for the low.

Visions of me looking out of project windows and seeing mom, and dad when they were young before substances took control.

Visions of my own kids leading themselves astray, away from the prism of what the creator unfold.

Lucifer's powerful hold control lost souls, those seeking fortune and fame, and the glitter, and gold.

Since the days of old I grew up, I growed.

17. No Love For This Side

Some say it's no love for the other side, in reality it's no love for this side. Brother's kill own Brother's to die. At the funeral momma cries, but she still continue to get high.

This side will look you straight in the eye and tell a bald face lie.

Shoe laces never learned how to tie.

Father was never by my side, to busy getting high.

Taught my own self how to drive down this bumpy road of being alive.

It aint no love for this side.

18. Thief

She came to me like a thief in the night.

My heart she stole, I sold my soul.

Her tactics were old, but new to me.

Although I'm from the city's streets, had been around numerous ladies, but she was, she really was something new to me.

She tricked me into being the man she wanted me to be.

Engaged to soon be married.

I love so much that our love affair was horrifying and scary.

Home alone I'd be Tom, she'd be Jerry.

This lady was like Christmas, very merry.

Come to find out she'd been with Tom, Dick, Harry, and even Larry.

Although living she made us all feel legendary!

19. She Had Game

She had more game than Milton Bradley.

Humanized Monopoly, schemed for money.

Each time a man landed on her property they'd have to pay heavily.

Those that was wealthy now lived in poverty;

She tricked them outta all they money.

She talked preacher's into being sinners.

She turned losers into winners.

Those that had finished were back at the beginning.

Her game came from all the things she'd seen.

She even turned filthy animals clean.

She was worst than a drug as men fiend.

Cold as ice the reality from a dream.

She made many men feel like kings.

For her venom was more poisoning than anything ever heard of or seen.

She really did her thing..... she had game.

20. Mexican or Puerto Rican

Didn't know if she was a Mexican or Puerto Rican.

She didn't speak any English.

But her body I was thrill seeking.

Late night creeping.

Away from others I wanted to be fleeing, around her is where I wanted to be in.

She was a beautiful human being;

Smooth creamy skin.

From her stride you could tell she had dignity and pride within.

Friendliness with no end.

Catholic life without sin.

I longed for her nights and days within.

Each time I'd tried to talk she'd say no comprende.

Didn't speak any English.

I wonder is she Mexican or Puerto Rican.

21. Advance

You see how they plotted on you in advance.
Wanted to disarm your successful circumstance.
Get within your wife's pants.
Overthrow you make you feel less than a man.
Wanted your life to come to an end.
Break bread with, hug, and show love, those you call
friends, plotted on you in advance, who knows what's
in the heart of men.....
Plots in advance.

22. Even Though

Even though I loved her so she had devilish tendencies

Like an embryo, anxious to grow.

More concerned with the way my cash flowed, fast instead of slow.

Some considered her a pro.

But as for me I loved her so.

In the cold of below zero I'd walk barefoot in the snow to her place down below.

Even though I loved her so other men have told that behind doors that's closed she was good to go.

Even though she's a pro I still love her so.

23. To Life

She brought things to life that brought the men out at night.

To life she'd show men just how tight.

Over her the guys would fight.

In her sight she'd see men lining up with money each night to bring things to life.....

24. Life and Death

God giveth life and only he should have the power to cause death.

As it shall be no penalties of death by the governor's estate.

No hoodlums shall create casualties of street wars in lives they can't take.

Fatality must rely through natural causes of faith.....

God giveth life and only he should have the power to take it away.

25. Paradox

A paradox of raging bills that spit.

On pull pits preacher sit scheming on ways to get rich.

Sick sexual cravings that's obviously evident.

Those that prey on those without street sense, common sense, tricking off money spent, young ladies that turn out to do whatever they are sent.

A paradox of nasty dirty old man looking for flesh of teenage kids.

Watching for the police as crimes they commit.

Throwing bricks at the pen begging for a way in.

Curse kids cause of lives of bastard parents sin.

Many men shall burn within the heart of devils firely skin.

This is the life we shall never change, never give in.

Murdering childhood friends, lil grammer school girls pregnant with twins by grown men.

A positive test of H.I.V. as your life shall end.

"This is your brain on drugs," as real brain cells are frying.

Witnessing testifying, grown men crying, the jail cells they shall die in.

Starvation and mayhem.

Puddles of blood new borns lie, and die in, continuous crying.

Ladies bodies perverts buying, in this paradox of eternal life I shall live and my soul shall never die in.....

A paradox of continuous crying.

26. Out of Order

A body of contaminated water.
Missing my daughters.
Affiliated headquaters.
Drugs imported, that customers ordered.
Plans unafforded.
Kids aborted.
Legislative men were extorted.
No law and order.
Immigrants deported;
but Mexicans steady crossing the border,
out of order through the dessert thirsty for holy water.....
Out of order.

27. Blazed

Blazed it with fire, tooking hire.
Stimulational desire.
Clientele grew, as workers continued getting hired.
"Who working, who got that loud fire."
In line mass amount of cash crop buyers, wanting to blaze to be taking higher.
At a young age they felt like they had retired.

Women and men would blaze and stick out their chest
as if they'd conquered a quest.
It was their choice for the best, loved it to death,
blazed it until it was no more left.

28. Said and Done

It was said that she'd love me breathing or dead.
Choice me first before any other men instead.
She did whatever I wanted in the bed.
Eased my mind, relieve stress from my head.
She even spent time with my mom when she was sick in bed.
Had been together through years that past.
One cold day reality had came to drag, code red, code
red as she left me as soon as I got snatched by the feds.
Jumped ship, left town with my money filled in bags.
Done the opposite of what was said.

29. Romance

Around the house topless she'd prance and sometimes tap dance as we'd romance.

At times she'd get on her knees and say I think I can, I think I can, I think I can.

To her I was the world's greatest man;

A God of the ancient Africans as we'd romance.

I was the perfect gentlemen; a lover and a friend.

We'd hold hands and I'd show her off around the men;

No egotistical stuff building within.

I treated her better than any men did or can.

We shall be together to the bitter end, capotilizing

On a romantic and erotic blend.....

A romance that will never shorten, as the completion

Will never begin or even give in.....

Romancing to the end.....

30. Publicize

Highly publicized.

A musicianist that played the saxophone in jazz.

Within comparison and contrast had more than a little class.

With a body that made me fantasize.

I'd see her on stage, in magazines, in newspapers next to ads.

She was a blast from the past.

Even in the future she'd last.

Famously she was publicized for the attributes she had.

She wrote down expectations, in a pad.

Then brought them to reality publicly as she publicized.

Parts of a Book of Poetry published by Alan Hines,

The Words I Spoke

1. Listen

In addition never graduated, didn't listen to the ministers intuition which was to be in a powerful position.

To be a misses instead of a mistress.

Be observant, and do your own surveys, and general statistics.

Yet and still she didn't listen as he told her education was the key to success within existence, to study King James version limited edition.

Once she got older she sat reminiscing, all five of kidsfathers missing.

Public housing living, check to check living.

Doing strange things to feed her, and her children.

Now she wish she would've listen, while the minister was telling her of premonitions.

2. Dignity and Pride

She had a good sense of pride that wouldn't let her inner soul cry, or die.

Felt as she could extend her arms to reach the sky.

Never questioning why.

Couldn't feel the heat from fire, soothing inside.

Champion of mountains she'd climb.

A leader with followers always by her side.

Held her head up high as she glide.

Would never accept a prize could see angels in her eyes.

On her day of birth she was baptized, worship God with dignity and pride.

3. A Different Time

A different time, a zone, a frame of mind.

A new world order was design.

Enemies leading ally troops from behind to the blind.

Addicted substances controlled minds.

Reenacting the massacre of St. Valentines.

Pedophiles in grammer school lines.

Bootlegging liquor turned back to a crime.

Boston taxes on tea recently inclined.

Living hundreds of years in lifetimes before dying as B.C. times.....

A different time.

4. Jesus Christ

I know he died for our sins.

If time repeats itself I know he'd do it again.

His blood lies in the heart of men.

No creature on earth could cast the first stone, because we all have sinned,

some will even do it again.

The son of men.

He died for our sins.

5. A Shaded True of Knowledge

S he sat under this shaded tree, couldn't see the entire truth of
knowledge,

this tree shaded her from problems, the dimness of the sun
only shined a bit of the truth of knowledge.

She couldn't see upcoming conditions that wouldn't be so marvelous.

Crying babies with no fathers.

Venereal diseases that had no cure for regardless.

Those content with receiving W.I.C. and section 8 apartments.

In summers women half dressed wearing garments.

Those with problems mainly because they didn't make wise
decisions regardless.

Her future couldn't be prosperous because she sat under the shaded
tree that shaded her from the truth of knowledge.

6. Count From One Through Ten

1. One is for the people that create problems as a sequel, evil.

2. Two is for those fools that dropped out of school, disregarding knowledge as a powerful tool.

3. Three is for those that didn't even attempt to experience life, and better things to see.

4. Four is for those that wasn't focused to walk through opened prosperous doors.

5. Five was for those that used, misused drugs O.D. and died.

6. Six, six is for gang members that showed false love to a sense had minds playing tricks.

7. Seven is for those that were slayed for sins they shall see hell instead of heaven.

8. Eight is for those with natural life, and shall never exit the prisons gate.

9. Nine is for those constant standing in dope lines, little kids getting killed dying, while the pastor profits off lying.

10.Ten is for those that did a stretch, ten or fifteen within, got out and start selling dope again....count from one through ten.

7. Continue

I'll continue to tell you what's on the menu.

There's been a change of venue.

Jobs that will suspend you.

Friends with no helping hands, no money to lend you.

Some never been where I been, do what I do.

Terminal illness that will effect those as easy as the flu.

No more red, white, and blue.

Wild animals break up outta the Zoos.

Confused not knowing where to go or what to do.

Words that will definitely offend you.

False instead of true.

Not even having a clue.

Doing you, but listen to me as I'll continue to tell you what's on the menu.....

8. Controlled Fates

Controlled all fates.
Demonic demons being pushed and kicked out of heavens gates.

The evil that body and souls do theirs no escape.

Violence some can't wait.

Setting dates for crimes of hate to take place;

burning of crosses to this day.

White sheets took away but in hearts racism shall forever stay.

The lake of fire where adolescents souls shall forever lay for the committed offenses against God's scriptures he created.

Easy used devil's bait, deniros, and pornography on first date.

Stuck in prison, once a month state pays.

Awaiting on appeals, and outdates, and some will forever stay until death take them away.

Lucifer paved the way, having things his way, and contolloing fates.

9. Engulf

Engulfed in flames.
Yelling of insanity using Jesus Christ name in vain.
Insanes playing mind games.
Trouble came, lions preyed on human beings.
Constant bodies being slain.
Militant devil worshipping gangs, that love to gangbang.....
Imagine being engulfed in gasoline then in flames.

10. Breadwinner

A breadwinner that's one of the many reasons I made her my bottom.

Met her on one of the sensational days in autumn.

She read all my books of poetry and I said I was heaven sent, a prophet.

Little did she know I felt the opposite, to me she was inspirational, marvelous, helpful with knowledge.

Smarter than those with those P.H.D's in college.

Loved me regardless.

She knew how to make an honest prophet.

A breadwinner my bottom.

11. Never Hopeless

Never Hopeless, concentration,
never losing focus.
The one that wrote a magical hocus pocus.
Like a friendly ghost.
Traveling coast to coast.
Striving for most.
A celebrated toast.
An everyday party host.
Stuck in a match on the ropes, but once off the ropes,
winnings and accomplishments shall overload.
Keeping the faith within hope.

12. Darkside

A darkside where 24hrs. a day 7 days a week there was no light outside.

Both teams didn't coincide.

No love for the other side.

They were murdering and getting killed no one naturally died.

You could ride pass and look to see the flaming fires of wickedness in eyes, those that hated and despised.

Like Vampires thirsty to see blood, and take away lives.

Laugh out loud at funerals, no cries.

Separated family ties.

As God children were killed didn't naturally die.

Lucifer's legacy inclined.

Gave Lucifer a new life in which he didn't seek or find.

It came through crime.

Still alive.

The darkside.....

13. In Vain

Visualizing those that tried to put me to shame, cause me pain, using my name in vain.

Those addicted to heroin and crack cocaine.

Eternal fire on earth as it flames.

Screaming demons giving birth to men.

Acid being poured on skin.

Bit by those I loved and considered as family and friends.

German Shepherds that eat away at my flesh then within.

Crying inside to finally meet a true friend.

Flashing faces of those that plotted against me in sin.

Behind my back with knives ready to dig in.

In vain they used my name and will do it again.

14. Views

Went out amongst protestors to voice her political views.

Nurtured children that had been abused.

Alcohol, tobacco, and drugs she never used.

Convinced drop outs to get back in school.

Used the King James bible and Qur'an as a tool.

She was super smooth, felt as if loyalty ruled.

Those that had issues she walk in their shoes,

giving advice on how to take away the rough edges and cruise.

She told people depend not on their own understanding because

God has authority over lifetime jewels.....

Through it all she went out and shared her views helping others to improve.

15. Mind

In the back of my mind I be internally crying wondering why people gotta do time.

Family members, and friends steady dying, witness, witnesses testify, signs of the devil's eternal fire, souls crying, usage of drugs as brain fries, little kids that backslide, and masters in lying.

Funeral of crying, puddle of blood babies drown, lie, and die in.

No holy water lives of sin.

Poking knives in the hearts of men,

can't even trust my next of kin.

in the back of my mind I wonder how long will I live without dying.

16. Reactions

Chemical Reactions
Kidnapping
Fainting and Collapsing
Overlapping
Backtracking
Factoring
Satisfaction
Relaxing
Cause and effect of reactions.

17. Based

I t was based on real life events.

Was never a real friend, bit my right hand and let
venom poison flow end.

I always wondered where your time and

money was being spent;

you was going against.

Covered up your real intent,

you did a good job to pretend.

You had ill intentions to begin,

in the center within you schemed from my Bejamin Franklin's skin,

literally stabbed me in the back in the end.

I should've paid more attention to the obvious sins of men.

Besides I met you over a state tray while I resided in the belly of the
beast within.

18. Tendecies

Murdering tendecies.
Never committed any crimes but
life long felonies he'd loved it to see.
Fantasies of misery, and loved company.
Mental attitude of burns, third degree.

Happily married.
Went to church every week, but still allowed demonic spirits to be free.
No one on earth can live perfectly.

Gave him a badge,
pass the police academy.
In the line of duty killed a thirteen year old in the streets falsely,
and then a second badge of honor and promotion he received.

19. Poetic Lines

Poetic lines, love and happiness combined.
A stimulant for minds.

Love at it's prime.

The best of it's kind.

Space age, that of another time.

Words that coincide as ryhmes, a freed mind.

Alphabets that come together and grind to enhance clues and visions in minds.

Reading, writing and reciting poetry lines.

20. Disguised Blessings

Bad experiences, and painful learned lessons in reality was disguised blessings.

Learned how to cherish gifts, and value sessions.

Repass of past aggressions brought forth smiles without questions.

Loving opposites genders presence.

Genuinely giving without expecting back commandments,

never forgot when I didn't have it.

Never went back as freedom became everlasting.

21. Just Remembered

They was gone through october, november
and all through september.
No love in the coldest of winters.
When it was no heat, cold air through cracks in walls,
and windows.
A genuine friend a sacred place of rememberence
I don't remember.
But I just remembered sick grown men molested children.
Project living.
Senseless killings.
Grade school children can't even get to school,
to much gun fire by civilians,
to many customers in lines of dealings surrounding buildings.
I just remember the chaos that suspended
through october, november, and through the rest
of the months until september.

22. Delicately Refined (Jean Hines)

Delicately refined, intellectual mind.

Forever placed in her prime.

She was before her time.

Spoke to people about reading the holy bible

to ease minds.

Spiritually inclined.

Read the word for those to go forward not being in the blind,

left behind of God's grace and mercy that was in

reach not hard to find.

Stayed on my behind letting me know that she loved me all the time,

and that through her teachings I shall someday shine.

Provided timeless jewels that would last a lifetime.....

I called her momma, but her name was Jean Hines.

23. Variation

I t be a variation of fiendish things that aint what they seem.
Survival tactics all revolved around schemes.
Living our own American dream.
In denial of certain things we've heard, done or seen.
Replica or clone is what is seen, but in reality it's the real thing.
Affiliants crowning themselves as kings,
in reality our father whom are in Heaven is the king of kings;
to get to him you must go through his sons name.
Cravings, fiending, and desiring a variation of things.....

24. A Rhyme, A Word

A rhyme, a word, a melody, a tempo, a poetic vibe being felt, and heard.

A mic of spoken word that came from Psalms, and Proverbs.

A vitalize of animated nerves.

Respect earned and deserve.

A love for hers.

Unconditional rhyme stirs, lost in love for the play of words.

A strategic path that sometime curves.

A rhyme, a way with words.

25. Contrary Beliefs

Contrary to popular beliefs.
She was more great than the Great Barrier Reef.
She was someone I just had to keep.
Was a part of me, pave the way for love to be, to see.
Kept me focusely.
Some would tell me bad things about her in deceit;
others would tell her bad things about me.
I forgot what others think I shall be with that special someone
I love whole-heartedly, complete, and feels the same way about me,
and that was she.
Contrary to popular beliefs, I loved her and she loved me.

26. Right Hand

My right hand is to Allah father of the universe,
my left hand is Satan Dragon of the beast.
My right hand shall crush my left hand, the beast.
As I face the east saying a prayer for those that's deceased,
those stuck in poverty, those that will never see the streets.

New laws unfold as crime didn't decrease.
Some use drugs, and pop pistols as a way,
a way of being free.

A product of their environment is what they came to be.
Nieve to power of knowledge, and education, years studying
to get a degree.
Wouldn't have to see jail cells, forever free.
Bank accounts of legitimately hard earned money,
no drug sells to see.

The serpent in hell planted bad seeds that ruined
the streets.
Death and destruction is all we see.
Kids being murdered daily.

Riots of firely burning souls,
those with no where to live, stuck in the cold.
As DCFS kids moms and dads strung out on cocaine, and blows,
controlled substances that turned out lost souls.

Violating parole in and out prisons doors.
Violent cases constant being caught as
animinalistic human beings refuse to fold,
refuse to let go of street life,
even when some grow old.
Stuck in time of dungeons and dragons in which the
beast controlled.

27. *Pitiful*

P itiful cries, could never whip away tears from eyes,
burning flames of fire,
    and everyone shall be killed or die.
Hypes that steady getting high.
Sanctified saints that hold they head down praying to the sky.
Hoping one day their kids and grandkids will seek the truth
instead of living in a lie.
Praying to see Heaven in the sky after they die.
Never questioning the Lord why,
but faithfully serving him down on earth as it is
in the sky.

Pitiful cries of people that will never be baptize earthly
devils without disguise,
utilize criminal enterprise,

seeing demonic spirits in eyes.

Meeting The dragon of the beast before and after we die.

Nightmares coming to reality in lives.

No steady flow of income hustle to get by since 1965.

Still aint taking advantage of dedicating to

grow and climb.

Constant mayhem,

and pitiful crying.

28. Present Eyes, Future lies

Caught up in a repetition of lies,
where scandalous ones come with surprise,
kidnapping, torchering, to die.
Saints often ask why?
Why must these people achieve a rush a rise off sick crimes,
never stopping as they get worser each time.
Causing insanity in minds.
Saints constantly visioning burning of mankind,
Satan inclined.
Those being set out and rotten like a fruit or vine.
Came to find, that the Myans was lying the earth didn't
come to end at that date, and time, but people steady dying,
revolutionary, revelation times;
the bible was the truth as state attorney's getting convictions
off lying.

But in time God's true followers shall see the bright light
that shall ever shine.

Outta the dark comes the light of lime.

Earthly bodies shall frequently see the dark within their life
time, but after death dark alleys, or night time doesn't exist
in Heaven's enterprise.

Heavenly souls cannot begin dying,
life has just begin as an everlasting light shine forever
blessed with eternal life without dying,
those that followed faithfully and didn't stay behind;
shall bare witness to the paradise that lies.....

Present Eyes, Future Lies.

29. Love and Respect

With me it's all about love, and respect.

Showing love, dispite of, to never forget.

Wanting and needing, never let.

Being there when times are worst or best.

No change of wearing sides of hats.

I'm with, those that are against, reject, protest, and don't rotate with.

The ones I know break bread with.

Not the ones that was fake, and pretend;

true colors came out of what had always been within.

Love, loyalty, and respect is a built within me as a men until the very end.

30. Silent Mind

Sometimes in my silent mind I feel peace as those that had won The Nobel Peace Prize.

Others times I feel like a horror story that came alive.

Sometimes I be watching her from behind thinking of the right words to get her to be mines, to see what's underneath the fabric designs.

Sometimes I be wanna write love poems that ryhme;

other times I be wanna write fiction about a killer that lost his mind.

Sometimes I take memorable drifts through my own mind, back to the future, present day in time, or futuristic optimist prime.....

Some try to read me and draw off signs, but you don't what's going on in my silent mind.